THE EVIL MEN DO

TITLES BY JOHN McMAHON

The Good Detective

THE EVIL MEN DO

JOHN McMAHON

G. P. Putnam's Sons
New York

Iosco - Arenac District Library
East Tawas, Michigan

PUTNAM
— EST. 1838 —

G. P. Putnam's Sons
Publishers Since 1838
An imprint of Penguin Random House LLC
penguinrandomhouse.com

Library of Congress Cataloging-in-Publication Data

Names: McMahon, John, 1970– author.
Title: The evil men do / John McMahon.
Description: New York : G. P. Putnam's Sons, [2020] |
Identifiers: LCCN 2019052508 (print) | LCCN 2019052509 (ebook) |
ISBN 9780525535560 (hardcover) | ISBN 9780525535584 (ebook)
Subjects: GSAFD: Mystery fiction.
Classification: LCC PS3613.C5843 E95 2020 (print) |
LCC PS3613.C5843 (ebook) | DDC 813/.6—dc23
LC record available at https://lccn.loc.gov/2019052508
LC ebook record available at https://lccn.loc.gov/2019052509

Printed in the United States of America
1   3   5   7   9   10   8   6   4   2

BOOK DESIGN BY KATY RIEGEL

For Zoey and Noah, my ferocity and my heart.
Who's got it better than us?

THE EVIL MEN DO

1

The little girl knew things.

Her mother said it was because she was a good listener. Not just to the words that adults said, but to the words "in between the words."

The girl noticed small facial contours that telegraphed an adult's lie. She tracked changes in the music and cadence of a voice, like when someone left the room and those remaining decided that enough time had passed and it was safe to talk about that person.

But mostly—she'd just always known more than girls her own age.

At her old public school, the teachers had moved her ahead one grade. Then another.

The school recommended a third, but her mother said it was unnatural for an eight-year-old to be in junior high, especially with how petite she was.

And so the girl had easily noticed the car that had been following them.

A Toyota truck.

White, with one headlight out.

Her father had changed lanes twice in the last ten minutes, and still the white truck remained behind them. Hanging back by ten or twelve car lengths.

The girl sat in the back of her family's Hyundai, playing Minecraft on her iPad.

She had calculated that she would need one thousand planks of wood to build the house she wanted in the video game. And she knew that each oak log produced four planks, so she set out to cut down two hundred and fifty pieces of oak. A simple task, all thumbs and fingers.

That was when the truck began accelerating.

Eight car lengths back.

Six car lengths.

Four.

The driver made a strange move then, speeding up, yet leaving the road and driving onto the shoulder. And it didn't make sense to the girl. Until the front left corner of the Toyota swerved in and made contact with the back right corner of her family's car.

Her world spun.

She saw the dark shortleaf trees of the Georgia forest at the roadside. A glimpse of the Tullumy River, far down the incline. And the metal of an oncoming guardrail.

Her mother screamed. The girl was thrown against her window. And then there was one last image.

The face of the man in the Toyota.

Focused and steady. Not at all panicked. Staring right at her.

And then her family's car lurched off the road.

2

My finger tapped the trigger on my Glock 42, and four rounds of .380 flew through the air.

Pop, pop, pop, pop. All before I could let out my first breath.

It was a Tuesday morning in May, and my partner, Remy Morgan, and I were in the Georgia Safe, a gun range three miles east of Mason Falls.

I took off my brown sport coat and hung it over the divider wall between me and Remy. Placed my gun atop the small weapons ledge, pointing down-range.

Through the open air, I could smell scrambled eggs and chicken-fried steak, floating over from the gun range's office. The owner, a retired patrolman named Cooz, had never met a gravy dish he didn't like. He had the figure to prove it.

"So, Rem," I said. "You never told me about your date."

Remy was dressed in one of her go-to outfits: tan pants and an ironed white blouse that contrasted with her dark brown skin. She wore bookish glasses, which I've always thought was a ploy to play down her good looks.

"Saturday?" She shrugged. "We went to Forest Oaks."

I glanced at my partner. Mounted a new target in my lane and hit the button to send it away. "He took you to a cemetery?"

Remy hung her target in the next lane over. "We saw *Blade Runner*, P.T. They show old movies there. It's a thing."

There were a lot of things that were *things* now, but I didn't know a thing about them. Maybe that was me, not wanting to get used to what passed for my new life. My life since my wife and son were gone.

I loaded a magazine into my Glock. "We don't go to the morgue enough times a year? You gotta visit gravesites for date night?"

Remy rolled her eyes. My partner was twenty-six, more than ten years younger than me. "Don't be an old man, P.T."

She put cans on her ears, and slammed the six-bullet magazine into her weapon. "Plus, old people usually aren't good shots," she hollered. "The eyes start to go."

I grinned. "We betting on this? 'Cause as far as I can remember, your partner's still the best shot in the department."

My cell buzzed in my pocket, and I took it out. Typed a quick response to the message and put the phone away.

"Loser buys dinner," Remy mouthed. "Best out of twenty? Four rounds of five?"

I got into a fighting stance and aimed my Glock 42 at the target. My partner can be a little chesty sometimes. The kinda person who can start an argument in an empty house. Then again, that's what I like most about her.

I tapped—one, two, three, four, five. Hit the return and faced Remy, not even looking as the paper target came back.

"I like steak places, you know," I said. "Expensive steak places."

The paper target stopped, and I lifted a corner of the printed silhouette. "Five out of five, rook."

Remy *wasn't* a rookie detective anymore. Which was why I said it.

She placed her right foot toward the back of her lane and extended her right arm straight. Her left arm supported it with a bent elbow. This was a different shooting stance than mine. It was called the Weaver and was taught to cadets in the last decade.

Remy threw her hair out of the way, over her left shoulder. My partner had the sculpted cheekbones, dark skin, and wavy curls of a fashion model. She exhaled and took aim, letting out five quick blasts. *Bam, bam, bam, bam, bam.*

She hit the return button with her open palm, and the target drifted toward us. "Tofurkey," she said.

The corners of the paper fluttered in the air-conditioning inside the range.

"Tofurkey?" I mouthed.

Five out of five shots were in the center of Remy's target. Two were inside a white area called the "inner ten." The center of the center.

Remy inspected her own results. First round in the books, and we were even.

"There's a really good vegan place off 85," she hollered at me. "When I beat your ass, we'll drive down there. Great tofurkey."

My phone buzzed again, and I glanced at the screen. Scanning the two texts sent to me in the last few minutes. My partner wasn't even vegan. She was just busting my balls.

"Rain check." I held up my phone, showing Remy a text from the chief.

We packed up and hurried outside. And I squeezed my six-foot-two frame into Remy's red '77 Alfa Romeo Spider.

My name is P. T. Marsh, and Mason Falls, Georgia, is my town. Lately we top out at a little under 130,000 souls. It's that interesting size—small enough for families to feel like they've escaped the sprawling urban buzz that is Atlanta, but large enough to keep a four-detective homicide squad overworked and underpaid.

"What does it say?" Remy motioned at my cell.

"To drop the rookie off. Despite her shooting skills, grab a more experienced detective."

Remy shot me the bird with her free hand, and I glanced down at my cell.

"Chief Pernacek has a friend," I said.

Remy smiled. "It's good he's making friends."

Jeff Pernacek had become chief of police back when I was a rookie, but had retired about a decade ago. With our recent chief having left office, Mayor Stems had called Pernacek back in as the interim boss.

"Is his friend dead?" my partner asked.

While Remy's point was that we worked homicide, it was also true that Pernacek had reentered the department with a specific opinion: that we'd become sloppy in his absence. We needed orders, and a lot of 'em.

When I saw his first text, asking if we could drop by a citizen's house to do a welfare check, I'd typed back a short note.

"Did you tell him we were getting weapon certs renewed?"

"I did," I said. Staring at my text exchange with the chief.

"What'd he say back?"

I showed Remy the chief's response, which was three words:

Order equals structure.

Which meant: Do what the hell I say—even if you think I'm sending you on some boondoggle errand.

Remy put her foot to the floor, and out the window a forest thick with loblolly pines flew by. In the foreground, weedy green kudzu climbed out of the Georgia mist, covering the pine trees like an old sock.

While she drove, I rang up the chief, who told me that a close friend hadn't shown for a monthly bridge game.

"Before you make some smartass remark, P.T.," Pernacek said, "it's worth noting that the mayor and I have played bridge with Ennis Fultz for ten years. Same restaurant. Second Tuesday of every month."

"And he's never missed one?"

"Not without calling," Pernacek said. "But Ennis can be a little eccentric, so I don't want to send some blue-suiter I don't know."

"Sure," I said.

The interim chief was a political animal of a specific type. When the mayor said "frog," he jumped. But it was good to be trusted by the chief. A quick welfare check, and we'd be back at the range.

Ten minutes later we exited SR-906, and my partner accelerated up a gravel road that was never intended for a late '70s Italian sports coupe.

"Well, we're not in the middle of nowhere," I said.

"But we can see it from here." Remy finished my thought.

She slowed, and the dust caught up to us like a tan canopy. Through the haze, a home came into view.

The house was two-story and custom-built, constructed log-cabin style, out of red oak. But the way it was positioned was odd. Unless I had the geography wrong, the Condesale Gorge was two hundred feet to the north and offered a gorgeous and expensive view.

But whoever had built this place had made a decision to face the road.

We parked in a gravel area out front and got out. Knocked on a large wooden door.

"What's his name again?" Remy asked.

"Ennis Fultz," I said.

I scanned the trim line of the house. No security system. No doorbell with built-in camera. And no gate coming off the highway and onto Fultz's giant plot of land.

I walked back to the gravel area where the Alfa was parked while Remy headed around back. East and west of the house stood a line of ponderosa lemon trees with green branches and waxy white blooms. Beyond them, the forest grew thick for half a mile in each direction, curving with the natural topography of the gorge.

"P.T.," Remy hollered.

I rounded the corner of the house and glanced up. A stairwell ran up to a small second-floor landing, where my partner crouched.

"Come look at this."

I walked up the steps and found Remy by a second-story back door. Her fingers ran along the wood near the doorknob.

The molding had been torn apart, a slice made in between two pieces of wood. It was a common way to break in, using something simple, like a painter's five-in-one tool.

I banged on the back door. "Mr. Fultz?"

No answer.

A couple hundred feet behind us, the land curved down at a slight angle at first, and then dropped precipitously into the canyon.

"It's not exactly exigent circumstances," Remy said.

Sure, I thought. But the chief had been calling his buddy all morning.

I held the doorknob at the edges and turned. The place was unlocked.

"Mr. Fultz?" I called out.

No answer.

I took a few steps inside a home office. The place was wall-to-wall wood, ornately carved from oak and stained an espresso color. A box beam ceiling. Built-in desk and cabinet.

I passed through the office and onto a second-floor landing. A large open space was downstairs. A combined kitchen and living area with no expense spared. A Sub-Zero fridge. A Wolf range.

As I turned back to Remy, I saw the door to the other upstairs room was ajar.

A man who looked to be in his late fifties lay there, buck-naked and faceup on a king-sized bed. His freckled skin was the color of an iridescent pearl.

"Damn it," I whispered. Not looking forward to a call to the chief.

I walked outside and shook my head at Remy.

"Bullshit," my partner responded. The day had started pretty lighthearted, and now that was over. A man was dead.

I called up the precinct. "Put me through to the chief."

While I waited on hold, we walked back down the stairs and around to the front. In the distance, dust kicked up into the air. A car was coming.

"You expecting someone already?" Remy asked.

I shook my head, holding the phone to my ear.

The car slowed as it got closer. It was an old beater from the late '90s. A faded yellow Mazda Protegé.

Chief Pernacek came on the line. "What is it?" he said curtly, as if he'd forgotten why he sent us here.

"Jeff," I said, "I hate to tell you this. But we're out at the gorge. Your friend is dead."

3

According to DMV records, Ennis Fultz was sixty-eight, a good decade older than I'd guessed from the brief glimpse I'd caught of him upstairs.

By ten a.m., a squad car had parked in the open gravel area next to Remy's Alfa and the yellow Mazda. As did a white van that read *Medical Examiner* on the side.

As it turned out, the Mazda that drove up belonged to Fultz's cleaning lady, a redhead in her late fifties named Louise Randall. She went by the name Ipsy.

Sarah Raines, the local M.E., hustled up the steps with her gear, and Remy opened the front door for her. Sarah was dressed in a bulky one-piece disposable jumper that matched her blue eyes but didn't do much for her thin figure.

"Morning," she said to me and Remy, her eyes hanging on me. Sarah and I had been seeing each other for about five months.

We moved inside, heading up to the bedroom, where I got my second look at Ennis Fultz. He was five foot ten with short white hair and two days of growth on his face. A sheet covered half his body, but his upper frame was muscular, his biceps and chest toned.

We took pictures of the body, circling the bed to see the victim from each angle.

"Look sixty-eight to you?" Sarah asked.

"More like fifty-eight," I said.

An oxygen tank stood between the bed and the wall, a tube snaking its way out of the tank and ending in a clear plastic mask, the kind with a strap you wrap around your head.

"The positioning of the tubing." Remy pointed.

The mask sat three inches from Fultz's outstretched right hand.

I picked up an inhaler from off the nightstand.

"Budesonide formoterol," I read off the side.

"Goes by the brand name Symbicort," Sarah said. "It reduces swelling and irritation in the airways. Could mean anything from asthma to a serious respiratory problem."

Remy and I let Sarah have some time with the body and split up inspecting the upstairs.

My partner checked out Fultz's home office next door while I moved to the attached bathroom. In the trash, I found a Trojan package and a used condom.

I bagged them for evidence, staring at the rest of Fultz's prescriptions. Promethazine for a chest cold three months ago. Lipitor for cholesterol. A bottle of Viagra, two pills left in the bottom. Nothing jumped out as suspicious.

"Estimating time of death as Monday, May sixth," Sarah said into a handheld recorder, referring to yesterday. "Ten a.m. to two p.m."

"You got a cause of death?" I asked.

Sarah hesitated, pulling her shoulder-length blond hair back into a hair tie. She was an eye-catcher, sure, but I had seen up close how good a person she was. The kind I needed around.

I followed Sarah's eyes to the man's right hand. The skin at the ends of Fultz's index finger and thumb had turned a dark blue.

"Let's wait for toxicology," she said.

Sarah put the recorder down and grabbed a camera. Her tools of the trade were housed in a repurposed tackle box, and I caught a glimpse of myself in a mirror inside the lid.

My wavy brown hair was uncombed and my blue eyes bloodshot. Sarah had shaken me awake twice this week in the middle of the night. Screaming in my sleep again.

I'd promised her that the problems I had last year weren't coming back.

I crossed the hallway to Remy. My partner had the back door open. The same door we'd come in earlier. On the floor near the jamb were fifteen or twenty splinters of wood, right where the molding had been sliced apart.

"The cleaning lady came twice a week?" I asked.

"Tuesday and Friday," Remy said.

"So if she cleaned this area Friday, it could give us a timeline as to a potential break-in."

I opened the door and glanced down the back steps. A half-dozen bags of Marathon grass seed were piled at the bottom.

I stepped back inside.

The walls in the office were plastered with framed covers of real estate magazines that featured Fultz's face. THE MASTER OF

THE DEAL, one called him. THE MOST HATED MAN IN GEORGIA, another read.

"We need to know more about this guy," I said.

Remy and I passed the body and headed downstairs to talk to the housekeeper.

Ipsy Randall was wire thin, and her red hair showed dark roots. She smelled like a mix of Lysol and Marlboro Reds.

"How long have you worked for Mr. Fultz?" Remy asked.

"Sixteen years," Ipsy said. She explained how she'd followed the Fultz family from one house to another. She'd seen them separate and divorce. Their son go off to college.

"We found a condom in the trash," I said. "Was Mr. Fultz living with a lady friend?"

"Or a guy friend?" Remy asked.

"Ha ha, goodness. He would laugh at that," Ipsy said to Remy. "Ennis was a charmer for sure, but I never saw any woman here on my two days."

"But the condom?" Remy pointed upstairs.

"Almost always one in the trash on Tuesdays," Ipsy said.

Remy and I shared a look. *Did the old guy have a regular girl?*

I leaned against the wall. On the opposite side of the room, a twenty-foot-wide custom fish tank was flanked by natural stone.

"What do you know about Mr. Fultz's health?" I asked.

Ipsy described breathing treatments Fultz would do in the mornings using the oxygen tank, but told us he'd been doing them for years and was active. "He'd be gone walking lately—half the time I got here."

"So you have a key to get in?"

Ipsy nodded, producing it, and I thought about the blue fingers. "Cyanosis" was the technical term. The coloring could mean a lot of things. Even a natural death, if the body sat long enough.

We asked Ipsy about the deceased's family, and she gave us an address on Ennis Fultz's son, Cameron, who was in his thirties. Fultz's ex-wife, Connie, was Ipsy's age.

"So the wife's ten years younger than him?" Remy confirmed.

"More or less." The housekeeper pointed at the front door. "I told the patrolman, by the way. Y'all might want to lock the house down after you leave. Mr. Fultz had a habit of hiding cash near-about everywhere."

"What do you mean 'hiding'?" Remy asked.

"I found ten thousand dollars in the toaster oven a few months ago," Ipsy said. "I'd see him walkin' out back with a paper bag and a shovel."

Ten thousand bucks was a good enough reason for a break-in. We walked Ipsy up to the office and showed her the wood splinters by the back door. Asked if she'd mopped the area the last time she was here.

"When I left Friday at three, you could eat off that floor."

Ipsy led us to some of the places Fultz might've stashed money. As she moved through each one—a safe in his closet, a shelf full of empty shoe boxes—they were all dead empty. The safe door, ajar.

"Do you know anyone who'd want to hurt Mr. Fultz?" Remy asked.

Ipsy hesitated.

She looked out the big glass doors that led onto the main floor balcony. "Do you mind if I smoke?" she asked. "It's been a helluva morning."

We followed her out to the balcony. There was a salmon-colored motel ashtray out there, alongside a pack of Virginia Slims. I imagined this was *her* spot to relax, rather than Fultz's, since he was on oxygen.

She lit her cigarette. Exhaled. Her teeth had yellow tobacco stains that were older than my partner. "Do you believe people can change, Detective?"

I wasn't expecting that kinda question.

"If they want to, sure," I said.

"Well, Mr. Fultz went into the hospital last year. And he came out a different person."

"In what way?" Remy asked.

Ipsy took a draw on her cigarette. Made a small O with her mouth and blew out.

"There was this couple," she said. "When Ennis built the house here—they'd been living on the land. In a little structure at the edge of the property. The woman, Indian, maybe her family lived here forever. The man as white as you."

"Okay." I nodded. "Did they get thrown off? Were they upset?"

"No, it ain't like that," Ipsy said, picking at a white skin tag on her sun-wrinkled arm. "Ennis left them alone. The man—he'd been maintaining the trails along the edge of the gorge. He kept doing that."

"All right," I said.

"But after Ennis came out of the hospital, he helped the couple adopt a child. Used his influence in the city. He did the same with me. Came out with a brick of cash one day. Back pay, he called it."

"How much did he give you?" Remy asked.

"Six thousand dollars." Ipsy stubbed out her cig. "You're gonna hear some awful stories about Mr. Fultz," she said. "How he was a real son of a bitch."

"Was he?"

"To people in business, I guess," she said. "But if someone broke in that door and hurt him?" Ipsy pointed upstairs. "As far as I'm concerned, that person oughta fry."

The housekeeper grabbed her pocketbook, a bulky leather number that looked about twenty-five years old. "I gotta lay down now."

Remy gave Ipsy a business card. "Don't forget your smokes," my partner said.

Ipsy shook her head. "Oh, those aren't mine. I was just worked up and needed a hit."

My partner bagged the cigarettes. Even if Ipsy's prints were all over them, they might have other value.

Sarah had established a pre-autopsy time of death as ten a.m. to two p.m. yesterday, and I thought about the amount of activity, out here in the middle of nowhere.

Six bags of grass seed had been dropped off at the back steps. Someone may have broken in the back door. And a mystery woman had sex with Fultz. We had no idea when half these events had happened, but the last seventy-two hours seemed pretty busy for a guy in his retirement.

Chief Pernacek arrived, and he met us on the balcony.

In some counties, the police are called to all manners of death, whether natural or homicide. Mason Falls wasn't one of those places. But if you were rich, famous, or suddenly dead, you could still get a house call from two detectives and their boss.

"I assume you're thinking it's natural," Pernacek said—more to me than Remy.

"I dunno," I said. Thinking of the blue color at the tips of Fultz's fingers. The damage to the back door. Then again, the old man needed oxygen just to breathe.

"Since you know the victim," Remy asked, "did you want to talk to the family yourself?"

Pernacek was tall and unusually slender, an Ichabod Crane sorta look. He smiled at my partner. "I think it's great that girls are on the detectives' squad now, Morgan," he said. "Brings a whole different perspective. But I ain't done a notification since the late '90s."

Remy held the chief's gaze.

This was classic Pernacek. Big bark over the phone. Backhanded compliment done good-old-boy style in person. And I couldn't remember the guy at one damn crime scene when he was in charge before.

I thought about the magazine headlines that Fultz had framed in his office. "Anything we should know about Ennis?"

"He was a good man," Pernacek said. "The bad lungs finally caught up with him. I assume you'll handle this respectfully. Contact his ex-wife and close the case up right quick?"

"Of course," I said. Even though I wasn't so sure I agreed. Either about Ennis being a pillar of the city—or about the death being natural.

Pernacek turned and walked out. And I glanced out at the dust coming up from Ipsy's old Mazda as she drove away.

The home wasn't designed with its best view in mind. The place was a garrison. Waiting for trouble coming down that road.

"What are you thinking?" Remy asked, her eyes tracking mine.

And the thing is—what I think about most when I'm at a murder scene is why *I'm* here. I don't mean some esoteric "why are we all here" type crap. I mean *me*.

I've attended the funerals of my wife and son. Been left for dead in the middle of a highway. And somehow, I keep waking up. I keep breathing.

But not this guy.

Ennis Fultz was old, but fit enough to get laid. He'd apparently been a real estate magnate, but built a custom home facing away from a million-dollar view. And if he'd known about the break-in, he didn't reach out to his friends at city hall.

A detective's job is straightforward. Line up the pieces that fit together into a story. And look for the ones that don't.

If Fultz's death wasn't natural, and this *was* murder, it meant a killer broke into his house in between a half dozen other visitors. And snuck out somehow. Putting himself in plain view. A small person in a big open space.

"You thinking the chief's spot-on?" Remy asked. "It's a natural death?"

I hesitated. "You know what I'm thinking, partner?" I said to Remy. "Some people have balls."

"That's a fact, boss," she said.

"But if this is murder . . ." I stared out at the road in front of us. "And there's only one way in and out of this place? Then the killer needs a wheelbarrow to carry his around in."

4

The girl opened her eyes, and everything was upside down.

There was a wobbling noise. Like something spinning on an uneven axis.

Her seat belt was pulled taut around her body, and the polyester material ate into her shoulders. Her head, which hung upside down near the ceiling, felt woozy.

She held her eyes closed for a moment.

"Too much imagination can be a bad thing," her mother had warned her last week.

The girl opened her eyes. Was she dreaming?

The Toyota driven by the man was pulled over along the bridge, its rear lights a block of orange against the blackness of night.

She'd seen the man's face. A calm look.

The wobbling noise stopped, and a creaking replaced it.

The girl turned her neck and looked to the front seat.

A twist of metal from the bridge's guardrail had speared the front window and was holding the Hyundai in place—keeping the car from sliding down the hill and into the river.

She looked back at the Toyota. The truck's lights shone in bright red now. It was backing up. Coming toward them.

The girl gasped.

The man had hit them on purpose.

And now he was coming back to finish the job.

She tried to scream, but her chest burned and no words came out.

5

While Remy got ahold of Fultz's family for the notification, I drove downtown and found my way to the second floor of the Lee F. Skirter Criminal Court Building.

In the year after I lost my family, I sunk deep into a swamp.

As I climbed out of the muck, I stumbled across the biggest case of my career. And as part of that, I killed a man named Donnie Meadows.

Today his sister had come down to the court building to hear how much the city would pay for my misdeeds.

I sat beside Liz Yugel, Mason Falls's district attorney, in a wood-paneled meeting room. Yugel was in her thirties and her conservative blue dress looked more like something she'd wear to an interview.

Two women sat across from us.

"Detective Marsh." The older woman smiled. "It's a pleasure to have your company again."

Catherine Flannery was known in her professional life as Cat the Tiger. The nickname was a piece of trivia that Liz Yugel had shared with me about the fifty-five-year-old attorney, along with a piece of advice she repeated multiple times the night before. *This is a settlement meeting, P.T. Act polite. Look reasonable. Say nothing to Cat.*

The case against the police department was for excessive use of force.

Mason Falls PD had a written policy on how to apprehend a suspect. The policy just wasn't clear on what to do if that suspect was seven foot one, three hundred pounds, and holding a cop underwater for extended periods of time.

The woman seated next to Cat Flannery was Tusila Meadows, the dead man's sister.

At six-two and weighing three bills, Tusila was the smallest member of the Meadows family that I'd met. And I'd met a few.

DA Yugel got right to it.

"We were asked to come here by Judge Crocket and present our best pretrial proposal."

She slid a folder full of paperwork across the table. "I have a binding offer for $150,000. I've also included police evidence tying Donnie Meadows to two counts of kidnapping, one count of murder, and three counts of attempted murder."

Cat the Tiger didn't even look at the folder.

"You know what I love about the *practice* of law?" she said. "When you *practice* law and win, you win. And when you practice and lose, you lose."

Cat took the offer letter out, but slid the rest of the papers back toward us.

"But when a cop plays executioner, we don't get our day in court to see if Donnie was, in fact, guilty."

I sat up straighter.

Donnie Meadows *was* guilty. We had him dead to rights on at least three of the five charges, including one murder and two attempted murders.

Tusila reached for a ballpoint pen on the table. She was wearing a purple dress with tiny fleur-de-lis prints. As she turned to the second page, DA Yugel pulled a set of papers from her folder.

"We'd also expect that Ms. Meadows signs a standard non-disclosure agreement," Yugel said.

Tusila put the pen down. She had a square face and a jaw like a horse. "What does that mean?" she asked her attorney. "I can't tell my friends? Who know what I've been going through?"

"The city doesn't want the public to know what they pay for settlements," Cat explained.

Tusila hesitated, her eyes meeting mine. "Then I want an apology."

"In writing?" the DA asked. "We can't put *anything* in writing, Ms. Meadows."

"I'm not talking about one of your papers." Tusila glared at Yugel. "I want a goddamn apology from him."

I felt my face flush, and under the table I made a fist.

A formality.

That's what the DA had called this meeting. Because Cat Flannery had already gotten an email with this settlement offer. She'd passed it on to her client, who had agreed to it last night.

DA Yugel blinked. "Are you not signing the document?"

"I dunno," Tusila said. "I gotta think about it now."

The DA glanced at me.

Yugel was a prosecutor. Her job wasn't to defend cops. But Mayor Stems knew she was familiar with the case, so he'd asked her to settle the matter quickly. The other choice was to bring in outside counsel at $350 an hour for each attorney.

Cat the Tiger smiled, enjoying the chaos. "You must be a blast to be married to, Detective," she said, "if you're this reticent to say 'I'm sorry' with just the four of us in an empty room."

Tusila shifted in her seat. Like others in her family, she was a mix of Samoan and German. "I think my cousins would want to hear you apologize too," she said.

Cat's eyes never left mine.

"I just remembered," she said. "You're *not* married any longer, Detective. That's what put you into this rage, right? You saw that young black girl that Donnie was with as a surrogate for your dead wife? And you saw red. Stopped thinking about things like due process. Or evidence."

A bead of sweat formed along the back of my neck.

As a detective, you meet victims on the worst days of their lives. And you catch suspects who are the lowest society has to offer. And that's the day to day of it, right? Morning to night. Over and over.

But once in a while, a case is more than that. Once in a while, you're confronted with true evil.

"I understand the importance of resolution, Ms. Meadows," I said. "And your brother—he got mixed up with some bad people."

"That's what I keep saying." Tusila threw up her hands.

Out of the corner of my eye, I saw DA Yugel nodding.

Say it, her body language screamed. *Apologize.*

"But there's a couple with no fifteen-year-old son because your brother murdered him," I said. "And that's before he put a bullet in my partner's arm. And tried to drown me."

I met Tusila's eyes. "So there is zero friggin' chance that I say 'sorry' to you. Here. Today. In court. Ever. That money's the best you're ever gonna get."

The room went quiet for a moment, and Cat turned to her client. "Did I tell you how this would go if you tried to get a simple apology?"

The attorney pushed the papers back. "One-time offer, Liz. Make that two hundred grand, and I'll recommend Ms. Meadows signs the papers right now."

"You know I'm not authorized to do that," Liz Yugel said.

Cat turned to her client. "You ready to go?"

Tusila Meadows stood without signing the papers. And I recalled something. The lawsuit was against the department, but the DA had told me that if the case didn't settle quickly, I'd be next. Personally named in a civil suit.

Tusila glared at me. And I sensed a brief moment where I could make this thing disappear. I could utter a handful of words, and she would sit back down. Grab the pen and sign.

But at the end of the day . . . we are who we are.

"Go on now," I said. "If you're not signing, what're you doing here still?"

And Tusila and Cat walked out of the room.

6

By two p.m. I was back at the precinct and found Remy parked in a chair in the lunchroom with a salad and her iPad.

"What's the latest?" I asked.

"The tox screen came back," she said. "Negative for drugs in Fultz's system."

"You do the notification?"

Remy . "Ennis Fultz's son, Cameron. He'd just come back from vacation. I caught him pulling into his driveway from the airport. The guy broke down. Started bawling."

"Jesus," I said. "From where?"

"Jacksonville," Remy said. "Nice guy. Thirtyish. Athletic." She consulted her iPad. "Spent the last four days at the Sawgrass Marriott with his girlfriend."

"When's the last time Cameron saw his dad?"

"Two weeks ago Friday. Said the old man had COPD, chronic obstructive pulmonary disease."

This explained the inhaler medicine. And the tank of O_2.

"Apparently the old man used oxygen to sleep a couple days a week," Remy said. "Also after his daily walks along the gorge."

"What did the son say about his mom?"

"Fultz and his ex split two years ago." Remy looked down at her notes. "Not on speaking terms. 'Acrimonious' was the word he used."

I thought about the condom in the trash.

"Girlfriend?"

"Cameron had no idea his dad was seeing anyone," Remy said. "And Sarah needs 'til end of day on cause of death."

I nodded, taking this in.

We could push the sex angle harder with the family. Figure out who'd been up at that house. Then again, if Fultz's death was natural, we had to be careful we didn't smear his good name in the eyes of the chief and his buddies at city hall.

"I'll look quietly at the ex-wife," I said. "Basic research we can do without a subpoena. If Sarah comes back with a natural cause of death, then I think we're done here, partner."

Remy got up. Tossed the rest of her chicken salad. "And me?"

"Confirm the son's alibi. His whereabouts since Sunday. Basic financial profile."

I moved back to my office and pulled up my internet browser.

Connie Fultz was an easy woman to research, and nearly always appeared in an evening gown. There were galas tied to the university in Athens. Charity benefits with the mayor and the former chief of police Miles Dooger.

She was tall and wore her brown hair up, highlighting the kind of jewels around her neck that set you back four or five digits.

And, in a good half of the pictures, there was Ennis Fultz, by her side. I scanned through pull quotes from Ennis and Connie and got the idea that Connie's mission was philanthropy, and Ennis deferred to her—at least at these events.

I thought of the break-in, if there was one, and Fultz's habit of hiding cash. The area out by the gorge was deserted. *How the hell would anyone know to drive out there in the first place?*

I pulled up a map online and starting clicking east and west of the property.

About a mile away, I saw a Valero gas station. I walked over to Remy's desk and had her pull up the same thing.

"If someone broke into Fultz's house," I said, "odds are they drove by this station, right?"

"If they came from town, yeah," Remy said. "You think the Valero's got security cams?"

"It's been a full day," I said. "If they do—might be erased soon."

Remy slid open the desk drawer where she kept her piece. She grabbed her Glock, and we headed out to the car.

"So the son looked clean?" I asked.

Remy nodded, explaining she'd made calls on Cameron Fultz's alibi.

"He and his girlfriend, Suzanne, went to restaurants in Ponte Vedra. The spa. He golfed each morning in a foursome, including on Monday at eleven-thirty a.m. during the time of death."

Remy floored the Alfa, and I heard that throaty guzzling sound come from the exhaust.

"What's he do for a living?" I asked.

"Works for a logging cooperative. Consultant of some sort.

Lives north of town in an older home. Makes a lot and spends most of it. Construction lien on the house. Nothing special."

A half hour later we were sitting in a tiny back office with the manager of the gas station.

Tamara Bradley was tall, with dark skin and green and yellow beads braided into her hair. She queued up the tape from Monday morning and left us alone to look at the footage.

About ten minutes in, I asked Remy to hit pause. There was no audio. Just a picture of a brunette, standing at pump number four, filling up a white BMW 7 Series.

Connie Fultz.

She was fifty-nine according to our records, but in shape and looked younger. Even in black and white, you could see her Rolex sparkle.

The time code read *10:18 a.m.*, the beginning of Sarah's four-hour block for time of death.

"Well, don't tell the son," I said. "But I think we just found out who Fultz's regular girl is."

Remy tinkered with the software until she pulled up a different angle.

Connie got in her car and drove off in the direction of Ennis Fultz's home at 10:19 a.m. Monday. The day Fultz died.

The manager came back into the office. "If you want, I can burn that to a DVD," she said. "We do it all the time for insurance. People drive off with the hose still in their tank."

"Thanks," I said.

We got the DVD, and Remy joked that now we just needed to find a computer that still had a DVD drive, to watch the thing.

As we walked out, I turned to my partner, pointing in the direction that Connie Fultz had driven off in.

"What else is up that way, Rem?" I asked.

"Except for her ex-husband's place?" Remy flicked her eyebrows. "Nothing you can't get to faster going on the highway. Problem is—it's not enough to pick up the ex-wife. Especially how *these* people are connected."

"Who said anything about picking her up?" I said. "Her ex-husband's dead. Consider it notification number two."

7

At three p.m., Connie Fultz showed up at the precinct, and Remy loaded her into Interrogation Room B. I stood in the small observation area that looked in on rooms A and B.

Connie wore white slacks and a pink scoop-neck blouse covered in a light sweater. Like on the gas station video, her face and body looked closer to fifty than fifty-nine, a figure probably maintained by expensive personal trainers and Pilates classes.

Remy opened the door to Observation, and I turned to my partner.

"Let's not talk in there," I said. "She doesn't have a lawyer, and we don't have a C.O.D."

I moved past my partner and opened the door to Interrogation. "Sorry," I said to Connie. "We're under construction, and there's a lack of conference rooms. I'm Detective Marsh."

Connie Fultz got up and shook my hand.

"We were gonna walk out to the park and get a snow cone," I said. "You mind joining us? We can talk out there."

"Sure," Connie said, and I pointed the way toward the lobby.

We walked out the front door and down the sidewalk.

"I'm sorry about Ennis," Remy said.

She looked to my partner. "You were the detective that spoke with Cameron?"

Remy nodded, and we crossed the street to a park near the precinct.

"I grew up in a time when a husband was the center of your universe," Connie said. "And Ennis was mine for thirty-nine years."

There's a subset of Southern women—well-bred, rich, or both—who have learned to stretch out a specific set of words. They pronounce "sweet" like "swate" and "time" like "tahm." The effect is that of being wooed by a debutante from a bygone era.

"What was he like?" Remy asked.

"Ennis was charming." Connie hesitated. "He was handsome." She smiled gently in that Southern way. "And he was a son of a bitch."

We crossed to an area that had been covered with that spongy material made from recycled tires—so kids didn't get hurt when they fell.

"Where did you two meet?" I asked.

"At Georgia," she said, meaning the university. "I was set to go to this brunch freshman year. In my best sundress and waiting like a fool outside the dining hall for a good hour."

"You got stood up?" Remy asked.

"I did." Connie nodded. "Then along came this handsome man in his late twenties. Asked me if I was okay."

"Ennis was older?"

"A twenty-seven-year-old freshman." Connie smiled. "He'd worked nine years on his dad's farm after high school."

This accounted for their age difference.

"What happened next?" Remy asked.

"The rest is history," she said. "He took me to the brunch, and I felt like Cinderella at the ball.

"After college we got married and moved to Atlanta," she continued. "Ennis had this theory that cemeteries were moving out to the burbs. The land was too valuable in the inner city."

"He was right."

"We ended up in the cemetery business on the outskirts of town and the commercial real estate business in the city. By the time I was thirty, we owned a hundred buildings. Ennis liked the cemeteries better. 'Dead tenants rarely complain,' he'd say."

We got to the cart where the guy sold snow cones, and I pulled out a ten spot. The vendor took three of those pointed paper cups and filled them with ice.

Remy got grape, I got cherry. And Connie picked sour apple.

Rapport was important, but we'd shot the shit long enough.

"We've been asked to dot some i's and cross some t's as it relates to Ennis's death," I said. "As you know, he was important to the community. Both of y'all are donors to great civic causes."

"I appreciate that," she said.

"When was the last time you saw your ex-husband?" Remy asked.

Connie took a seat on a nearby bench. "Probably a month ago."

There it was. Ever since I'd gotten my detective's shield, there was the one consistency. Everyone lied.

"And what was the occasion?"

"Some papers for a charity that Ennis had to sign."

"You and Mr. Fultz were divorced two years ago," Remy said. "Can we ask how it ended?"

Connie offered a half smile. "We grew apart, like a lot of couples."

I paused, weighing my options. The wife was well-connected in the city, but she was also bullshitting us. "Your ex-husband died on Monday between ten a.m. and two."

"Oh," she said.

I held out the photo of Connie taken from the video at the Valero gas station. "This was taken at 10:18. A mile from his house."

Connie stared at the picture.

As the wind picked up, she pulled her sweater tight and a pair of ruby-throated hummingbirds dive-bombed a hedge of foxglove behind her.

"So maybe we should start over," I said. "When was the last time you saw your ex-husband?"

Connie stood up. "Wait a sec." Her posture shifted. "He was fine when *I* left."

"When was that?"

"An hour or so later." She pointed at the picture. "Maybe less."

"What were you doing there?" Remy asked.

"We needed to talk."

"About?"

"We'd pledged money for the children's wing at the hospital. Two hundred thousand dollars over four years."

"Was there a problem?"

"Ennis hadn't paid," she said. "That was the problem."

"Was there a reason?"

"He told me his priorities had shifted. Problem was—they'd

already carved our name onto the building. The Fultz Wing for Children."

"So you fought?" Remy asked.

"Women of my stature don't fight, young lady," she said. "We argue, sure—"

"You're a nurse, right?" Remy interrupted her. We'd seen a picture of Connie in Fultz's house, from decades ago, in a white uniform.

"What?" she said, confused at the question. "Yeah, when I was young."

"So you know about dosages?" Remy asked.

I glanced at my partner. A couple blue fingers were far from proof that Fultz was poisoned.

Connie squinted at Remy. Started moving past us. "I'm gonna talk to your coroner. Find out what y'all are implying."

"Ma'am, did you sleep with your ex-husband that morning?" Remy asked.

"Rem," I blurted out.

The ex-wife turned, her face pale. "How would you—"

"I know this is delicate," Remy said. "But we found a condom in the trash."

Connie's nose scrunched up, and she looked madder than a hen dipped in water.

She pressed her green snow cone against Remy's white blouse. "There's a thing called decorum, young lady. Look it up." She dropped the paper cone and stormed off.

Remy looked dumbstruck, and I hustled after Connie Fultz.

I thought about the amount of grief we might walk into with the chief. If Connie knew Pernacek as well as her husband had.

"Mrs. Fultz," I hollered.

The ex-wife turned. But her face was different than I expected. A woman scorned.

"I haven't used protection with my husband since I was nineteen," she said.

Connie Fultz hit her key fob, and a white BMW convertible at the curb nearby chirped.

In my head, a synapse fired.

Connie hadn't denied having sex with Ennis. Yet the condom wasn't hers.

There was another woman in that house. After her.

She got in her car. "So I guess you're clear now—why we split up. I got tired of drinking to get over the women he was with. And he got tired of buying me the wine."

She hit the start button on the car, her door still ajar.

"But you know the saddest thing, Detective," she said. "I lied because I was embarrassed. I still love the son of a bitch. But after I left—" She shook her head. "Unbelievable."

Connie yanked the door shut. "He was a shitty husband and even worse of a father."

I tried to calm Connie down. "Listen—"

"You want a lead, Detective?" she interrupted me. "Look for some little gal who's into bondage. If you smell leather—you're headed in the right direction."

Connie pulled the wheel hard, and her BMW flew out into traffic.

Remy caught up with me, the mark from the snow cone a fluorescent green smear across her white blouse.

"Jesus H. Christ on a grain of rice," I said to my partner. I turned across the street toward the precinct. Remy followed me, knowing I was pissed.

"I realize I pushed her, P.T. But we got information, right?"

We walked into the station house.

"We don't have a cause of death," I said. "And Chief Pernacek is just filling in, Rem. Something like this blows back on him with the mayor. It blows back on us."

"But the DVD from the gas station, P.T. I had tech services put the footage on my laptop. We have a second camera on the road up to Fultz's house. If there's another woman, we're gonna find her now."

I considered what Connie Fultz had said. About leather and bondage.

If the ex-wife *wasn't* the killer, our window on time of death had just shrunk to the two and half hours after she left. Eleven-thirty to two p.m.

We stepped into my office, and Sarah was waiting there.

"I found something," she said, an excited tone in her voice. "Acidosis. Hypoxia."

"English," Remy said.

"Fultz was poisoned. But not in the usual way," Sarah said. "*Nitrogen* poisoning."

"That's a thing?" Remy asked.

Sarah nodded. "The only problem is—how do you get someone to breathe in nitrogen?"

The oxygen tank in Fultz's bedroom.

Someone had tampered with it.

8

Ten minutes later, Remy and I were in my truck and headed out to Fultz's house.

As police, we have a duty to preserve key pieces of evidence. At the top of that list is any weapon used to perpetrate a homicide.

If the oxygen tank had been tampered with—if the container had been refilled with nitrogen, lying in wait for Fultz to inhale— we needed to get that tank into our lab.

I got off of 906 and drove more slowly this time toward Fultz's house, taking in the stretch of land between the highway and the Valero. A logging project had stripped the area of trees, and low-lying creeping jenny grew horizontally, moving through the scrub brush like a water moccasin.

We found the gravel road that headed up to Fultz's house. Broke the evidence seal on the front door and headed up the stairs.

The metal container was larger than I realized, and we wrapped each end of the tank in a clear oversized plastic evidence bag, so as not to leave any of our prints on it.

As Remy lifted it up, I stared out a side window. The sun was dropping fast, and a three-wheeled all-terrain vehicle was parked just east of the house.

"Who the hell is that?" Remy said.

A young girl in a sundress sat on the ATV seat. Eight or nine years old, with black hair that fell to her shoulders.

"Probably that family who lives on the property," I said. We still needed to follow up with the couple that Ipsy had told us about.

We headed down, loading the tank into the cab of my truck before moving around to the side of the house.

As we walked over, the girl looked up, and we introduced ourselves as police. She had a striking look that was a mix ethnically. Half white and the other half maybe Hispanic or American Indian.

"What's your name, sweetheart?" Remy asked.

"Alita." The girl's eyes moved down to my partner's firearm, clipped at her waist. "Is that a gun?"

"It is," Remy said.

I stared around. *Is she out here alone?*

"Have you ever shot anyone?" Alita asked.

I interrupted her questions. "Are your folks around?"

"Dad!" she screamed in a voice that could be heard a quarter mile away.

A man broke through a hedge of brownish-green arborvitae. He wore a red and white flannel and held a cordless hedge trimmer in hand, the kind with teeth for contouring bushes.

The man dropped his headphones to around his neck. Introduced himself as Bill Lyman.

"Ipsy mentioned you live on the property," Remy said. "This is your daughter?"

"Yes, ma'am," the man said. He was white and in his thirties with a scruffy brown beard. Looked like the type of guy who knew how to change his own oil.

"You heard about Ennis?" Remy asked.

The man nodded, looking to his daughter and then back at us. A parental glance that told us his daughter knew that Fultz had died, but put us on notice about what to say in front of her.

"When's the last time you saw Ennis Fultz?" I asked.

"Last Thursday," Lyman said.

"And how about yesterday?" Remy asked. "Were you around the property?"

"I leave around six a.m. for work. Get home by five."

Lyman explained that he operated a crane in a sand and gravel pit north of town. I wondered whether he had access to nitrogen.

"And your wife?" Remy asked.

"She's a vet tech. Works with animals two days a week and two overnights. Mondays she's on days."

"I saw Mr. Fultz Saturday," the little girl volunteered.

"You saw him how?" Remy asked.

"He's my friend," she said. "We walk the trail each weekend."

Remy crouched. "And did Mr. Fultz *seem* sick?" she asked. "Was he breathing heavy?"

"No, ma'am," Alita said. "When we first started walking, he would take his tank with him. Roll it down the path."

"But not Saturday?" I asked.

"Not the last month," she said. "Mr. Fultz had lost twenty-six pounds. He does magic, you know. Sleight of hand tricks."

Bill Lyman looked down at his daughter. "Why don't you go home, hon. I'll finish up with the police."

The girl raised her eyebrows, a half smile. "Should I take the ATV?"

"Walk," her dad said.

Alita took off like a herd of turtles. Looking back at us twice as she meandered slowly down one of the maze-like paths through the scrub brush.

"Have you seen anyone suspicious around the property lately?" Remy asked Lyman.

The man shook his head. "I thought Ennis died in his sleep."

"We're keeping all options open," I said. "His housekeeper mentioned you lived here before he did. What was the arrangement, officially? Did you rent from him?"

"No," he said. "I know it sounds weird, but at first he just let us stay here, and I kept up what I was already doing maintaining the trails. No charge."

"At first?"

"Last summer, he asked me if I could start a project for him." Lyman motioned at a utility wagon attached to the ATV that was loaded with scrub brush. "I do fifteen hours a week."

"Of what?" Remy asked.

"I've been creating a series of pathways. Kinda like an English garden, except in the mountains. There's trails. Benches."

"For the public?"

"That was the idea." Lyman shrugged. "Eventually."

I thought about Fultz's changing priorities. "So what happens to your arrangement now?"

"I dunno," he said. "I called up his son, but haven't heard back."

He looked down the road, to where his daughter had gone. "I better head home," he said. "Make sure Alita gets there okay."

Remy took out a card and told him we'd follow up.

We turned back to my truck then and drove to the station in silence.

Ennis Fultz being poisoned meant we officially had a homicide on our hands.

It also meant that we'd discovered that fact a full day into the traditional forty-eight-hour window in which murders were statistically solved, if they were ever gonna be.

I felt the tension building. The kind that comes with the first long night of every investigation.

Because in our line of work, when you're chasing a case, there's no tomorrow. There's no time for anything but the lead. And if you're good at your job, it's obsessive in that way.

In my mind, I saw the possibilities lining up. Connie Fultz. The Lyman family. And some woman who Fultz had hooked up with after his ex-wife left.

But mostly there was the tank.

Someone had tampered with Fultz's oxygen. Someone who had access to it. Who knew how to unhook the tubing that led to the mask and connect it with a different, more dangerous substance. Someone who wanted Fultz dead.

9

Outside my office window, the sun fell out of the sky, and the silhouettes of banana palms moved in the darkness.

Remy tracked down a phone number for Travis Thorpe, the man who left the six bags of Marathon grass seed by Ennis Fultz's back stairs. Thorpe told us he'd talked to Ennis in person around four-thirty or five Sunday night. That was the afternoon *before* Fultz died, and we pinned this visit as the earliest moment that we trusted in our timeline.

"And he looked fine to you?" Remy asked Thorpe on speaker.

"Couple twinges in his hinges as he moved around, but nothing unexpected for a guy his age."

We thanked Thorpe and hung up.

Remy rolled the large portable whiteboard from the conference room into my office. Then we spent the next four hours with Remy pausing the DVD from the Valero station and me jotting down each make, model, and license plate of car that passed by the gas station.

I stared at the whiteboard when we got to the end. "Eighteen cars and two work trucks." Not an impossibly long list.

We focused first on the vehicles that drove past the Valero between ten a.m. and two p.m. Monday, the exact time slot that Sarah had estimated for Ennis Fultz's death.

We saw Connie Fultz's BMW head south toward the interstate, pinning the time she left the house at 11:08 a.m.

"If you believe her story," Remy said, "she was with Ennis a little under an hour."

Remy slowed the DVD at the time marked *11:45 a.m.*

A dark sedan flew by the gas station heading east in the direction of Fultz's house, hitting the green light by the Valero in stride. One of three cars and one truck that we'd listed as "miscellaneous" because we couldn't see a license plate.

"I think *this one*"—my partner pointed at the dark sedan and fast-forwarded the DVD to a later time—"is the same as *this one* coming back the other way at 12:40."

Remy swiveled her laptop screen so it faced me, and I stared at this later time.

A woman pulled into the Valero station, but didn't gas up. She got out and started unloading stuff from her back seat. Papers. Fast-food trash. She dumped everything in a garbage pail in between the gas pumps. Then moved to the other side of the car, continuing to do the same, cramming the two trash cans in between the pumps.

The woman had pulled into an area that was hard to see from the camera. Judging by the height of the car, she was petite. She wore a crop top and a black skirt.

"Is she white?" I asked, staring at the black-and-white video.

"Asian, I think," Remy said.

The woman walked over to the pump and typed something in. Then took a paper back to her car and pulled around the back side of the gas station.

"The hell's she doing?" I said, more to myself than my partner.

Remy took a screenshot of a particular angle on the car. She opened the screenshot in Photoshop and zoomed in on a corner of the woman's plate.

"B-Z-T-Eight," Remy said. "Those are the first four digits. Looks like a Honda."

Remy popped downstairs to have the late-night guys in Booking run the license plate.

While she was gone, I picked up the phone and called the Valero station. I got ahold of the same manager who'd helped us before.

"Tamara, what's behind your station?"

"How do you mean?" she said.

"Is there an air pump? Water?"

"We have an automated car wash."

"Can you buy a ticket for the car wash at the pump without getting gas?"

"Absolutely," she said.

"And your trash from Monday?" I asked. "Is it still around?"

"Gone like the water," Tamara said. "Picked up this morning."

I thanked her and hung up, staring at the paused video.

Remy walked back in.

"Falls Automotive Imports is the owner of the Honda," my partner said.

I knew the name. A used-car lot east of downtown.

"A 2008 Civic," Remy said. "And get this—"

"The title on the car is a day old," I said.

My partner shook her head. "I hate when you do that."

I pointed at the paused video. "She cleaned out the car. Got it washed. And then sold the thing. You check who the owner was the day before?"

"Suzy Kang," Remy said. "Thirty-two years old. Five foot three. Hundred and ten pounds. DMV lists her as Asian or Pacific Islander."

I studied the image.

"So maybe Ms. Kang went out to Ennis's place," Remy theorized. "Poisoned him after having sex. Cleaned him out. Then pulled into the Valero. Took every scrap of shit out of her car. And sold the old beater. What does that make her? A pro?"

I stared at the woman in the short skirt. Including drive time, she'd been in the house less than an hour. Which didn't give her a lot of time to dig up cash in his yard.

I reflected on what Connie Fultz had said about her ex-husband's proclivities with women. "She have a rap sheet?"

"Something sealed from juvenile," my partner said. "Nothing as an adult."

A condom in the trash every Tuesday, Ipsy had said.

"She might've been Fultz's regular girl," I said. "Maybe the ex-wife was the unexpected guest that morning."

I stood up. Looked at my phone. The date and time glowed in white: *May 8, 12:46 a.m.* We didn't have enough evidence to get a search warrant for Suzy Kang's home. At most right now, she was a person of interest.

"I can hardly keep my eyes open, and I gotta be at court in the morning," I said. "Why don't you go first thing and try to get a peek at her juvy record."

Remy's eyes tracked mine. "Officially?"

"Unofficially," I said. "Someone in Records must owe us a favor. We can meet here by ten."

I got home in fifteen minutes. Sarah's Acura was in my driveway and the house was dark. She was asleep already.

As I crossed the street, a light nearly blinded me. It was the rectangular shape of a mid-2000s Mustang's headlights, flashing on.

"Jesus, buddy," I said, putting up my hand to block the light. I didn't recognize the car as one of the neighbors.

The person flipped a U-turn and took off.

Inside, my house was quiet. I picked up Purvis's leash, and my eight-year-old bulldog heard the noise and came trotting out to the entry.

Instead of a walk, I loaded him into my truck and drove for ten minutes, slowing along the bridge at I-32, beside the Tullumy River.

To observers, Purvis is just a brown and white bulldog with a bad underbite. But he's something else to me. When I get out of sorts like I did last year, Purvis speaks to me—in a voice that resembles English. A voice that sounds like my own, but healthier—with enough added sanity to keep me alive on bad days.

I got out of my truck and climbed up so my legs dangled over the side of the bridge, pulling Purvis onto my lap.

The night air was cool, and it carried the lemon scent of sweet bay magnolias downstream, from some bank where they were planted a century ago.

I was forever linked to the water here. When I was six and hadn't yet learned to swim, I was dared by a friend to walk out onto a rock. I slipped on a slick of algae, fell in, but by some miracle, clung on to a piece of plywood that happened to be floating by.

Serendipity, my mom called it. The river gave life.

Thirty years later, my wife Lena's Jeep went into the Tullumy, and she and Jonas never breathed again.

I flipped open my wallet to a picture of my son sitting on my wife's lap on the front steps of our house. Jonas had beautiful honey-colored skin and a short reddish Afro that was a mix of my unkempt brown wavy hair and his mother's beautiful black curls.

I put the picture away.

"Happy birthday, Lena," I said.

I climbed down from the railing and got in my truck.

On the way home, I called Marvin, my dead wife's father, who I knew stayed up late and had been trying to reach me.

I got his voicemail. Which was my voice talking back to me, since I'd set up his iPhone last year.

"Marvin," I said. "I got your message, but I couldn't understand what you were saying. Call me."

At home, I parked in the empty spot where the Mustang had been earlier.

Inside, I wandered into the kitchen and stared out the window. A group of slash pines was planted by the neighbor's side yard, but in the darkness, they were just vertical shapes—invisible almost—brown lines against the blackness of night.

A friend of Sarah's had left a bottle of cane rum in the cupboard, and I poured a single shot to calm my nerves.

As I stared at the rum, Purvis sauntered into the room. A bead of drool hung from his mouth, halfway to the floor.

For real? my bulldog huffed. *We're doing this again?*

See, I told you he talks to me.

I dumped the shot down the drain, grabbed Purvis, and headed into Jonas's room.

I pulled my son's old comforter over my head and faded to sleep.

10

The girl was frozen.

She could reach up—in this upside-down world—and
release her seat belt. But her father had told her never to do this.

She remembered this moment—maybe a month ago. She'd
dropped her iPad while they were driving and un-clicked her seat
belt to grab the tablet. The car made a beeping noise, and Pop
hollered at her. He yelled like others had yelled in places she'd been
before.

She looked back at the Toyota. Her car was dangling at the side
of the road, and the bad man's truck moved backward toward them.

Suddenly, there was a light in the distance.

It flickered—"oscillated" was a word she'd recently learned—
getting brighter and then softer again.

She felt a sticky liquid along her face, and her throat pulsed.
Something had slammed against her neck when the Toyota truck
had hit their car.

The brightness got larger, until she saw it was a pair of lights *from an enormous truck. The high beams of a semi, pulling over onto the shoulder behind them.*

"Someone's coming," she whispered.

But from the front of the car, there was nothing.

No sound from Pop. Nothing from Momma.

Just silence. And danger. Because with adults, danger came. It always had.

11

By nine a.m. Wednesday, I made my way over to the criminal court building on 5th Street.

The Meadows case was moving ahead with no settlement in sight, and DA Yugel had asked me to sit in on the practice deposition of Detective Abe Kaplan.

Abe had been my partner years earlier, but was now paired with an older guy named Merle, who I occasionally bumped heads with. In the case that involved Donnie Meadows's death, Remy and I had folded Abe in as our third, to help out.

Abe was seasoned in the courtroom, but with Cat Flannery stepping it up, the DA had told me it was "good conditioning" to observe a couple practice depositions in advance, so that nothing shocked me in court.

I got to the second floor and found the meeting space that Liz Yugel had reserved.

Abe sat at one end of the room and Yugel at the other, about fifteen feet apart. A video camera rolled on the interview, and I slipped into the back of the room.

"Patrolman O'Conner reported that you and Detective Marsh got into a fight that night at approximately one forty-five a.m.," Yugel said. "Is that true?"

Abe wore a salmon-colored linen jacket with a mint-green shirt underneath. "I wouldn't call it a fight," he said.

"You weren't in a fight?" the DA asked, playing the role of Cat the Tiger. "Was the patrolman lying?"

It was certainly true that Abe and I had gotten into a spat during the last few hours of that investigation.

"We tussled a bit," he said.

"You *tussled*?"

"We rolled around in the dirt for a few seconds," Abe said. "It was no boxing match."

Yugel removed the blue button-down sweater she wore over her tan dress and consulted her legal pad. "What was the fight about?"

Abe ran a hand through his hair. He was half black and half Russian Jew, and he had a broad muscular chest and an Afro that grew patchy in places.

"There was a misunderstanding," he said, underplaying the details.

"Detective Marsh accused you of being a dirty cop?" Yugel asked, pushing the button that Cat the Tiger would push.

"Tempers were running high," Abe said.

"We're here today because of a potential overuse of force by Detective Marsh. Was he acting outside of police procedure, in your opinion?"

"I couldn't tell you."

"You don't have an opinion?"

"I wasn't at the cave where he and Donnie Meadows squared off. When I saw him, it was a half hour later."

My phone buzzed, and I looked down. A text from Remy told me the chief wanted an in-person update on Fultz. We'd sent him a note regarding Sarah's poisoning finding earlier that morning.

I stood up to go, but Yugel shot me a look.

"Did Detective Marsh seem out of control?"

"No."

"Yet he punched you in the jaw?" Yugel said. "So that's Detective Marsh *in control*? Just so we have a baseline on what's normal for him."

"His partner had just been shot, ma'am," Abe said. "Sometimes adrenaline runs high, and boys will be boys, you know. We push each other around. Tussle. No harm, no foul."

Yugel paused the camera and took a note in her yellow legal pad.

"I like that," she said to Abe in a different tone. In her own voice. "I think this 'down-home wisdom thing'—'boys will be boys'—it's a good instinct, Detective."

Abe ran his tongue over his lip. I knew my old partner well, and he didn't like his personal style being referred to as some act.

"Unless you got more for me," Abe said, getting up from the chair, "I've done this a hundred times, Liz."

"Sure," Yugel said. "You're ready."

Abe grabbed the twenty-year-old briefcase he always carries

around. Walked over to me. "Remy said this Fultz case is officially a homicide."

I nodded. "If Merle can ride solo for a while," I said, referring to Abe's partner, "we could use your help."

"We're slow," he said. "Consider me on the team, brother."

Abe nodded to the DA without speaking and walked out.

Yugel faced me. "You and I are gonna need a *full* day," she said. "For your prep."

I didn't want to do any prep.

"Tell me the time and place," I said. "Be there with bells on."

Yugel grabbed her briefcase and packed the camera in its bag. "Who is Vonte Delgado, by the way?"

"Why?" I asked.

"Cat Flannery requested his police file."

Cat the Tiger was browsing old cases of mine.

"He's a dirtbag who imprisoned his own daughter," I said, realizing Cat's strategy was to paint me as a recidivist killer. "Before your time, Liz. And just so you know, I shot him before the DA back then could show the world how guilty he was."

The DA nodded, understanding Cat's approach.

"I get it that you don't want to be here, Detective," she said. "But don't make the city overpay a murderer's family."

She headed past me, reciting the type of lines we'd practiced that I was supposed to say. Lines that proved I didn't have a death wish when I went after Donnie Meadows. "You were looking forward to your next vacation," Liz said.

"I was looking forward to my next vacation," I repeated.

"You were buying Christmas presents," she said and walked out the door.

I stared out the window at a pair of sago palms as they fluttered in the wind.

This was a line I couldn't force myself to say. There were only two people I ever loved shopping for at Christmas. And I'd lost both of them.

12

Remy and I briefed Abe on the Fultz case, giving him the details we'd gathered so far on Connie Fultz and Suzy Kang. Then we left him with the murder book and the DVD from the Valero and headed out to find Suzy.

"You drive," I said to Remy.

"Sure, hold on," she said, taking out her phone.

My partner is one of the smartest people I've ever met, but she rarely knows where her damn car keys are. Recently, she bought these GPS locator thingies and attached them to everything she owns.

I heard a chime from deep within the folds of my office couch.

"Got 'em," Remy hollered, closing the app on her phone.

We headed out then into what cops call the numbered streets, a three-by-six-mile quadrant where half the crimes in Mason Falls are planned, if not carried out.

Remy had an address from Suzy Kang's Honda Civic registration, and we hoped Ms. Kang could tell us what she was doing at Ennis Fultz's place. If in fact she was out there.

My partner looked over at me as she drove. "It was a no-go on seeing Suzy Kang's juvy record, by the way."

"Who'd you try?"

"Fescue," she said, naming a clerk downtown.

"Text Abe," I said. "He'll get the info."

Remy turned at 23rd and slowed. A green and white two-story motel from the 1960s had been converted into apartments. The address on the registration read #103.

We got out and Remy took her long dark hands and flattened the wrinkles out of her pants. She motioned at the structure in front of us. "Feels a little low-rent for a woman consorting with a multimillionaire," she said.

Outside number 103, a woman sat on a white plastic lawn chair, a pack of Parliament cigs on the ground beside her. She looked like forty miles of bad road.

"Is Suzy Kang around?" Remy asked.

The woman was white and in her thirties, her face wind-burnt and dirty. She looked past Remy, and her eyes landed on me.

"What do you want with her?"

Remy flashed her badge. "Her 2008 Honda Civic was stolen," she lied. "We think we may have found it."

A nearby teenager on a skateboard planted his feet wrong. The board smacked hard on the sidewalk and flew out from under him.

"Someone stole that piece of shit?" The woman grinned, showing off a missing tooth on the right side of her mouth.

"Does Suzy live here?" Remy asked.

The woman crushed out her cigarette against the concrete. "Nah, but maybe I got an address for her somewhere. C'mon in."

The woman held the door open, and Remy entered. I followed behind her, catching the screen door and leaving it ajar.

Inside, the furniture was threadbare. Only a few lights were on. The woman took off her pea-green army coat, and the smell of body odor moved toward us.

"What's your name, darlin'?" I asked.

"Patty," the woman said.

I saw a notice from superior court on the kitchen counter. The envelope was a half-inch thick and unopened. Addressed to a Patty Snade.

"When's the last time you saw Suzy?"

"Maybe two months ago," she said.

"So she *used* to live here?" Remy asked.

"Nah, it's her brother that does," the woman said. "Him and me dumpster-dive together. Suzy just uses the address for mail. She comes by and grabs it every month. When she's flush, she gives us a few hundreds for our trouble."

"Where's she working these days?" Remy asked.

The woman didn't answer. She stared at me, and I thought of what Connie Fultz had said about leather and bondage. And now Patty describing Suzy as "flush" with "hundreds."

I took a chance on something.

"Is Suzy dancing still?" I asked.

Patty smiled. "Nah, she didn't like it much. She's not like us, you know?"

I cocked my head. "No, how do you mean?"

"I don't mean us, us." She motioned at me and Remy. "She wasn't like me and Wyatt, her brother. She's classy, y'know? She didn't like guys touching her for small bills."

"Yeah." I nodded. "I get that."

Outside, the skateboard hit the sidewalk again, and we waited. Remy and I had this silent thing where we stare around and stay awkwardly quiet. We call it "STFU time"—and generally, when we shut the fuck up, people start talking.

"Well, I'm guessing she'd want to know if y'all found her car," Patty said finally.

"That's why we're here," I said. "You heard of 'protect and serve,' right? This is the serve part."

I pulled out my phone. Found the picture from the gas station video. I zoomed in, past the point where you could see Suzy Kang, to where it was just the car.

"This is the car we found." I turned my cell for Patty to see. "Some dirtbag unloaded the Honda at a used-car lot. Thing is, once the dealer sells the car, it's gone through too many hands to get it back to Suzy. Y'understand?"

"Sure," Patty said. "Makes sense."

"So you have that address?" I asked.

"She's got a place she stays at in downtown Atlanta," Patty said. "Guess I don't got the number, but her brother says it's easy to find. You know those bars where you gotta wear a ski jacket? They make 'em cold on purpose?"

I looked to Remy.

"I've been there on a date," she said. "It's called Sub Zero Ice Bar. In Little Five Points."

"Well, Wyatt said she lives right across from that."

I wanted more info from Patty. I motioned to the superior court envelope. "Everything okay?" I asked.

"I dunno," she said. "I reckon so."

I pulled out a business card. "You get in a corner and need help with the DA, you call me, all right?"

Patty took the card, her smile showing off a second missing tooth.

"Suzy's car," I said. "It's odd. It being way up north here, while she's living in Atlanta. The car was found off 906."

Patty thought for a second. "Oh yeah, well there's some old rich guy she visits lately. She goes out to his house by the canyon and hangs out once a week. They talk." Patty gave me a look. "Do other stuff, I guess."

The pieces were coming together now—Suzy Kang and the old man. I thought of something my mom used to say. That there's no fool like an old fool.

"Classier way to make some cash, huh?" I said to Patty.

"Sure is," she said.

I pulled out two twenties and pressed them into her hand. "Stay safe, okay?"

"God bless."

We walked back to the Alfa.

"That was nice of you," Remy said. "Giving her your card."

"That was Merle's card," I said. "She smelled like his type."

Remy smirked at this and fired up the Alfa.

"Well, we know what Suzy does for a living," my partner said.

I nodded. "Let's get to the car dealer. Patty here hasn't seen Suzy in a month, but they did business with her yesterday."

13

Falls Automotive Imports was located on a corner lot off 7th Avenue and 31st Street, about five minutes away.

At 31st, I motioned at a parking lot, and Remy turned, pulling onto cracked asphalt. A low-slung white building was at the far side of the lot. In front of the structure, four cars had their hoods open, each one of them sporting a white cardboard sign with a single letter in red, the four signs spelling out the word *SALE*, visible at two hundred feet.

We parked and walked toward the building, but halfway there, a tall guy in a black polo shirt and khakis intercepted us.

"You looking to dump that old Alfa?" He smiled, and put out his hand to my partner. "Isaac," he said.

"Remy."

He was good-looking. In his twenties and white, a fade in the back and product slicking up his dark hair in the front. He dressed more like a caddy at a golf resort.

"Isaac," Remy said, "I'm gonna be buried in that car. No chance of me selling."

The guy turned to me. "So *you're* looking for something. Let me guess. Truck guy, right? Silverado? F-150?"

"Sedan," I said. "A 2008 Honda Civic."

Isaac stopped walking and smiled at the specificity of the model and make.

"Green," I said, flashing him some tin.

"Official police work, huh? I get that. I sell to a *lot* of cops."

He steered us across the lot in a new direction that wrapped around the back of the white building. "You tell me what you need for business." He flicked his eyebrows. "And the next time you're looking for a truck, maybe you come by."

"Sounds fair," I said.

Isaac slowed and pointed at Suzy's Honda, in front of us. "Now, I bought this free and clear, and I checked the title and her ID twice. Gave her a fair deal too."

"Mind if we look inside?"

"Be my guest."

Remy tossed me a pair of latex, and we gloved up.

"Now, y'all would tell me if this was used in a crime, right?" Isaac said.

We didn't answer him. Just flipped the doors open.

"We just vacuumed the car," he said. "We do a hundred-and-nineteen-point check on any car we take in. From brakes to tires to engine. This is a reputable place."

The good news was that the car dealership owned the vehicle, and Isaac had just given us consent to look inside. The bad news was that nothing we found would be usable as evidence. Too many hands had touched it.

The car was empty, which we expected since Suzy Kang had cleaned it out, and now so had Isaac.

"What can you tell us about the seller?" I asked.

"Korean gal," he said. "Wanted to upgrade to something fancier."

"So this was a trade-in?"

"Oh yeah, she got a used Mercedes E350. A 2010. Low mileage for that age. Forty-two thou. You know—if you're looking for a truck with low mileage—I can guarantee you—"

"She finance with you, Isaac?" I asked.

"Nope." He smiled. "That's the funniest part. This car—plus nine thousand dollars in cash."

Remy had been looking in the trunk, and she pulled her head around.

"Cash cash?" my partner said.

"Like a brick," Isaac said. "Had the money in her purse. Kinda freaked me out at first—that many crisp hundred dollar bills. But from her dress, ya know . . ." He looked at Remy, who had walked over.

"You don't have to mince words around me, Isaac," Remy said in this sexy voice she does. "I'm not shy."

"Well, let's just say her skirt was so short you could almost see to the promised land," he said. "And leather. She wore one of those white"—he motioned at his own chest—"strip things."

"A tube top?" Remy said.

Isaac nodded.

"So you figured, what?" I said. "She was a stripper? An escort?"

He put up his hands. "Hey, I just sell cars, man."

"She use all that brick?" Remy asked. "Or was the nine grand only part of what she had on her?"

"Oh, she had more in her purse," he said. "Maybe another six or seven. All in stacks, sealed in plastic."

"We'll need the details on that Mercedes," I said. "Plates, VIN number."

Isaac hustled back to the white building. I sat down on the passenger seat of the Honda and looked at my partner. "You thinking what I'm thinking?"

Remy had her phone out and was searching for something.

"That she cleaned out the toaster oven at Ennis's house?" Remy asked. "Got out the shovel and dug up Fultz's cash?"

"Not just that," I said. "She must've been a regular. To do all that. And get in and out so fast."

I opened the glove box. The original Civic manual was inside.

I flipped through the book. Stuck into a page were three or four copies of the same glossy pamphlet, the front featuring a picture of a woman's leg, covered in leather bindings. *Decadance,* the brochure read, along with an address in a suburb near Atlanta.

"The boss man doesn't look happy, P.T.," Remy said.

I looked up. Isaac was headed back, an older guy with him.

I flipped to the inside of one of the pamphlets. Decadance wasn't a strip bar. It was some private club. A sex dungeon.

"I'm on the car lot's website," Remy said. She held up her phone, showing off a photo of a white Mercedes E350. I heard the sound of Remy's phone taking a screenshot.

"The car Suzy bought, P.T.," my partner continued. "They haven't taken it down yet. I got the plates and VIN number right here."

I turned my back to the approaching boss and slipped one of the pamphlets into my sport coat pocket. Put the car manual and the other pamphlets back.

"Detectives," the older man said. "My name is Dave Kurtin. I'm the sales manager here. You have a warrant to search this car?"

"We don't," I said. "But your colleague Isaac was nice enough to give us consent."

The older guy turned to Isaac. "Well, let me revoke that. This is private property. If you want anything here, you'll need to make a formal request. I assume you know how to do that?"

I smiled. Some people just don't like cops.

"We're gonna get a warrant for the cash Suzy Kang gave you," I said. "We need to look at the serial numbers."

The older guy motioned at the small white trailer at the back of the lot. "You think we kept that much scratch sitting overnight in this neighborhood? That went to the bank the minute that woman left."

I looked around the place. Probably half their sales were in cash. If Suzy's money was already in the bank, it'd be mixed in with other deposits and impossible to legally connect with Fultz.

I turned away—no need for these two to see my frustration— but I kept in mind that at least Remy had the VIN number of the new car.

I turned back. "Thanks for your time, fellas."

"Come see me about that truck," Isaac hollered.

We got back in the Alfa and drove out of the lot, talking about what we had and didn't have on Suzy Kang. The reality was—she was the closest thing to a suspect. At the same time, she was

only a person of interest. And the main reason was that everything we'd lined up so far was based on assumptions.

We assumed Suzy was an escort, but she had no rap sheet.
We assumed she robbed Ennis Fultz, but had no proof that the
cash she bought the car with wasn't her own. And we assumed
that the theft of the money was the reason she killed the
old man.

"Well, if we're right," Remy said. "She's still got a bag of hundreds burning a hole in her pocket. Presuming Fultz took the
money out in bulk from his bank, they'd order new cash from the
central bank, right?"

"For high dollar amounts, sure."

"So either Fultz or his bank might've marked down the serial
numbers."

"Possibly," I said.

Meaning that if we found Suzy with that cash in hand, we
could trace those serial numbers to what Ennis Fultz had with-
drawn. Making her our thief and murder suspect.

It also meant that if we *didn't* catch her with the cash, we
were shit out of luck.

"So what would *you* do if you were her?" Remy asked.

"To clean the money?" I shrugged. "I'd go somewhere where
changing a lot of money doesn't pop on someone's radar."

"Casino?" Remy asked.

"It's a good thought," I said. "Change out the cash for chips.
Wander the floor a couple hours and then change it back.
Only problem," I said, "the nearest one's in North Carolina. Five
hours away."

There were other places to gamble, but unless you were a degenerate and knew the underground life, Georgia had been strict in keeping most gaming out of the state.

"Suzy's Korean, right," Remy said. "Korean Air flies out of Hartsfield-Jackson. If she lives in Little Five Points, the airport's twenty minutes away."

I saw where Remy was going. "Maybe she's got family overseas," I speculated. "Splits town? Exchange the money somewhere else—where no one cares or knows her?"

"It's a theory," Remy said.

"Then why blow nine grand of the cash buying the Mercedes?"

My partner shrugged, and I called up Abe, back at the precinct.

"What's up, podna?" he said, his go-to phrase from back home in Louisiana.

"You know any cops who work out of Hartsfield-Jackson?"

"Is a yard dog barefoot?" Abe asked. "You tell me what you need, and I'll get it going."

I motioned toward the airport, and Remy found the center lane, spinning the wheel left toward the interstate.

I asked Abe to check travel manifests. See if Suzy had booked a flight in the last day. In the meantime, we'd keep heading south. Both the airport and Suzy's place in Little Five Points were in the same direction.

Remy got on the on-ramp, and we passed a small roadside lake of fetid green water. A fifteen-foot skiff sat down one end, a tree trunk growing through the middle of the hull.

I checked my phone, and Remy glanced over. "You got somewhere to be, rook?"

I smirked. This was a line I used to say to her when we started working together.

"Hot date tonight?" she followed up with.

Which was what I always said next.

I had to laugh. "I'm afraid that's your territory," I said. "Sarah and I have kinda settled into a rhythm."

"Good rhythm or bad rhythm?"

Sarah worked with me and Remy on a daily basis, so as soon as I brought it up, I regretted saying a thing.

"New subject," I said.

But Remy was like me. And most bull terriers. She didn't let things go.

"You guys are together what—five months?" Remy said.

When I didn't answer, she gave me a look. "As women, you know, we have certain checkpoints."

"Meaning what?" I said.

"She's not living there, right?"

"No," I said. "Not officially."

"Not officially?" Remy shook her head. "That is such a man's answer."

"Well," I chuckled, "I am kind of a man."

"What's she got?" Remy asked. "A drawer?"

"She's got a whole dresser." I shrugged. "I mean, I got the space. Lena's sister came and took her stuff away in January."

Remy gave me this look. "You having fun with Sarah—getting some tail?"

Sometimes my partner can act more like a man than me.

"Don't be like that," I said.

"Well, *your* problem is that your house is a museum, boss. Sarah's a grown-ass woman. If you want to make it work with her—and she's over there even half the time—you need some 'you and her' things. Not old things."

My phone buzzed, and I happily changed the subject by putting Abe on speaker. "You find an airport cop?"

"I did one better," he said. "Suzy Kang bought a one-way ticket to Fort Lauderdale. Spirit Airlines."

The departure time Abe gave us was only twenty-five minutes away, so we hustled to the airport, connecting with a cop named Brodovic and running at full speed through the terminal.

We arrived at Gate D3 just after the plane left.

"Shit," I said, out of breath.

"At least we know where she is," Remy said, not at all out of breath. "We could get airport police on the other end to pick her up."

Brodovic walked over to us. He'd been talking to the lady at the Spirit gate, and his face was scrunched up.

"Guys, she ain't on that plane."

I squinted at Brodovic. "You sure?"

"They called her name multiple times. No-show."

I leaned against the large windows that faced out to the landing strips. Why the hell would someone buy a ticket an hour ago and not use it?

I thought about the airline choice and destination.

Spirit was a discount airline, and Fort Lauderdale was probably the cheapest ticket they sold.

"She was never flying out," I said. "She wanted access to the terminal."

"What for?" Remy asked.

"Is there a currency exchange in the airport?" I asked Brodovic.

"There's one right around the corner," the stocky cop said. He walked us over to the Travel-Xchange, which had a small kiosk built into the wall. We showed the lady at the counter a picture of Suzy.

"Yeah, she was in here an hour ago. Changed about six grand into Hong Kong currency."

I tried to picture Suzy moving through the airport.

"Did she head toward the gates afterward like she was leaving on a flight?"

The woman shrugged. "I didn't notice."

"The money she turned in," I said. "All hundreds?"

The clerk nodded. The money Isaac at the dealership saw.

"We're gonna need the serial numbers on those bills," Remy said to the teller. She motioned up at a camera angling down on us. "And that camera footage."

"Of course," the woman said. "But I'm gonna need a warrant."

Remy took out her tablet to get the paperwork started. I stood back, looking down the long walkway that led away from Concourse D.

If Suzy had a ticket to Hong Kong, Abe would've already found that flight.

I had started my career in burglary, years ago. Which was a godsend, because the best way to learn about people is to study thieves.

See, homicides happen for a reason: a grudge, a jealousy, and so on. But burglary is a crime of opportunity. The only way to solve it is to think opportunistically—like a criminal.

I turned to the clerk at the window. "Is there *another* Travel-Xchange in the airport?"

"Sure." The woman pointed. "Concourse E."

We headed that way, and like I'd guessed, Suzy had changed the Hong Kong dollars back into U.S. bills. She'd cleaned the money, in exchange for five points on the dollar.

Brodovic knew the woman in this second change window better and flirted with her. "Beth's a real peach," he said to us while he smiled at the blonde. "One of the good ones."

I decided to use his good standing with the teller to our advantage. "What do you say to giving us a peek at that camera footage?"

Beth looked to Brodovic and shrugged. "*I* can rewind the footage and look. If y'all happen to be standing here watchin' too, so be it."

She rewound the video, and we saw Suzy Kang standing at the window. She stacked the red and green currency on the counter and handed the money over to Beth.

"These two," Remy said as we watched. "With Suzy stealing and Ennis having sex with her *and* his ex-wife on the same day—they *belong* together."

"All the qualities of good dogs," I said. "Except for loyalty."

We hurried out to find Suzy at that address near the ice bar in downtown.

We had enough for Abe to get a warrant for the first exchange window. Which would get us the serial numbers on that cash.

With Suzy on video and what Isaac gave us at the car lot, all we had to do was find Suzy with one of Fultz's hundreds or the new cleaned money and she'd be wearing cuffs.

Game over. Case closed.

14

The girl gasped and her eyes flew open.

She was lying on a board of some sort. With a curved divot that ran down the middle.

A face appeared over her. It was the nice man from the semi. The one who'd pulled behind the Hyundai before the Toyota could get to them.

"The little girl's awake," the man hollered at someone.

The nice man leaned close. Blue and red lights flickered across his glasses. "Just hold tight, honey."

"There's a guy who hit us," the girl mumbled.

The nice man looked at the Hyundai and then back at the girl.

"I think your daddy just hit the bridge," he said. "But you'll be okay."

"I saw him," the girl said. "I know his face."

The nice man stood up as if he didn't hear her.

She heard someone say the words "field test" and yell for "another back brace."

Then another voice was talking. She heard the word "motorcade," and a fireman loomed over her.

"Easy now," the fireman said as her body was lifted up. "Easy. Easy."

The little girl tried to move, but orange straps were tied around her body, to keep her in place. And something puffy was around her face and neck.

They placed her down, and the nice man leaned over again. "I think you've had a concussion, little lady," he said. "Try to close your eyes and rest. You got bumps and bruises, but you're gonna be okay."

She closed her eyes like the man said.

In a moment she felt herself being lifted up again. She blinked and saw she was inside an ambulance.

A new voice echoed gruffly from outside. "Hey, I was just driving by. You guys need help?"

"Sure," the nice man said. "There's no cops around."

The girl tried to move her head. To see who owned this gruff voice, but she couldn't. She was locked in place.

Then the nice man walked away, and the gruff man leaned in to the ambulance for a moment. He made eye contact, and the girl saw the same face she'd seen in the white truck.

The man who hit them.

The gruff man disappeared then, and the girl tried to get up. To unstrap the belts that held her down. But she was locked in place, and her throat burned when she tried to speak.

"Say, where you fellas takin' these folks anyway?" the gruff voice asked someone. "They going to the county hospital?"

15

We had Suzy Kang, dead to rights. We just needed to locate her.

With Abe working on the warrant, Remy and I hustled along 85 toward Atlanta to find that ice bar that Patty back at the motel had mentioned.

While my partner drove, I used her iPad to read a file that Sarah had emailed us about Ennis Fultz's medical condition.

COPD was classified from mild to severe, the degree determined mostly by the results of a series of lung function tests.

In essence, the disease caused air to move more slowly through the body, which was bad news for the small blood vessels and air sacs inside the lungs. When all these vessels and sacs were gone, oxygen had trouble getting into the bloodstream.

"How's this thing end?" Remy asked. "Did Fultz have any end-stage symptoms?"

I looked to Remy. "It lists inability to do physical activity—"

"But he was walking three miles a day," my partner said.

"Low body mass index," I said. "But he was muscular. And severe shortness of breath."

"Meanwhile, he's banging hookers," Remy said.

My partner took the exit for Central Avenue, and I saw the golden dome of the Georgia State Capitol off to our right.

"So . . . what?" Remy squinted at me. "Fultz wasn't sick? This Kang woman murdered a healthy man?"

"He *was* sick," I said. "He just mustn't have let the disease get in the way of what he wanted to do."

The report concluded that if the tank had contained nitrogen in order to deliberately kill Fultz, that once he became incapacitated, the rest of the nitrogen would dissipate into the atmosphere inside the home. Undetectable.

My phone buzzed, and I put Remy's iPad down.

"Abe just texted," I said. "He's got Suzy's sealed juvy record."

"And?"

I clicked the attachment he sent. "She got caught selling nitrous oxide when she was seventeen."

"Whip-its?" Remy said. "People did that in high school. It's not exactly a high crime, P.T. They sell mini canisters nowadays on eBay. A buck a pop."

"'Cept here, there's the obvious," I said.

"She knows her way around a tank of nitrogen?"

I thought about the classic pieces of conviction: motive, means, and opportunity.

"She was at Fultz's house." I put up a finger. "She knows how to work with a nitrogen tank." A second finger. "And she stole and laundered his money." I put up a third.

The GPS on Remy's phone told us we'd arrived at the address of the ice bar in Little Five Points.

Remy pulled to the curb. Threw a police placard onto the dash.

The Little Five Points neighborhood had improved dramatically since I came here when I was young. Hipsters filled coffee shops. Old cotton mills and factory plants had been stripped back to their essence. And lofts rented for three grand a month.

Remy stepped out of the car, and we walked over to the front door of Sub Zero Ice Bar. I pressed my face to the window and noticed that everything inside was made of ice.

"You don't freeze your ass off in there?"

"They give you parkas," Remy said. "You sip vodka, and it's like you're outside in Siberia."

I rolled my eyes. "Sounds like I picked the perfect time to quit drinking."

I glanced at the building across the way. Ten stories of red brick. An old-style vertical neon sign read *Factory Lofts* down one side.

We entered the building's lobby and walked toward a slender man in a checked shirt and Dockers. He sat behind a white counter and wore a name tag that read *Xander*.

I flashed him my badge. "We need to speak with one of your residents. Suzy Kang."

"Of course." He nodded, typing some information into his computer. He squinted before looking up.

"Wait—we don't have any Suzy Kang here."

Remy pulled out her phone and showed Xander a picture.

"Oh, her," he said. "Yeah, she's a guest of Mr. West. Not a resident, but I see her all the time."

He started to punch some keys again, his head down. "She works out a lot." He shifted his gaze to see in between Remy and me. "Usually around lunch."

We turned to see what Xander was looking at. A set of glass doors led to a gym that faced Euclid Street, the other direction from the bar.

Inside, two women rose up and down on ellipticals.

A third was bent over, a towel draped atop her head.

"In pink," Remy said, motioning to the third woman.

The towel came off her head, and the woman looked up. She was petite and Asian. Looked to be about thirty.

We moved toward her, and she dropped the towel. Turned the other way.

We took off, swinging open the glass doors to the gym and threading around elliptical machines and treadmills, a sea of black and rubber.

An alarm sounded, and I raced toward the noise. At the far end of the room was an emergency exit.

I swung the door open, entering a stairwell. The steps led down for one floor to a parking garage. I cocked my head and saw a flash of pink above us.

"We just wanna talk," I hollered, taking the steps two at a time all the way up to the fifth floor before catching my breath.

Remy passed me by a stairwell that read 6 in orange lettering.

"I see her," Remy yelled. A moment later, she threw open the door to the roof.

Air conditioners sat every ten or fifteen feet, their turbines spinning. I hurried around the space, looking behind the AC boxes. No sign of her.

"Damn it," I said, my breathing heavy. "You think she got out on some other floor?"

"No way," Remy said.

I walked over to the far edge of the roof. Suzy was moving fast, arm over arm, down a fire escape ladder. Too far ahead for us to catch up.

She got to a rooftop area with a Jacuzzi and some outdoor chairs. Dropped the last few feet to the ground and sprinted into the building.

My partner stared over the edge, her eyes following Suzy. "Fucking cat woman."

"C'mon," I said. "She made us fast, but we'll get a BOLO on her Mercedes. We know where she lives. Let's get our paperwork done, and half the cops in Atlanta will be looking for her."

We took the elevator down and talked to Xander at the concierge desk. "Hank West," he said in response to inquiries about who Suzy stayed with. "He owns the penthouse on eight. It's half the floor."

"Let me guess," I said. "Ms. Kang visits once a week?"

"No, she's here every day."

I blinked. So this was Suzy's steady boyfriend, not a client. Remy jotted down Hank West's particulars, and we walked out to the Alfa.

Suzy had dumped her car and stolen the money, but she did both well before we even knew her name.

Was it possible she wasn't on the run and had simply returned to her daily routine?

I knew a detective named Mandelle Clearson who worked in

Atlanta Homicide, and we decided to head to the nearby precinct for assistance. Mason Falls is pretty rural compared to Atlanta, and I'd helped Mandelle hunt down this shitbrick who'd knocked off his wife three years ago and was hiding in our area.

"Marsh." Mandelle greeted me in the lobby of the precinct with a tough handshake. This would also serve as our official notice that we were working on a lead in what Atlanta PD called Zone 5.

I introduced Mandelle to Remy. He was a big guy in his late forties. Tall with wavy salt-and-pepper hair. I filled him in on the particulars, and he offered to run the name "Hank West" for us.

"Well, nothing criminal," Mandelle said as he ambled back from the printer with a DMV sheet. "One speeding ticket a year ago," he said. "Drives a Porsche 911. Name is familiar, though. I think he's an attorney in town here."

I asked Mandelle to put out an all-points on Suzy Kang, and he offered to go by Hank West's place on the way home from work. Chat him up if the guy was home.

I thanked him, and Remy and I walked out to her car.

I could tell my partner was frustrated, but this is the job. Long hallways with dead ends.

I pulled out the brochure I'd snaked from Suzy's car. "Well, there's this," I said. "Got it from her glove box."

Remy looked at the pamphlet. "Is it a strip bar?"

"Some sort of swinger's club," I said.

"What's the angle?" my partner asked. "The local cops are watching Suzy's apartment. The new car's got a BOLO. This is a safe place to regroup?"

"She had multiple copies of the brochure," I said. "And remember what Fultz's ex said about leather and bondage? My guess is Suzy works here."

I called Johnny Tobin in Financial Crimes and asked for a quick background check on Suzy Kang.

Tobin worked the financial end of any crime in Mason Falls. A former CPA turned detective, Tobin assisted in every area from homicide to burglary to sex crimes.

"A company called Deca LLC is listed as Suzy's employer," Tobin said. There was a nasal quality when he spoke, as if he were constantly stuffed up.

"What else?"

"Average credit. The address you already know at that motel. This 'Deca LLC' thing is probably as close as you're gonna get to a confirmation she works at Decadance."

I thanked him and hung up. Remy was studying the brochure.

"Boss," she said. "This place doesn't open until ten p.m."

Remy and I decided we'd take a two-hour supper break, and visit Club Decadance after sundown. Dinner and dancing, detective style.

As we headed back to Mason Falls, Remy talked about volunteering in the evenings lately with a few guys in the K-9 unit. This was a small group with three patrol cops working with dogs. They had been helping out with the County in the last month.

"This is after the dogfighting problem?" I asked.

"Exactly," Remy said.

In the wake of a recent scandal, Mason Falls Police Department had taken over supervision of Animal Services from County.

There was some talk that they might be looking to staff a couple real cops there as "Humane Law Enforcement Officers."

"What exactly are you doing?" I asked.

Remy shrugged. "Animal abuse cases . . . serving warrants on suspected puppy mills."

My partner had grown up in a rural area called Harmony and missed being with the four-legged. Then again, in homicide we dealt with animals all the time. They just shared more of our DNA.

Remy drove down Hannover Avenue, heading toward my place.

"So two hours and then back at it?" I said.

Remy nodded and pulled to the curb. "I've been thinking about Suzy," she said. "There's something you told me my first week on the job."

"What's that?"

"The guilty ones run," Remy said.

"Sure," I said. "And lucky us—we get paid to catch 'em."

16

I got out and walked across to my house. As I opened the door, I smelled garlic and basil. Purvis tore around the corner, and I crouched to let him climb into my arms.

Sarah was in the kitchen. A V-neck T-shirt and cutoff jean shorts, an apron tied over them.

"Dinner," I said. "Wow, this is a nice surprise."

"Figured we hadn't seen each other in two days, outside of a crime scene. Thought you might like a little chicken parm."

"From the smell of this guy's mouth"—I held up Purvis—"I think he likes a little chicken parm too."

Sarah gave me a peck on the cheek. "I might've given him a small piece."

I walked to the bedroom and jumped in a hot shower to clear my head. When I came out in jeans and a T-shirt, Sarah was in the small eat-in kitchen. The breaded chicken sat beside a pile of angel hair pasta covered in tomatoes.

She described how she'd been off work most of the day. She'd met with DA Yugel on the Donnie Meadows case in the morning and decided not to go back afterward.

"This was a practice deposition?" I asked.

She shook her head. "My stuff's all factual, hon. Amount of blood loss. Number of stab marks. It's considered bad form to coach us on whether there's twenty-five or twenty-six entry wounds."

Purvis moved underfoot, and I chuckled. "There weren't twenty-six entry wounds in Donnie Meadows's body."

Sarah stopped eating. "There were *exactly* twenty-six entry wounds, P.T. Tell me you're not gonna walk into court and deny that. Make one of us look like an idiot."

Yeah, tell us, hon, Purvis snorted.

I took a bite. "I'm kidding," I said. My head was spinning from how this number must've sounded at Sarah's depo. What cop in their right mind would stab Donnie Meadows twenty-six times?

Sarah sliced her chicken in one direction and then the other, until a four-year-old could eat it. She was fussy in that way. "I've been called by this attorney before," she said. "She's a hard-ass. But this time she showed up with a team of co-counsel. New to the case. Yugel looked surprised."

"Surprised in what way?"

"These guys wore expensive suits," Sarah said. "And they left in town cars."

I squinted at Sarah. Had Cat the Tiger brought on additional firepower? Another law firm?

"Other than that, it was business as usual," Sarah said. "Normal questions about the victim." She jumped up suddenly. "Crap, the bread!"

She opened the oven, and a plume of smoke filled the room. "Damn it," she cursed.

Sarah carried the tray out the side door with a pot holder, dumping the blackened garlic bread into the trash.

"Sorry."

She came back in and pulled her chair close to mine. "So I gotta come clean on something."

I looked at her a second. "Okay," I said, drawing the word out.

"Our show."

Sarah and I had been watching a detective series on Netflix—mostly at her place, but sometimes here.

"You wanna eat at the counter and watch?" I asked, pointing at a tiny kitchen TV.

About a year ago I'd put my foot through my main TV in response to a crime reenactment show that reminded me of my wife. All I had left was one of those little nine-inch jobbers.

"No, it's not that," she said.

Sarah looked down, biting her lip.

"You didn't?"

"I'm sorry." She grinned.

"You went by your place after the depo?" I said. "Watched without me?"

Sarah covered her face with her hands.

I shook my head. "Total binge-watch etiquette violation. How many episodes?"

"All the rest of them." She stuck the last bite of chicken with a fork. "Can you forgive me?"

"If you give me that." I motioned at the chicken.

Sarah started backing away, and I got up.

She screamed, and I chased her from the kitchen into the bedroom. As we got there, she stuck the chicken in her mouth and swallowed.

We both bent over, laughing.

"Hey," she said when she caught her breath. "I've been thinking. My lease is up next month. I'm over here a lot. Maybe I downgrade my two-bedroom to a studio. Bring my big screen over here. I don't need such a huge apartment."

I thought about me and Sarah. Whether I was treading water or moving forward. I'd been out at Tullumy Bridge the night before, on my dead wife's birthday.

"Maybe you get rid of your place altogether," I said. "Move in here."

Sarah smiled at me, but the moment got real. The mood, quiet.

"I don't know, P.T.," she said. "I don't want to screw this up."

"You just said—you're over here all the time."

"This is still your place—and Lena's," she said. "You guys decorated the rooms. It's got a lot of your . . . stuff in it."

Exactly what Remy had warned me about.

"So move some of your stuff in."

Sarah sat down on the bed next to me.

"You mean that?"

I thought about Cat the Tiger walking out of the settlement yesterday. And DA Yugel saying nothing to me since then.

My friend Pup Lang, at the start of this thing, had given me a piece of advice: *Get your own attorney, P.T. The city has their own interests in mind.*

But to do that, I needed to take a second mortgage on the house. Maybe I should be selling it, instead of asking Sarah to move her TV over.

"Yeah," I said. "Move in."

Sarah's wavy blond hair laid lazily at her shoulders, and her cheeks were red with sunburnt freckles. As she leaned in and kissed me, I smelled the lilac in her hair.

"I'd want to change a couple things, maybe paint a little."

"Paint away," I said.

The doorbell rang.

"Hold that thought," I said.

I moved out to the front, and pulled open the door.

My father-in-law, Marvin, stood there in a blue flannel and dark gray pants with suspenders. Lena's dad. I still referred to him as "Pop" seventeen months after my wife's death.

"Evening," he said. "How are you, Paul?"

"Good," I said. I invited him in, and he took his white porkpie hat from atop his short gray curls. Held it at his side.

"What's going on?" I asked. Purvis walked out from the bedroom, and I picked him up. "We've been swapping messages."

Marvin leaned against the wall inside the front door. He couldn't be more than a hundred and forty pounds these days. "Yeah, I got the one last night," he said.

"Is everything all right?"

"Oh yeah," he said. "I just wanted to check in. Haven't heard from you in a while. I worry, you know."

Sarah's voice got to us before she arrived. "Well—there's painting to be done for sure," she said. "But I'd say removing the kitchen wallpaper's job number—"

She rounded the corner and saw Marvin. "Oh hey."

"Evening, Sarah," Marvin said.

My past and present collided, and the air got sucked out of the room.

I jumped in. "Marvin, can I get you a water or a Coke?"

"I'm not staying," he said, his eyes on Lena's old blue and white apron, which Sarah had wrapped tight around her slender hips. "I was just in the area and wanted a quick word."

"Have you eaten yet?" Sarah asked. "I can scare you up something."

"Another time," he said, his hand bracing against my shoulder. He steered himself out the front door and onto the porch outside.

I carried Purvis out with me.

"It looks like you're finally moving on," Marvin said. "I guess that's overdue."

I followed Marvin's eyes into the window at Sarah, who'd taken off the apron. She was the best person I'd met since Lena passed, but I also knew how tough it was to compete with a memory. My dad used to say, you can't put one foot in two shoes at the same time.

"What's on your mind, Pop?" I asked.

"I could use a hand with something at the house," Marvin said. "No rush. Why don't you stop by one of these days. We can talk then more privately."

"Tomorrow," I said. "I'll come by after work."

"Great."

I hugged Marvin goodbye and went back in.

Sarah was in the kitchen, cleaning up, but the mood had shifted.

I grabbed my sport coat from where I'd left it. As I hung it up, I pulled out the brochure that I'd grabbed from Suzy Kang's glove box.

I looked at the time. I'd already told Sarah I had to go after dinner, and I walked out to the kitchen. "Time to get back to the case."

Sarah nodded, and I kissed her. I grabbed a leather jacket from the hall closet. There was no more talk about her lease or moving in. At least for now.

I glanced in the mirror. A new look. Less P.T. the cop. More P.T. the swinger. As if that were a thing. "I'll be home in a few hours."

17

Twenty minutes later I'd picked up Remy, and we were flying in my truck down 85 toward Atlanta.

My partner clicked through the private club's website on her phone. "They got some serious hardware, P.T."

Remy held up a picture of a bondage rack. The contraption looked like four metal posts that came up from the floor with chains on each side. A woman was tied to one corner.

"Geez, Rem, I'm driving here."

Carefully, I moved off the freeway.

"I gotta tell you. It threw me," I said to Remy. "When we saw Suzy Kang at that gym."

"Why?"

"Because it meant she wasn't running."

"So?"

"So why wasn't she?" I asked. "She'd dumped her car. Cleaned the money. Then she went home and worked out?"

The area shifted from commercial to industrial. "Yeah," Remy said. "I hear you."

"Unless she wasn't covering her tracks from *us* at the airport."

"Then why go through all the trouble?" Remy said. "Booking that flight. The exchange fees."

"I dunno," I said. "Maybe she cleans behind her. Maybe she has her whole life."

"Meaning what?" Remy said. "She's a sociopath? Or the opposite—she thought she made off clean at Fultz's and went back to daily life?"

"I dunno," I said. "There's just something about her . . . that's not tracking for me."

I took a right at Vernon Boulevard.

"Well, she knows we're after her now."

"Sure," I said. "That's why if we don't get her here tonight, maybe she's in the wind."

I turned at the next light and slowed my truck.

Decadance was in a large black building at the back of an industrial park, about five miles from downtown. The suburbs around Atlanta had become one big cluster, with each neighborhood growing into the next. Dunwoody closed in on Sandy Springs without invitation. Buckhead made headway into Brookhaven, unannounced.

I passed the building, finding a space on the street about three blocks from the door.

We walked down the dark street, hearing the pulsing of electronic music in the distance. The night air smelled like dirt and smoke. How all cities smell to someone who grew up in the country. The smog hangs low in the sky, and the fragrance of confederate jasmine and mountain camellia are replaced by an ash that stains the tiny hairs in your nose.

At the club's door, three or four couples stood, smoking. The women didn't match my fantasy of a sex dungeon, and I didn't get the impression the men matched Remy's. But hey, it takes all types.

A woman who called herself Miss Sheila came over. She was thirtyish and slender and wearing a bright yellow yoga top and black leather pants. I produced the flyer and said a friend had given it to us.

She pointed at the faded pamphlet. "How long you two been staring at that thing?"

"A couple months." Remy smiled shyly. "Gotta admit when it's your first rodeo, right?"

"Yes, cowgirl, yes," Sheila squealed, showing off a tongue-piercing.

We had enough on Suzy to scare or strong-arm the woman with our badges. A warrant in our pocket. But Remy and I had decided to play it differently, at least at the door out front. I wouldn't call it working undercover, but if you can't run with the dogs, stay on the porch, right?

"Well, it *is* couples night," Sheila said. "You buy one membership and get a second free."

I took out some cash and told Sheila our names without mentioning Suzy's.

"Is there somewhere private we could talk?" Remy asked. "About what we like?"

"Sure," Sheila said. "We'll find a place. Let me give you the five-dollar tour first."

Sheila grabbed my hand then, and I felt like a boy being led upstairs at a chicken ranch. We left the entryway and moved into a large area, with Remy trailing behind. Off to one side was a square parquet dance floor, but only three or four couples were dancing. At the far side was an L-shaped bar. The room was dark, but one of those gobo lights spun around, intermittently illuminating the floor and walls with yellow stars and dots.

"It's BYOB here," Sheila hollered over the techno music. "The bar just has mixers, so next time bring your favorite liquor and we'll tag it with your member number. Store your booze for you."

"Nice," I said.

She pointed to an area to our left, across from the dance floor. "That's our main play and watch area."

We moved under an archway and into a giant open room, with metal contraptions throughout. On my left were two cages, one of them containing a graying man in his sixties. A woman in a black leather tank top whipped at the bars from the outside, while the man cowered in the corner.

Had Ennis Fultz and Suzy Kang met here? And if so, how had that played a part in his demise?

"Let's talk in here," Miss Sheila said, and we moved into an area with a raised platform, covered in what looked like red wrestler mats. Two stacks of white hand towels sat on a shelf.

If the place was half bondage and half swinger's club, this was a sex room for the latter group.

Sheila closed the door, and the music from the dance floor muffled away. "So what do you want to talk about?" She raised an eyebrow.

Remy and I produced our badges, and her face fell.

"This is a members-only club," Miss Sheila said. "Everything done here is consensual. We're licensed, and you just signed our confidentiality agreement."

"We have a warrant for an employee of yours," I said. "So we did you a favor out there—not flashing metal and scaring away half your customers."

Miss Sheila took this in. "Okay. Who?"

"Suzy Kang," Remy said, holding up a picture.

"Is she on tonight?"

"She's one of our mistresses at large. Roams the club."

"Tell her she's got a special guest. Waiting for her in here."

"She's gonna get spooked. She *knows* her regulars."

"You'll figure out what to say," Remy said. "You don't want us walking the place, right? Coming back every night and standing outside? Maybe a patrol car at the curb?"

Miss Sheila took my number down and asked us to stay in the room, promising she'd text me when Suzy arrived.

"I'll bring your cash back." She flicked her eyebrows. "Assuming you don't want a membership?"

Within a half hour, the place was bustling. A heavyset man with red leather pants and no shirt came into the room. We told him to scram.

"I like to watch," he said, but Remy pushed him out the door.

Remy called for a patrol car, and told them to park a few blocks away.

About ten minutes later, Suzy came into the room in a silk white top that hung lazily at her cleavage and a leather skirt shorter than the one she had on at the gas station. She didn't recognize us from the split second in the gym.

"I heard you were looking for me."

Remy spun Suzy's arm behind her back, handcuffing her before Suzy realized what was happening.

"Damn it," she hollered. "Fuckin' Sheila."

"You're under arrest," I said. "For theft. Under Georgia penal code sixteen dash eight dash two."

"The fuck is this?" she said. "Theft of what?"

"And the murder of Ennis Fultz, under penal code sixteen dash five dash one."

"Wait a minute," she said, her voice becoming serious now.

I read her a full Miranda while Remy patted her down.

"He was dead," she said. "When I got there."

Sheila had requested we take Suzy out discreetly, and she'd loaned me a trench coat.

Remy led her out, with me trailing behind.

Near the exit, Sheila laid her hand across my shoulder. "Maybe you can come back sometime. A lot of clients would like to be handcuffed by someone who knows what they're doing. Some staff too."

"I'll keep that in mind," I said.

We walked Suzy out to a black and white waiting a block down. Put her in the back.

"Ennis was dead when I got there," Suzy hollered from the back seat. "Are you fucking listening?"

I motioned the blue-suiter to lower the window all the way. "You have sex with him?" I asked.

"No."

"Then what was the condom for?"

"Fine, so we had sex," she said. "I didn't do anything wrong. I got up there. And he was ready, you know?"

I met her gaze. The Viagra.

"Like a twenty-year-old," she said. "I put on a condom and got on top. A minute later he wasn't moving."

"So a minute earlier he *was* moving?" Remy asked.

"I dunno," Suzy said, getting quieter. "I swear I heard him talking when I came in downstairs."

We motioned the squad car to get going and walked back to my truck.

By the time Remy and I got to Mason Falls, Suzy had been booked and was in Interrogation A. She hadn't yet asked for an attorney.

Abe had gone home, but a note was taped to Remy's laptop. One of the serial numbers on the cash exchanged at the airport matched up with a large withdrawal Fultz made six months earlier. Fultz had asked the bank to make a copy of the top bill in each stack, and the manager still had a copy.

"One's enough," I said. Suzy was a thief. Her money was Fultz's money.

We turned and walked into Interrogation.

"We don't *need* to talk to you, Ms. Kang," I said. "We already matched the cash you exchanged at the airport to a withdrawal made by Ennis Fultz."

Suzy shrugged. "Ennis owed me eight grand. How else was I gonna get the money?"

"So what was the other seven grand for?" I asked.

Suzy hesitated.

"You're on camera at the gas station," Remy said. "We've been to the dealership."

You could see the wheels turning in her head. "So I bought a car," she said. "So what? Ennis and I would sit on the balcony when I smoked. He'd say, 'Why do you drive that piece of shit? Let me buy you a car.'"

"Just out of the blue? He's gonna buy you a car?"

"It's complicated," she said to me. "Me and Ennis."

I leaned against the far wall. "How'd you know where his money was?"

"He told me." Suzy shrugged. "Practically every week. 'Get the cash in the box in my closet. Get rid of that crap bucket you drive.'"

I glanced at my partner. Some people think we're dumber than dishwater.

"So why'd you go to the airport?" Remy asked. "If everything was aboveboard, why trade the bills for Hong Kong dollars and then back into U.S.?"

Suzy didn't answer.

"This is a waste of our time," I said.

It was late. If she wanted an attorney, she'd be waiting until morning.

I got up and so did Remy. "You know what I don't understand?" I said. "You cleaned up the car. Your prints aren't on the tank. But you left the condom there. Got your DNA on it."

"Why would I touch the tank?" she said. "He loved that thing."

"He loved his tank?" Remy asked.

"He talked to that damn triggerfish all day," she said.

Suzy imitated Ennis Fultz then, speaking to his fish. "'Let's see if old Sally agrees,' he'd say. 'When no one's around, I tell Sally everything. She knows where the bodies are buried. She watches my treasure.'"

"We're talking about his *oxygen* tank," I said. "Not the fish tank."

"What about it?"

"You switched it out and poisoned him," Remy said. "With nitrogen."

Suzy looked confused.

"We know about your juvy record," Remy said. "Nitrogen sales."

Suzy's face went pale. "I need my phone call," she said. "Lawyer. Now."

A blue-suiter hauled Suzy out of the room. There was no court open at this hour, so after her call she'd spend the night in lockup.

We sat in Interrogation Room A by ourselves for a minute, talking about the reasons people kill. The stupidity and simplicity of it. By morning, Suzy's lawyer would probably be looking for a deal. Offering some lame excuse why she'd taken Ennis Fultz's life.

There was a bright side. With the lawsuit against me, I needed a win. Within the department and publicly. And nothing beat that like a high-profile murder closed in seventy-two hours.

"Why don't you head home?" I said. "Suzy's not going anywhere. I'll start on the paperwork, and be right behind you within the hour. We'll finish the rest tomorrow."

"All right," Remy said. She grabbed her purse and gun and headed out. I went upstairs to my office and stood there, watching my partner from the window as she got into her Alfa and drove off.

But once Remy was gone, I didn't start on any paperwork.

I took the stairwell up to the fourth floor, where DA Yugel worked.

I had something to check into.

18

The girl flicked her eyes open and looked around.

She was in a hospital room.

Earlier, when she woke up here, she tried to figure out where she was, but something had affected her thinking. Had made her mind dull and the world around her shift strangely.

Now it was darker outside, and her mind was clear.

As she sat up, a pain shot down her elbow. There was a large window off to her right and a bathroom at the far end of the room. Another bed was next to hers, and a curtain hung halfway around it. A small boy slept in the bed.

The girl glanced down.

Her forearm and elbow were wrapped in a white gauze.

A bag of fluids was hooked on a metal holder beside the bed, and the girl traced the tubing down to an area below where the bandages ended, closer to her wrist.

The fluid bag was on rollers, and the girl got out of bed. The *floor was cold on her bare feet, and she slid the rolling holder with her. Finding her way to the bathroom.*

She stared in the mirror.

Her neck was bruised, a bluish mark running up and down, below her chin. And her eye. Black and blue, like stage makeup.

She touched her neck and winced. The window in the Hyundai. She'd struck the glass when the car was hit.

The girl rolled herself over to the window.

Outside, an ambulance was parked under a brightly lit awning that read EMERGENCY.

She scanned the rest of the lot until she noticed a white Toyota truck, parked in the second row.

Not every Toyota is the bad man, *she told herself.*

But the left front corner of the truck was crunched in, a smear of blue paint from another car across the bumper. Blue like her family's Hyundai.

19

There's a small library that Liz Yugel and the other district attorney use to research legal matters. The room might've been a large maintenance closet in some past decade, but in the last two years, Yugel and the others had put their legal books up on shelves in the room. Put diplomas and awards on the walls. Even painted the place a shade of tan that looked positively library-esque.

At dinner, Sarah had mentioned something about a new counsel on the Donnie Meadows case. I could ask the DA about it straightaway, but my gut told me not to.

Yugel had let me use the computer in the library for legal research a couple months ago. It was definitely a lend-out situation, versus permission to come back and research whenever I wanted. But the situation made its demands.

I found the knob and turned the door.

Locked. Damn it.

I crossed the empty office and found the desk of a woman

named Julie, who served as the admin for the DA and the other two city attorneys.

I sat down at Julie's desk and started looking around. Opening drawers to find any paperwork that signaled a change of attorneys in the litigation.

Sarah's words about the lawyer echoed in my head. *These guys wore expensive suits,* she'd said. *And they left in town cars.*

I found a blue folder with a tab marked *MEADOWS* in red Sharpie.

Inside was a form. Yesterday, a Notice of Association of Counsel had been filed, amending Tusila Meadows's legal team to include the law firm of Johnson Hartley.

I took out my phone and typed the name in, seeing Johnson Hartley was a firm with offices in Atlanta and Athens.

I clicked through their website, finding the descriptions were broad, probably setting the net wide enough to accept a variety of cases.

It wasn't unusual for one attorney to share costs or expertise with another. Maybe Cat Flannery's pockets weren't as deep as she let on. Or the new firm had a specialty in suits against municipalities.

I looked up Johnson Hartley's cases, but most were security or civil litigation. There was nothing to indicate they'd ever sued a police department or city.

I went to the firm's bios page and scrolled through the pictures. Nothing jumped out.

Then I got to one of the partners.

I stared at Lauten Hartley's photo, knowing I'd seen the man somewhere, but not sure where. In the picture, he wore a gray pin-striped suit with a thick black tie and thin-rimmed glasses. His hair was wavy brown, and he was ruggedly handsome into his late forties.

A vacuum cleaner started up somewhere on the floor, and I got up.

Scurrying down the stairs back to my office, I punched Hartley's name into the DMV database and saw a different picture of him, less suit-and-tie, but still familiar. Then again, I was in court twice a month for cases. It could be anything.

His home address was in Milton, a half hour away, and the adrenaline from sneaking around upstairs was coursing through my veins. Still, I had to be careful poking around in a case where, at any second, I could be named a defendant in a civil suit.

I clicked on my iPhone to make sure the battery had a full charge. Then I left the phone on my desk on purpose and walked out to my truck.

I got on the 903, heading to the town of Milton.

A second law firm on the Tusila Meadows case made no sense.

Tusila still had an offer for $150,000 in hand. She'd almost settled the case yesterday, and the city was now considering paying her the higher dollar amount that Cat Flannery had intimidated us with, $200,000.

Why the hell would her attorney bring on another law firm? If a settlement happened tomorrow, Cat Flannery would have to share her portion with them.

Twenty minutes later I got off the highway.

Tall electric lines towered over three-story Georgia pines— part of a recent infrastructure project in the northern part of the state. I moved deeper into the country and found Hartley's address. The home was a two-story Victorian, painted a gray color with white columns and black triangular turrets. A porch wrapped around the front.

I'd never been to this house before, and I couldn't put a finger on what case I might know Hartley from.

Sometimes my mind ran in circles, and sometimes it ran in place. It's an illness to suspect everyone around you.

I got back on the highway, and I suddenly felt bone-tired.

By the time I pulled up outside my house, it was past two a.m. Sarah was sitting on the porch with Purvis, and I got nervous. Something was wrong.

I moved quickly across the lawn.

"P.T.," she said. Sarah wore black Lululemon pants and a blue Michigan sweatshirt. "I've been texting and calling you for an hour."

I stared at my bulldog, but his eyes were cast down at the concrete.

Two midnight drives in two days, Purvis muttered. *Should I be concerned?*

"I left my phone at work," I said to Sarah. I didn't mention that I'd done it on purpose.

"It's Marvin," she said. "There's been an accident. An explosion out in Centa."

"God, is he okay?" I asked.

Sarah's eyebrows pinched together, and a line ran down the center of her nose. "I made a few calls. He's in ICU."

That quick, my brain was swimming in my head. My chest burned. We'd just seen Marvin a few hours ago.

"There was a gas leak in some mini-mall up north," Sarah

said. "Marvin was hanging with a military buddy. I'm not sure of the details."

I stared at Sarah, confused.

"P.T." She grabbed my hand. "They rushed him to Mercy Trauma here in town. Do you want me to come with you?"

"No," I said. "I'll go alone."

20

I don't remember driving to Mercy Hospital. Just some vague recollection of leaving my truck in a spot reserved for physicians. A security guard hollered as I ran by, but I ignored him. Hustled into the lobby and looked for signs that directed me to the ICU.

When my wife was alive, I sometimes skipped out on Sunday afternoon dinners at Marvin's house. It wasn't that the meal was ruined by drama. The family wasn't overly political or religious as they broke bread. It just wasn't something I grew up with. A big family. Passing food. Sharing stories.

My dad left when I was fourteen, and I hadn't seen him since. My mother was brilliant, a feminist who taught public health at the University of Georgia. She never felt the need to replace Dad with another man. And so I grew up eating quietly, the TV on ESPN on mute, and my mother across from me, silently reading a text on epidemiology or disaster management.

But in the last three months, Marvin and I had gotten closer

than before. He'd begun walking dogs in his neighborhood—
more to pass the time than for money—and sometimes I walked
with him on my lunch hour.

I'd learned about Marvin's youth in Savannah, a city that I'd
always imagined as a gem of the state, though of course it wasn't
always that way for people of Marvin's color growing up in the '50s.

And at last, on these walks, we talked about Lena and Jonas
for the first time since they'd passed. After the accident, there'd
been some confusion because Marvin had been called by Lena
to the roadside to help his daughter. And I'd blamed him for
things that were not his fault. Implicated him in how her car had
gone off the road. Said a lot of things that still needed apologizing for.

I got to the check-in nurse and flashed some tin. There was
no time to explain how we were related. "I need to know the status on Marvin Freeman."

The woman looked up his information. Told me he was in the
operating room now.

Ninety minutes later a man with red wavy hair and black
glasses found me in the hallway. His ID read *Dr. Burke*.

"What's Mr. Freeman's condition?" I asked, showing him my
badge.

The doctor wore light blue scrubs and had a smear of red on
his chest.

"Not great," he said. "We used barbiturates to sedate him. Put
him into a coma to relieve the pressure on his head."

I swallowed. Marvin had become my friend, but he was also
my connection to Lena and Jonas. If I lost him, what part of my
wife and son went with him?

"We found fluid in his abdomen," the doctor said.

"So he's bleeding inside?"

"We're taking him to CT to get a scan."

"A nurse said he was burned."

"A couple small areas," Dr. Burke said. "His right arm and leg. But overall, that's the least of my worries. The other man caught the brunt of the blast. I assume you know he was dead on arrival."

I remembered what Sarah had told me. That Marvin was in Centa with a military buddy.

"Detective," the doctor said, "if you're waiting to interview this Freeman fella, go home and get some rest. Odds are he's gonna be in a coma for some time."

I told the doctor that I'd wait for the CT scan first. And that Marvin was my father-in-law.

"Geez, I'm sorry," he said, embarrassed that he'd been talking so bluntly.

I waved off his apology. When my wife and son were alive, this would happen all the time—people not thinking I was related to Jonas or Lena.

I wandered out to the waiting area.

The space was a large L-shape, with four TVs, each positioned strategically so that most of the chairs could see them. Two of the screens played an infomercial for a kitchen utensil called the Chef's Thumb, which kept you from cutting your finger off while slicing tomatoes. The other two were rerunning old episodes of *Family Feud* with Steve Harvey.

I walked outside for some air. I had an urge to drive out to the mini-mall where the explosion had happened. But Centa wasn't my jurisdiction, and Marvin was here, with no one else to speak for him.

By five-thirty a.m., Dr. Burke shared with me the CT results, telling me that Marvin's internal bleeding was under control, but he was suspended in a coma.

My mind felt dull, like someone had stretched gauze over my eyes, and I was seeing only little bits of things, through stretched, webbed channels.

I don't remember leaving, but at some point my truck was rolling along at just five miles an hour down my own street. I parked a few houses away and stumbled out into the early morning light.

I wandered past a blue Mustang and down my driveway to the backyard, opening a side door that led into the back. Marvin had rebuilt our garage into a hobby shop the year we got married, with a big worktable in the middle and stools all around.

Reaching under the table, I pulled out a fifth of Jim Beam that someone had given me as a gift. Someone who didn't know I was recovering.

I turned the screw top and heard the tab break on the fresh bottle. The smoky smell of Kentucky bourbon filled the air around me.

Something behind my eyes went red with anger, and I picked up the bottle by its neck. Tossed it at the wall.

The glass smashed against the pegboard, and hammers and screwdrivers fell to the floor.

I grabbed an oversized monkey wrench and starting working away at the table, pounding the sides of it. The stools. Chunks of wood flew back at me, but I kept swinging the wrench and taking sharp pieces of shrapnel from everything I hit.

After about twenty swings, I was exhausted and fell onto the floor, the light above the table swinging from left to right, moving me into shadow and then back into the light.

I heard a door open and kept my head down.

I knew it was Sarah, but I was embarrassed to turn and look at her.

"It's never gonna be fixed," I said.

"All right," she said. "Let's get you into a hot shower."

"Not until I know what happened," I continued. "Not until I'm a hundred percent sure."

Sarah stared at me. Unsure what I was talking about. "C'mon," she said. "Marvin's gonna be fine."

I got up and went inside. Showered and crashed hard.

21

By ten a.m., I was back at Mercy Hospital.

Marvin's daughter Exie had driven in during the night, and she was asleep in a cigar chair by his bed, a yellow hospital blanket pulled tightly around her.

Exie was Lena's twin, and as she slept, I stared at the beautiful brown skin that she and my wife shared.

Sun through the window cast a glow on the side of Exie's face and turned her long frizzy curls a reddish brown. I never said it aloud, because there was no way to say it right. But I longed to touch Exie's skin. To run the back of my hand along her face.

Beyond appearances, the sisters were nothing alike. Exie was a free spirit who worked part-time as a psychic and had a penchant for stealing antiques. My wife, Lena, had been the sensible sister. Pragmatic. Practical.

Exie's sandals had fallen off the seat, and I pulled the blanket around her feet. I found a nurse to get an update on Marvin's condition. A few minutes later, Remy walked into the waiting area.

"How's the old man?" my partner said.

I gave Remy the latest.

"Jesus," she said.

"How was your meeting with the chief?" I asked. I'd seen a text to me and Remy, but had skipped the meeting to come here.

"Short," Remy said. "The DA was there. And another guy. Observing."

"And?"

"Suzy Kang was arraigned and released on bail this morning," Remy said. "First on the docket."

I had hoped that Suzy might be held without bail as a flight risk, since she'd run from us. She'd also booked a plane flight out of town, even if she didn't get on it.

"She posted a fifty-grand bond. Surrendered her passport and driver's license, and agreed to wear an ankle monitor."

On most days, this was a win. We'd know exactly where Suzy was at all times.

"So why do I get the feeling you're about to tell me bad news?"

"Her attorney talked to the DA," Remy said. "Apparently Suzy's got a copy of Ennis Fultz's will. Fultz gave the document to her for safekeeping."

"And?"

"And in it, Suzy gets twenty grand in cash, specifically for a new car. Tax-free gift. Plus, fifty grand. And the fish tank."

"The fish tank?" I said. "That big-ass one?"

I took a step across the waiting area. *Fultz had put an escort in his will. Then given her a copy of the legal document. Why?*

"Suzy's lawyer argued that the Fultz family would screw her over, so she took a portion of her money now."

"For real?" I said.

Remy nodded. "Her lawyer put the cash in an escrow account until the case is cleared up."

"What's left of the cash, you mean," I said. "She already bought a car."

I walked over to a machine that served free coffee and hot chocolate. I hit the button, and a cup fell down.

We had Suzy driving away from Ennis Fultz's house. She'd parlayed the cash into a car sale. Then laundered the money at the airport. We'd convicted serial murderers on less. Then again, the case was all circumstantial.

"So what's *her* version of things?" I asked. "She took what was hers and never touched the guy? And we're back to square one?"

"Fultz paid her two grand a week. Apparently she deposited the cash religiously and never touched it. Except for the last month. He told her he'd get her the eight grand later and she trusted him."

Remy gave me a look. "I did my best at the meeting, P.T. But the word was that you and I got tunnel vision on the easy answer. Old rich guy and young deceptive escort."

"And what?" I said. "Disregard her and just find some new suspect?"

"'Be more open-minded' were the chief's words."

I shook my head. "Was the undertaker pissed?"

This was one of the nicknames for Chief Pernacek. Based on his slender and pale look.

"Hard to tell." Remy shrugged. "This civilian was watching, so maybe he was holding back. I dunno. But the chief wants us to talk to some guy." She looked down at her phone. "Quentin Reed."

"Who the hell's he?"

"Some real estate expert. Apparently when the city needs land or buildings—and the city *often* needs land or buildings—"

"This is the guy they go to?"

Remy nodded.

"How well did he know Fultz?"

"Very well, the chief said." Remy put up her hands. "I can go alone. His office is walking distance from here."

I took one sip of the coffee and dropped the crap into a nearby wastebasket. I was doing nothing here. The doctors had purposely put Marvin into a coma. And if Suzy wasn't our poisoner, someone out there had killed Fultz and was laughing at us. Nothing drove me crazier.

"I could use the fresh air," I said. "I'll come along."

22

The area west of Mercy Hospital was the part of town that the city put on brochures with copy lines about Southern charm. A neighborhood of multicolored Victorian homes from the '30s had turned into bed-and-breakfast places and small businesses, architects and landscape design firms.

Remy and I walked west for six blocks before turning to the south at 8th Street.

Beyond this cute area was "downtown" Mason Falls, which was a collection of twenty or so two-story buildings, among them a handful of cafés, independent bookstores, and dress boutiques that catered to women over forty.

"So what exactly happened with Marvin?" Remy asked.

"I'm still trying to figure things out. There was an explosion. They say a gas leak."

"The other guy's dead?"

"Some military buddy," I said. "I don't know him."

We approached the address at the corner of 8th and Gentry.

"Fultz's last will," I said. "You get a copy?"

"In a few hours, the DA said. Right now they're hesitant to confirm that Suzy's copy *is* the final."

"Fultz changed his will recently?"

"Well, her copy is dated a month ago."

I shook my head at this, still not grasping the relationship between Fultz and Suzy Kang. "Any other surprises Yugel knows about?"

"From what the DA saw, Fultz's money gets split: seventy percent to his son, Cameron, and thirty percent to the ex-wife. Suzy gets the cash I mentioned and the fish tank."

"We need to talk to Suzy," I said. "If the escort just took the money that was coming to her and left other cash behind . . ."

Remy nodded. There was no money in Fultz's house when we got there, so if Suzy only took a chunk of the cash, someone else might have taken the rest.

We crossed the street.

"And did Abe already check the alibi on these Lyman people for Monday?" I asked, referring to the family who lived on the property.

"Bill Lyman was at work," Remy said. "So was his wife. And the girl was at school."

The building we'd arrived at was made of gray brick and had four decorative wrought-iron beams that ran from the edge of the sidewalk to an ornate overhang.

"Was Chief Pernacek sore?" I asked. "Fultz was his friend."

"He's just spinning," she said. "'Cause we're spinning. He just wants the ride to stop."

I pulled the heavy door open. "Him and me both."

Inside, the lobby looked like a sitting room built for 1920 debutantes to wait for prospective husbands. There were five couches spread out, each with overstuffed pillows in bright patterns and coffee tables covered in glass. In the center of the space was a wooden desk from the antebellum period. A late twenties blonde in a pencil skirt sat there.

"Good afternoon, officers," she said.

Remy looked at me. We were in plain clothes. *Receptionists were making us now?*

"I was told you were coming," the woman said by way of explanation. She motioned at an elevator at the far side of the room. "Why don't you take the lift up to four. Mr. Reed's expecting you."

The office on four was the width of the whole floor, but was broken into three areas. One held a large black desk, another a seating area, and the third a conference room.

Quentin Reed was white, with capped teeth and a full head of hair that was half gray and half sandy brown. He was probably early fifties, but his face looked younger, his body seemingly preserved through the power of plastic surgery.

"You must be Marsh and Morgan," he said, putting weight into his handshake. "The M Squad. Have a seat." He directed us over to the area with a love seat and two Eames chairs.

I took one of the chairs, and Remy sat on the other. "We understand when there's a question about real estate, you're the guy with the answer," I said.

"Well, all towns are small towns," he replied. "I started coming to this office when I was this tall." He motioned at his knee. "So . . . you get to know people and families . . ."

"Did you know Ennis Fultz?" Remy asked.

"Everyone knew Ennis," Quentin said. "Shame he passed so early into his retirement."

"What was he like?" I asked.

"Solid guy," he said. "Made his investors money."

"What about outside of business?" Remy asked.

"Gave to charity." He nodded. "Part of the city trust."

I stared at Quentin Reed. I was, at the moment, simply too tired for this shit.

"Mr. Reed, we know Ennis was tight with the mayor and the chief. But we're not here looking for character references. We gotta solve crimes whether we like the victims or not."

I held his gaze, and he didn't look away.

"What's really helpful," Remy said, "is the unvarnished truth, dirty or clean."

Quentin squinted at us. "I heard Ennis had a heart attack. The way you're talking—"

"We know Mr. Fultz was a dog with the ladies," Remy interrupted.

"We also know he rubbed some folks the wrong way," I added. "But we don't know the man."

Quentin got up. Poured himself three fingers of Belle Meade Bourbon from a rolling wooden cart nearby. As he passed me, I noticed his neck lacked a single wrinkle. There was little chance he wasn't banging the secretary downstairs.

"The thing you gotta know about Ennis," he said, "was that he could sell two milk machines to a farmer with one cow. Ya understand?"

"He was a good talker," I said.

"But right when you thought it was just talk," Quentin said, "turned out he knew something you didn't."

"And how *did* Fultz know things?" I asked. "He spread money around?"

"Nope."

"Was he well-connected?" Remy asked.

"It wasn't about networking with Ennis. People like me, Detective Morgan—we think of money like farmers think of fertilizer. If you don't scatter enough around, the cash ain't doing what the good Lord intended."

"So what was Fultz's philosophy?" Remy asked.

"Ennis would outwork folks. He'd spend weeks downtown at County Records. He'd go block by block and acre by acre to see who owned every goddamn parcel in this county," Quentin said. "Drive over and introduce himself. Looking for some angle. Some advantage on the rest of us."

"And then he'd spring it on you?"

Quentin shook his head at Remy. "No, ma'am. See, Ennis was a real sandbagger. Let's say a piece of land was held in a family trust. Ennis would know if the son had a gambling problem and needed cash the minute his daddy died. And old Ennis'd hold on to that info for years, playing dumb, waiting for the right moment to use it. He might even be ready with a good tip on a pony race."

"Did he have enemies?" I asked.

"Ha, a line of 'em." Quentin put up his hands. "Commercial agents. Farm owners. Institutionals. After a while, his last name became a damned expression."

I squinted. "How do you mean?"

"If you thought you were on top of somethin'," Quentin said, "but it turned out you were missing a piece of information—you got Fultzed."

I had to smile at this. Thinking about Fultz, who wasn't originally from Georgia, coming here for college and outworking these good old boys whose daddies handed them their portfolios. It made me like Ennis.

"So who got Fultzed the most?" Remy asked.

"Well, if you're saying he didn't die natural," Quentin said, "I'd look at those farmers out by Paradise Grove. Sorrell is their last name. He did a sale and leaseback with those boys, and Ennis got 'em coming and going."

Quentin explained that a sale and leaseback was a real estate transaction in which Fultz bought the farmland off the Sorrell brothers to help them reduce debt they'd built up during a bad season. Then he leased their former property back to them to operate it like they had before.

"There was a lot of that going on with peach farmers a couple years ago," I said. "The winter crushed the crop and they were left with nothing to bring to market."

"Problem was," Quentin said, "when Fultz decided to retire and liquidate all his properties, he wanted to get rid of that farm too."

"He offered the land back to them?" Remy asked.

"In a manner of speaking," Quentin said. "First he offered to sell to a large conglomerate. To draw up the price. But when all was said and done, the conglomerate got forty-nine percent, and the Sorrell brothers fifty-one. But they had to pay Ennis twice what he paid them. Word was they threatened to kill him."

"He never went to the police," Remy said.

"No, I doubt he would," Quentin said. "See I think he liked it. The threats. The danger. Kinda gave Ennis a high."

"What do you know about his wife?" I asked. "You ever speak to Connie?"

"We jawed up a patch," Quentin said. "At charity events and such. A stand-up woman. Bullied Ennis into giving a quarter of his money to charity. Meanwhile, he'd bring women in their thirties out to properties he owned. To show off. Get some play on the side."

"Connie knew?" Remy asked.

"A wife always knows," Quentin said. "Ennis was the sorta fellow who liked to sow his wild oats. Then pray for crop failure. You know what I mean, little lady?"

My partner ignored Quentin's leering. "When's the last time you talked to Fultz?" she asked.

"A real conversation?" Quentin shrugged. "Last summer in County Records. And it was odd. Because he was out of the business. I mean complete liquidation."

"You ask him what he was doing there?"

"Did one better," Quentin said. "I circled back after—to see what he was looking at. The old boy out at Records said the property was right by Ennis's house—way out by the gorge. It may've been his own deed, so I guess it was nothing."

"But you stayed away from any deal out that way, huh." I smiled. "Afraid of getting Fultzed?"

"Fool me once," he said, finishing his drink.

We thanked Quentin Reed and got up from the sitting area.

"Just out of curiosity," I said. "What are these Sorrell brothers like?"

"You mean are they peckerwoods?" he asked.

I didn't answer.

"One of them's tolerable," Quentin said. "Even smart. But the other one? Watch your back, Detective."

23

The girl heard a noise.

Someone was coming down the hallway.

She glanced at her arm, and saw that the IV tubing was connected with a plastic piece that could be unscrewed.

She turned the plastic. Lefty-loosey, the man who was a plumber had said. He was a nice man, but that family couldn't keep her for long.

But that was all in the past. She had a family now.

The plastic piece popped off, and the liquid dripped onto the floor. She carried the IV holder into the shower, so the floor would stay neat. Left it there.

The girl opened a tall wardrobe closet in the room and climbed inside then, pulling her knees to her body. She only had her underwear on under the gown, and the cold wood of the cabinet pressed against her skin.

She heard the door to the hallway open. Saw through a sliver of the open closet that a man had come in.

He wore a white lab coat and looked around.

A doctor.

He walked back to the door and grabbed some paperwork attached to a clipboard. Glanced at a medical record file before placing it back in the holder.

The man walked over to where the boy was sleeping. Pulled the sheet off of him and turned. Stared over at the girl's empty bed.

"Can I help you, Doctor?" a female voice said.

A nurse stood at the door. She had blue gloves on, and the girl looked at the man's gloves. They were purple.

It was a small detail, but she had a memory of being rolled into this hospital room a few hours ago. All the doctors and nurses wore blue gloves.

The doctor turned, and the girl saw his face through the sliver in the door.

Her throat tightened.

The bad man.

"I'm following up on a surgery," he said. "But I'm clearly on the wrong floor."

The nurse glanced around—looking at the empty bed herself. Then followed the man out.

"What patient are you looking for? Doctor? Doctor?"

24

The Sorrell family farm was located southwest of Mason Falls by a good twenty miles.

"What'd you think of that guy?" Remy asked as I drove. She meant Quentin Reed.

"My daddy used to say, 'There's one thing lower than a dog. And that's a dog's belly.'"

Remy looked over. "You and those damn expressions. What the hell does that even mean?"

I started cracking up. "I dunno." I smiled. "Guess I should've asked the old man before he walked out the door."

Remy had an attitude in her voice since we'd left the hospital, and I was trying to figure out why. Had the chief laid into her? Uttered one of his usual chauvinisms? Was she mad at me for no-showing at the meeting?

"What's going on?" I said. "You're pissed."

She held a beat before speaking. "You weren't upset."

"About what?"

"Suzy Kang," she said. "Your reaction at the hospital—normally you'd be upset she got bail."

I scrunched up my face. "You saw the email that Abe sent on fingerprints at the crime scene, right?"

This report had come in via email late last night. Suzy Kang's prints were on the cigarettes on Fultz's balcony, but all the prints on the oxygen tank were Fultz's.

"Sure," she said. "But if Suzy was there—"

"Either her prints would be on the tank's knob if she tampered with it," I said. "Or she'd have wiped the container down and there'd be *no* prints."

"She could've placed Fultz's hands on the tank, after wiping it down."

"Or wore gloves," I said. "But there's the other issue. We only found one tank in the house. If she came with a bad nitrogen tank, where's the good oxygen tank she took with her?"

"She could've dumped the oxygen along the way," Remy said. "Any trash can or dumpster."

"True," I said. "But everything else got tossed at the Valero station or the car dealership, so why not toss the tank there? Suzy didn't know she was on camera."

Remy nodded, but her face still looked hurt.

"Don't be sore," I said.

"We're partners, P.T. You don't hold back. We're supposed to be . . . you know . . . simpatico."

"I shoot low, you shoot high?" I said. "I duck left and you kill the bad guy the other way?"

She looked off, away from me. "Something like that," Remy said. "Point is—you're not supposed to hold back. Not from me."

I nodded, as my way of apologizing. "Well, Suzy's not out of the woods as a suspect yet, Rem."

We slowed at a break in the picket fence, and turned down a dirt road that led to the Sorrell brothers' farm. In the distance, thick green rows of leaves were dotted with tiny red marks.

"Tomatoes," Remy said, the main crop of the farm.

The phone rang, and it was Abe on speaker. I'd texted him to start checking out the Sorrells.

"What've you got so far?"

"Greer Sorrell's got no record," Abe said. "But the other brother—Nesbit, he's got two D&Ds."

A D&D was a public safety violation. A drunk and disorderly.

"Nothing criminal?" I asked.

"No," Abe said. "But you know how I set up Fultz's cell phone to forward to me?"

"Something caught in your trap?"

"A BMW dealership in Athens," Abe said. "The manager called ten minutes ago to see if they should go ahead with the repairs on Fultz's car. Apparently, they towed his BMW over there Friday night. Three days before the old man was killed."

"What kind of repairs?"

"I just sent their estimate to Remy's phone," Abe said. "It's twelve grand of someone beating the shit out of a 2016 528i. Windows smashed. Both back quarter-panels. Looks like rage."

Remy pulled up the body shop estimate, and she squinted at a black-and-white photo on the second page.

"Are you seeing it?" Abe asked.

Remy didn't say anything, and Abe continued. "There's a chunk of baseball bat they found inside Fultz's car."

Remy held up a picture. The piece was a couple inches around, part of the rounded barrel of the bat—the end of it—farthest from where you hold the thing.

"There's an end cap to most baseball bats," Abe said. "If you look carefully, there's some letters burned onto the wood chunk the guy left in the car. NS9 and then part of an 01."

"Wait—Nesbit Sorrell is the N-S?" Remy asked.

"He was a big star locally," Abe said. "Pro prospects even. One year at Texas and flamed out."

Remy was typing something into her phone. She turned her screen to show me a picture of a blond kid in a baseball uniform.

"The internet never forgets," she said. "Meet Nesbit Sorrell, eighteen years ago." Her thumb zoomed in on his uniform number, which was a nine. As in NS9.

"And the 01?" I asked.

"Judging by his age," Abe said, "2001 was his graduating year."

I shook my head. The idiot had left a piece of his high school bat inside Fultz's BMW. The same bat he was holding in the picture online.

"You get an affidavit started?"

"Already underway," Abe said.

In Georgia, this was the fastest way to get a warrant in hand. An officer writes up a sworn statement listing the offense, the place of the crime, and the criminal code violated.

In this case, we'd bring Nesbit Sorrell in for damage of property over $500, a violation of code 16-7-23. While we had him, we'd push for more, until we got him talking about Fultz.

"Judges are light today, P.T.," Abe said, "probably take all afternoon. You wanna wait before you go out there?"

I looked at the gravel driveway leading onto the farm. A boy, about fifteen, was bent over a row of plants.

"We're already here," I said. "You talk to the dealership?"

"Sure did," Abe said. "Fultz knew about the bat. And the NS9 marking."

Which meant the old man knew who smashed his car up before he died.

I wondered what happened next. Did he call Nesbit? Was there a confrontation?

"There's something else," Abe said. "Your girl Suzy Kang came here with her hotshot attorney. Talked with Yugel again."

"Did you find out if she left cash behind—or cleaned him out?"

"Suzy thinks there was other cash hidden. Places she didn't know about."

"This attorney, Hank West," Remy said. "He's her boyfriend, and he's sticking by her. Knowing she was banging Fultz?"

Abe made a noise with his nose. "Morgan, I met Hank West. He's not anyone's boyfriend. Except maybe his boyfriend's boy-friend."

So Hank West was only a roommate to Suzy. And now, her lawyer.

"All right," I said to Abe. I didn't want to come on too strong with the Sorrells like we had with Suzy. "We'll play it easy with these farmers. Call you in a half hour."

I pulled onto the gravel at the edge of the property, and we got out, the teenager glancing up as we closed the doors to the truck.

His strawberry blond hair was cut into a short fade, probably with a number two clip. He wore jeans that barely hung on his thin frame and a blue Mason Falls High baseball shirt.

"How you doin'?" I asked, getting out of the truck.

The boy looked to Remy and then back at me. "All right."

I flashed him some metal and introduced ourselves, telling him we were detectives. "What's your name?" I asked, keeping things friendly.

"Cooper Sorrell."

We knew there were two Sorrell brothers, Greer and Nesbit. The kid told us his dad was Greer. Also known as the older, smart brother. Not the one with the baseball bat.

"Is your old man around?"

Cooper nodded, walking us up a dirt road that threaded in between two fields. Remy mentioned she grew up in nearby Harmony, which was all farmland. She asked him about the crop this year.

"Well, the sap beetles ate half the sweet corn," he said. "So now it's hand-to-hand combat for the tomatoes."

Sweet corn was what locals called a trap crop. You placed a row of sweet corn in between every ten tomato plants because the corn attracted the worms that might eat your tomatoes.

"You don't spray?"

"There's natural sprays you can make for aphids. Leaf spray. But when the worms or caterpillars get onto the plants, we pull 'em off by hand."

The main house was white with cedar shake siding that had been stained darker than its natural color, but had faded to a gray. Rust marks ran from where the drainpipes were attached— down to the edge of the porch.

The kid asked us to wait out front while he went inside.

We looked around at the fields that surrounded the house. The farm was larger than it looked from the road, and in the distance, you could see what was probably eight hundred single pine stakes, jutting up into the air, each holding the stem of a single tomato plant.

In the other direction, weedy triangular-leafed plants without stakes covered the south hills.

"Cucumbers." Remy pointed.

A minute later a man in his forties came out. He had light brown hair the color of wheat stalks and a paunch. His T-shirt read *Freedom Ain't Free* in big blue letters, along with an American flag.

"What can I help you with, officers?" Greer Sorrell said.

Cooper slipped around his dad and took a seat on a wicker love seat on the porch. We mentioned we were looking into the death of Ennis Fultz.

"We understand Mr. Fultz did business with you," Remy said.

Greer flicked his eyebrows, which were thick and wiry. "If you call it that."

"Did you know he was dead?"

Greer nodded. "I heard somethin', yeah."

The shutters above Cooper's head were painted a shade of green that had sun-faded to a light mint color. Beside the boy, on the porch, a single citronella candle sat on an overturned paint can, to ward off mosquitoes.

"When's the last time you saw Mr. Fultz?" I asked.

Greer hesitated, his hand resting on his big pappy, as if he were a reflective pregnant woman. "In person, a month ago maybe."

"We heard about the sale and leaseback," Remy said. "That sort of two-handed dealing's enough to make a couple fellas angry."

Greer looked at his son. *Is he wondering if the kid told us something?*

"Well, we were pissed about the ownership change, sure," Greer said. "But ever since we expanded in '15 and loaded up with debt, we were destined to sell off some chunk of this place. One way or another."

"So you weren't upset with Fultz?" I asked.

Greer sat down on the wicker beside his boy, his foot up on the porch railing. He wore dark clodhoppers, with mud caked under the soles. "We might've been a little sore," he said. "But there ain't no way any of us is committing murder over it, if that's what you're thinking."

"Who said Ennis was murdered?" my partner asked.

The evening news, in fact, had called his death natural.

Greer paused. "My son said you were homicide."

I took this in. On the walk up, we *had* mentioned this to Cooper.

"Is your brother, Nesbit, around?" Remy asked.

"Nope," Greer said.

"And where were you both this past Monday?" I asked.

"I was here," Greer said. "I do twelve hours a day outside. The Lord's work."

"And Nesbit?"

"Right by my side. Hundred guys'll alibi us."

A hundred employees scared to lose their jobs.

I considered the nitrogen tank. "What kinda chemicals you use on the property, Mr. Sorrell?" I asked. "Nitrogen? Oxygen?"

Greer shook his head. "We're certified organic. Can't use a bottle of Roundup if we want."

I thought about the damage to Fultz's BMW. "We'd like to talk to your brother. Can you tell us where to find him?"

Greer looked at his son. "Well, he was just here, wasn't he, Coop?"

"Probably missed him by five minutes," the boy said.

What a bunch of shit we were collecting here. And the thing is—you get a lot of this as a detective. People think they're smarter than us, and we have to bide our time.

"Y'all are welcome to come back tomorrow," Greer said. "But if you wanna go interviewing a bunch of hardworking farmers, I expect to see some paperwork in your hands. Warrants and such."

I held the shitbag in my gaze. We'd have a warrant on Nesbit in two hours.

"So Ennis Fultz," I said. "He never came by here in the last week, huh? Talking to you or your brother?"

"Not me. You'll have to ask Nesbit yourself."

"And where does Nesbit live?" Remy asked. Abe had an address for the brother already, in a trailer park across town. We just weren't sure if the information was accurate.

"Ya know, I don't know where he's staying lately. Some girl's house, I think."

I stared at Greer. "You sure you wanna play it this way?"

"I didn't realize we were playing," he said.

"Thanks for your time," I said.

Remy and I walked back to my truck.

Per a text from Abe, the warrant process would take another hour to get a judge to sign off.

I let Remy out at the precinct and headed over toward Mercy to check on Marvin.

As I drove, I stared off in the distance, thinking about how dire Marvin's situation might be. And here I was, wrestling with asshats like Greer Sorrell.

Up on a bluff above the hospital sat a series of enormous homes. I knew one of them was owned by the mayor. I'd been invited to a reception there last year, but hadn't shown, preferring to spend time with Purvis over a night with politicians.

In the battle for my time, it was dogs one, snakes zero. But maybe if I'd been nicer to people like the mayor, I could call in a favor and make sure the best doctors were taking care of Marvin.

As it stood, I had to hope for the best.

And like they say, hope is a good breakfast, but a pretty lousy supper.

25

Up on the ICU floor, Garva, the nurse who'd helped me last night, was back on shift. She wore pink scrubs with purple triangles, and her black hair curved around her neck and hung in a single braid across her scrubs' V-neck.

"Hey, darlin'," I said. "Just checking in on Marvin."

She looked up and smiled. "Well, good news, Detective. His breathing is improved."

Yesterday, I'd been told that one of the concerns of a barbiturate-induced coma was the increased risk of infection. With Marvin specifically, there was a concern with his lungs, since he'd just gotten over pneumonia.

"His oxygen levels are up?"

Garva moved over to a computer and punched in a few keys. "His PaO_2 is eighty-seven. Oxygen saturation, ninety-seven. For his condition, that's great."

Her eyes scanned the screen for other data. "His heart rate is good. I think it's just a wait and see at this point."

I saw the nurse's eyes shift over my shoulder. Someone was waiting behind me.

"You gonna sit in with Marvin?" she asked.

"For a few minutes," I said.

I glanced back at the woman behind me. She was white and in her late sixties, with salt-and-pepper hair tied in a ponytail. She wore a scoop-neck T-shirt and carried a mason jar with flowers in it. Azaleas mostly.

"I assume you two know each other," Garva, the nurse, said.

We didn't, so I put out my hand. "P. T. Marsh."

"Raye-Jean Griffin."

Raye-Jean handed the flowers to Garva. "This is just a thank-you," she said. "For the time you let the family stay here with Lucas's body."

"I'll put 'em right here." Garva motioned at the nurse's station.

The nurse cocked her head at me. "Raye-Jean came in with Marvin and Lucas."

"Oh my God," I said. I hadn't known who Marvin's buddy was. The one who'd died in the explosion. "I'm sorry for your loss. Marvin's my father-in-law."

"How's he doing?" the woman asked.

"He's in a coma," I said. "I was just about to see him. You wanna join me?"

"Sure."

We walked down the hallway and entered Marvin's room. Exie had left for the day to take care of her son.

My father-in-law wore a blue hospital gown, and the white bedsheet atop him was tucked around his waist. Snaking its way across his chest was a thick plastic tube that was taped to his mouth.

I motioned for Raye-Jean to take a seat. "I'm sorry about your husband. I didn't know him, but I heard what happened."

"Oh, Lucas Royster wasn't my husband," she said. "I worked for him for the last ten years."

I blinked. "But you weren't in the office when the explosion happened?"

"Thankfully no," she said. "It was after nine p.m., and these days Lucas is rarely there himself, let alone at night."

"Where did he serve?" I asked.

The woman squinted at me. Her face had ridges in it, almost like the bark of an ash tree.

"Marvin was in the 199th," I said, having learned most of what I knew about my father-in-law's youth in the past three months as we walked dogs together. "He was light infantry in Vietnam. The Iron Triangle."

"Oh, Lucas wasn't in the service," she said. "I think, draft-wise, he fell into that hole right after Vietnam. He was younger than Marvin."

I nodded, sitting in silence for a moment, the only sounds the beeping and whooshing of the equipment.

"I'm sorry, Raye-Jean," I said. "How did Lucas know Marvin then? I thought they were army buddies."

"Lucas was working a case for your father-in-law. He was retired, but once a year someone would find him and ask him to take something on. Officially he didn't have his license anymore."

"He was a P.I.?"

"When he was younger," she said. "Down in Atlanta. The work I did for him was bookkeeping on the mini-mall. He bought that ten years ago."

Out the window, a line of sugar maples shuddered in the wind, their canopy of leaves crowded with yellow and green flowers that hung in clusters.

I looked back at my father-in-law, peacefully sleeping. *What case was a P.I. working on for Marvin?*

"Was he trying to find someone?"

"I'm sorry, Mr. Marsh. I just took the checks in from the tenants. Paid the bills."

I sat forward. I'd met a dozen P.I.s in my time, and they usually specialized in certain types of work. Missing persons. Judgment recovery. I pinged Raye-Jean on Lucas's area of expertise, back when he was working.

"He used to do a lot of marital work," she said. "Some background for a stable of attorneys in the city. But I just picked that up in conversation. It was before my time."

"Do you know how Marvin found Lucas?"

"No."

Raye-Jean stood up and stretched. My questions were bothering her. She was the bookkeeper. Nothing more.

"I'm sorry," I said. "I'm a detective. The questions are an occupational hazard."

After a few minutes, she patted me on the arm and left. I pulled my chair closer to Marvin's bed. Maybe he was trying to *find* an old army buddy. Maybe that's what Sarah had heard when she first got the call.

My phone buzzed, and I looked down at a text.

Remy had the warrant for Nesbit Sorrell and an address in the numbered streets.

I rang her up. "How sure are we that this is Nesbit's place?"

"Address is off DMV records," Remy said. "Tags renewed two months ago. A place called Happy Aisles Mobile Home Park."

I had been called out to Happy Aisles a couple times, back when I was in patrol. I remembered a place that was a little rangy. Trash outside the front doors. Rock gardens with cars up on blocks.

"I can go alone," she said.

I thought of a moment last year when Remy had acted rashly and been suspended. Even though she wasn't a rookie anymore, it was my job to keep her safe.

"No," I said. "His brother, Greer, may have tipped him off. Wait for me, will ya? I'm on my way."

I moved out to the nurse's station, my mind still on the conversation I'd had with Raye-Jean. About Marvin hiring a P.I.

"The stuff my father-in-law came in with," I said to Garva, the nurse. "His clothes and personal items. Where are they?"

The nurse grabbed a key and walked me back into his room. She unlocked a drawer at the bottom of a tall wardrobe. Inside was a green plastic basket with a ziplock bag. Marvin's name was scribbled on the bag in Sharpie. Inside were his keys and wallet.

"I was in Critical Care when he came in, Detective," she said. "His clothes were cut from his body. Some were burnt."

"And this is all he came in with?" I held up the basket. "What about his phone?"

"That's all he had."

Marvin's wallet was a weathered brown leather number with two credit cards, his driver's license, and twenty-three dollars in fives and ones. On the inside, a single flip of plastic held two photos: one of his wife, the other of his twin daughters, Lena and Exie. Lena was carrying Jonas, who was a year old at the time.

I stared at the photo of my wife, remembering when the picture was taken. It was after Easter service, a few years after we were married. Lena was wearing a yellow blouse that was striking against her dark skin. God, she was a beauty.

"Thanks," I said to the nurse.

I patted Marvin's leg. "I'll be back in a couple hours," I said. "Start getting better."

I headed into the lobby, but before I could leave, a voice called out my name.

"Detective Marsh."

I turned to see a man seated on the arm of a waiting room couch. He was white and in his fifties.

"You're a tough man to find." He put out a thick hand. "Dana Senza."

I shook his meaty paw but had no idea who the guy was.

"I'm in kind of a rush, Mr. Senza. Can I help you with something?"

"I'm the new chief," he said.

I took a beat. Examining him a second time. Senza had a wide-barreled chest and black hair with gray streaks. A day of growth on his face.

"Chief Pernacek'll work the rest of the week," Senza said. "With me shadowing him. Next Monday I start solo, and he can get back to fishin'."

This was the guy Remy had thought was a civilian. He had a nose that looked like it'd been broken a couple times.

I pointed toward the elevator. "I'm headed to meet my partner."

"I'll walk out with you."

In the elevator Senza told me that the mayor had hired a search consultant, who found him in Alabama.

"You're not a Crimson Tide fan, are you?" I smiled. "That's not gonna go well with the boys on patrol."

"Auburn actually. Played defensive line there myself. More than a couple years ago."

We left the lobby and walked toward my truck.

"I won't delay you," Senza said. "Mostly I wanted to meet the big hero. I heard about the case last year."

I shrugged. Playing it down. "We caught some good breaks on that case."

"I also heard that you refused to say sorry to some woman who's suing us. So now we gotta cough up an extra hundred grand from the city budget."

I hadn't talked to DA Yugel in the last day about the status of the Meadows settlement.

"Chief," I said. "It's a complicated situation—"

"I'm sure you got your reasons, Marsh." He put up his hands, which were substantial in size. "I'm the new guy. I just wanted to let you know in person—that's not my idea of heroism. Money puts more cops on the streets. Lack of it puts cops in harm's way."

I stared at him, saying nothing.

STFU time.

Except he knew the same trick and stared back.

"I think if I told you the details," I said. "Tusila and Donnie—"

"No need," he interrupted me. "Just keep closing cases. Connie Fultz met with me and the mayor this afternoon. Afterward, I assured Mayor Stems that Detective Marsh won't fail us like he did the other day in the courtroom. He's our best guy."

I smiled at this. What a prick.

"Welcome aboard, Chief," I said. "I won't let you down."

"I'm glad we're on the same page now," he said.

I walked out to my truck and sat there. Thinking about me and Remy going in circles on Fultz. How maybe we'd been sharpening our axes before we'd treed the coon.

I called up my partner.

"Let patrol go by the mobile home park, Rem. If Nesbit Sorrell is there, any blue-suiter can pick him up."

"Where are *we* going?" Remy asked.

"The same guy who busts a car up with a baseball bat," I said, "he doesn't carefully plan a break-in. He doesn't sneak around carrying a tank of nitrogen. Switch it out with oxygen and slink into the shadows."

"Nesbit Sorrell isn't our killer," Remy said.

"I'm sure he's a real shitbag," I said. "But we got a poisoning with no poisoner."

"What's our move, boss?" Remy asked.

"Back to Fultz's house," I said. "Go over it again with fresh eyes. We missed something on day one."

26

I left the hospital and found the interstate.

The afternoon clouds hung low in the sky. The honeycomb-shaped stratocumuli above me looked like someone had taken an artist's knife and flattened puffier clouds, smearing in some blues and grays.

I found the road that led to Fultz's house, overlooking the Condesale Gorge, and drove more slowly this time. Now I noticed that the driveway was a strip of gravel with thigh-high weeds on each side for two hundred yards.

I parked and waited 'til Remy arrived five minutes later.

Inside Fultz's place, the air was stale. We walked the house once over and found Ennis Fultz's triggerfish floating at the top of his immense fish tank. Or should I say Suzy's? I tapped my hand on the glass near the yellow and black beauty, but it didn't move.

Remy gloved up and began inspecting the cabinets, one by one. Taking the place apart.

I walked back out to where I'd parked my truck. From there, I moved around to the back of the house, staring up the staircase we'd seen on day one. If someone had broken through that door, this was most likely the path they took.

I stepped over the bags of grass seed and glanced out at the gorge as I climbed the steps.

In the '70s, the Army Corps of Engineers had dammed up a portion of Tullumy River that flowed into the gorge, directing most of the water into the fingers of June Lake. This left barely enough precipitation to keep the gorge green, and killed the hunting and fishing that once was popular here.

At the top, I crouched as if I had a five-in-one tool in my hand and opened the door. From my vantage point outside, I could see through the office and onto the interior landing that fed into the bedroom. I walked slowly, my feet never squeaking on the floor, counting the steps. At ten, I was on the upstairs landing and looking in at the old man's bed. At fifteen I was crouched by the bed and ready to switch out the oxygen tank for a nitrogen one. I could be in and out in thirty seconds.

I thought again of the clouds I'd driven under on my way here, how they made me think of paint on a canvas. A murder scene is like the most exquisite painting you've ever seen. You notice the brushstrokes. The smudges. They all reveal something about the artist, some unconscious pattern. But when there's just silence screaming back at you, there's another way to go. You take the one piece of the picture that *isn't* there—Ennis Fultz—and understand him better.

Remy had gotten ahold of Fultz's official last will while I was at the hospital, and I grabbed it from her bag. Sat down and started reading the document from page one.

The big winners, like the DA had said, were Connie and Cameron Fultz.

The ex-wife was to continue to maintain the Fultz Family Foundation, and enough money would be carved off the top to handle all the existing commitments.

The rest of the assets were split, with seventy percent going to Cameron Fultz and thirty percent to Connie, the ex. This didn't include the land and house we were sitting in, and a couple other properties, all of which were held in a trust.

The assets in the trust eventually went to Cameron, the son, but not yet. First they passed to Anna and Bill Lyman, the guy we'd met two days ago—cutting the hedges.

Remy made it up to the second floor.

"The date on this thing's pretty recent." I held up the will.

"Abe confirmed what changed. Just the temporary passage of the land to the Lymans. We assume it's just this land here. But it's complicated. The trust owns a series of joint ventures and partnerships—to shelter tax. The other partnerships may hold other land. Abe's checking on that still."

"Are the Lymans even aware they're getting the land?"

Remy shook her head. "Today's the day they'd find out. The will becomes public."

I flipped back to this section of the document. "I've seen these setups before," I said. "Rich families use them with nannies and caregivers for the elderly."

"They let the caregivers stay on the property?"

"Long after the elderly person dies," I said. "It's a thank-you for taking care of them. Eventually when the caretaker passes, the property reverts back to the family."

"But Lyman wasn't taking care of Fultz," Remy said.

"Yeah." I nodded. "This one is more complicated too, because the Lymans are around the same age as Cameron, so there's a provision that when they die, the trust goes to Cameron. But if Cameron is already dead when they die, the assets get donated to the Tullumy River Preservation Society."

"The environmental group?"

I nodded again, putting the will down and standing up.

"Have you looked out in this direction?" I pointed out the window from the stairwell.

"No."

"Well you can see all these trails that Lyman's been making. There's two that lead along the bluff. Where Fultz walks. But the ones cut into the scrub brush out toward the bluffs and the highway . . . they're pretty amazing, Rem."

My partner looked out the window. Ten or twenty winding paths had been cut. They terminated in circles where someone had placed decomposed granite on the ground. The circles led out to other paths. It looked like a maze in an English garden, except with brown scrub pines and arborvitae instead of boxwood.

"I'm not finding shit downstairs," Remy said. "Maybe we should've stayed on Nesbit Sorrell."

I thought about a different way that we might understand Fultz better.

"Let's go for a walk, Rem."

"A walk?"

"Step into the old man's shoes," I said. "Walk the gorge. It's the one thing they all said about him. The housekeeper—Ipsy—she said he'd be walking when she got here."

"The girl, Alita, walked with him every Saturday," Remy said.

We took the stairs down, finding a trail that led through a lightly forested area. In a minute, the path became a dirt hiking strip no more than eighteen inches wide, set in between two slanting pieces of rock.

As we walked, we got into the basic X's and O's, to get us back on track with the investigation.

"For motive," Remy said, "the killer's gotta know the money exists. And that the quantity is substantial enough for the risk."

"If money is actually the motive," I said.

Remy blinked. "If not that, what?"

I shrugged. "Something we haven't found yet."

"The killer's gotta know how to break in," Remy said.

"And have access and knowledge of how to work with a tank of chemicals. That's why I still like Suzy."

To our right, the canyon sloped downward at a steep angle and then leveled off about forty feet down. At the bottom of the gorge was a bed of rocks the length of two football fields.

"I've been thinking," my partner said. "Maybe our timeline is off."

"I had the same thought," I said.

Everything we theorized about Fultz's death was based on two points of data, in reverse order: (1) when Fultz strapped on the tank Monday and inhaled the nitrogen; and (2) when Fultz last used the tank *before that point*—and normal healthy oxygen came out.

If the second moment wasn't the night before he died—if Fultz had gone three days, for instance, without using oxygen—this meant that a killer could've planted the tank three days earlier. And the same of two days. Or five days.

"From Ennis Fultz's medical records," I said, "he didn't always use oxygen to sleep. So when else would he have strapped on that mask?"

"After walking the gorge," Remy said.

"Ipsy said he did that every morning."

"Except on Monday the ex-wife showed up," my partner said. "Unexpectedly. Maybe he skipped his walk."

The trail we were on came to an end in a rock wall, so we turned around and headed back, still walking through the details.

Off to our right, the canyon walls were striped with tannish-green streaks of limestone, and shortleaf pine grew on small ledges where the rock stopped and the dirt began.

"So maybe Fultz didn't use the tank Monday morning at all," Remy said. "Because instead of walking, he got his exercise with Connie, in bed."

I smiled. "I see where you're going with this. You don't think a sixty-eight-year-old could manage two trysts in one day?"

"If I'm Fultz with COPD," Remy said, "and I hear Suzy coming in downstairs, I strap on my mask and start inhaling. To get my strength up for the escort. Get my money's worth."

"And if it's nitrogen, he's coming up empty," I said.

"Sarah mentioned it would burn," Remy said. "Making Fultz need air even more. Eventually, he passes out. Right as Suzy gets on top. That would track with Suzy's story about hearing him downstairs."

"And if he leaves the tank on, the rest of the nitrogen dissipates into the room," I pointed out. "Which means only one thing about the bad tank, Rem. If we agree, he didn't use it to sleep Sunday night."

"It was already there," my partner said. "The day before."

Remy stopped walking for a moment. "I got a question," she said. "What are the bags of Marathon seed for? You put that on your lawn. Where we parked, he's got gravel. Around the side, decomposed granite. Even among all those trails, there's no lawn. No sprinklers out here."

"You got the grass guy's number?" I asked. "Thorpe?"

While we walked, Remy called him up. Asked if Thorpe could pay us a visit out here.

We kept heading back to Fultz's house then. And Remy started pinging me with questions. About if I was resting enough. How I felt.

"What are you getting at?" I asked.

My partner hesitated. An awkwardness that was abnormal for us.

"The other night," she said, "I grabbed a cheeseburger from Jack's after work. And I'm worried about you. So I drive by your place to talk. It's late, but I know you'll be up. I get there and Sarah's car is there. But you're not."

I squinted at my partner.

"The next night," she continued, "you tell me to go home early 'cause you're doing paperwork, but I hang down the street. You get on the 903 fifteen minutes later, heading south."

"I was probably heading to the hospital. Got on the interstate the wrong way."

"This was *before* the hospital," she said. "Before Marvin."

I thought about where I'd gone the last few nights. The lawyer's house in Milton. The trip out to the bridge on Lena's birthday.

Neither were active cases.

We came out into the clearing between the back of the house and the gorge.

"I supported you last year," Remy said. "When you were drinking. But this year—"

"Whoa." I put up my hands. "I'm as dry as a goat's ass, Rem. I haven't touched a drop in four months."

A white cube truck pulled into the gravel drive in front of us.

"I was looking into something personal," I said to my partner. "Will you believe me?"

"Sure," Remy said. But I wasn't confident that she did.

Thorpe got out of the truck. He was black and muscular and wore one of those tan floppy hats with the mesh in the back, the kind hikers wear.

We led him around to where he'd dumped the Marathon bags at the back steps.

"Did Mr. Fultz give you any idea what these were for?" Remy asked.

"Have you been down the hill?"

"No," we said.

Thorpe led us in a new direction. Beyond a thick hedge was a series of twenty or so flagstones, each set about two feet apart, lower and lower, bringing us down the hillside in a different direction than we'd just walked.

"Is all this Fultz's land?" Remy asked.

"From what he told me," Thorpe said.

About fifty feet down, the area leveled off into a huge meadow of saw grass. Not rocky like where we'd been walking ten minutes ago.

"This is what he wanted the seed for?" Remy asked.

Thorpe nodded.

"But it's a meadow," Remy said. "You don't plant grass seed in a country meadow."

Thorpe smiled at her, looked to me and then back at Remy. "Well," he said, "there's no accountin' for the whims of . . . you know—"

"Don't say 'white people,'" Remy said.

"*Rich people* is what I was gonna say."

Thorpe walked across the meadow until he got to the center of it. There, the grass was a darker brown. Dead. An array of rocks, each six or eight inches around, along with two large boulders, lay there.

"Mostly we talked about this," Thorpe said.

I cocked my head. "About what?"

"These boulders. He wanted them removed. The small rocks too. And grass planted again."

I crouched by the larger chunks of rock. There was nothing special about them. Pieces of limestone mostly. They were angular and sharp, stuck into the ground.

"The old man said these rocks are new," Thorpe said. "He had proof too. Showed me a picture of this meadow, full of wild grass, from nine months before."

I looked up at the cliff face above us.

"Well, I'll bite," Remy said. "Where'd they come from?" She pointed up at the cliff. "Earthquake?"

"If you believe Fultz." Thorpe pointed at the gorge below. "They came from down there."

"How?" I asked.

Thorpe smiled. "The old guy started rambling about oil exploration. He was pretty sore about it too. More than that, he was pissed about the timing of it. Said it happened when he was in the hospital last year."

Thorpe walked us over to another area. The same spray of rocks interrupted the grass. But if no one had told us, we would never have guessed that it wasn't the grass that grew up naturally, around the rocks.

Thorpe looked up at the setting sun, as if to judge the time. "Look, I gotta get going. I got a delivery to make. Not sure if this helped you, but good luck."

We thanked him and began climbing the flagstones back to the house.

It wasn't like most cases didn't present us with a number of suspects, but it had been a while since I'd seen this many dead ends. We were seventy-two hours into the case and still spinning.

"Mr. Thorpe," I said. "You dropped those bags off on Sunday around five p.m. How well do you remember the delivery?"

Thorpe tapped at his head. "This is a steel trap."

"You see anyone out here when you came or left?"

Thorpe huffed a little on his way up to the top. "It's usually empty out this way. But as I got on the highway to leave, I passed a delivery truck. Remember seeing it in my side mirror."

"Coming from the direction of the gas station?" Remy asked.

Thorpe nodded. We'd looked at two camera angles from the gas station video. We'd focused mostly on Monday morning, but had started at the moment Thorpe's truck passed, Sunday night.

"We had one truck unaccounted for," Remy said. "What color was the vehicle you saw?"

"White," Thorpe said.

"A white truck blew through the light without us seeing the plate," Remy said. "Must've left the opposite way, because we didn't see it go back toward the gas station."

"Did you see what the truck was carrying?" I asked.

"Nope."

"But you said it was a delivery truck. How did you know?"

"Safety stickers," he said. "Had 'em on the back bumper when I saw it in my side view after it passed. Like hazardous waste or something. Those little flammable icons."

We let Thorpe get on with his evening, and I stood there, thinking about whether this was a clue or another random detail.

"Rem," I said after he left. "The safety stickers . . . Could the bad oxygen tank be delivered by the chemical delivery company itself? The place that refills 'em?"

"No way," Remy said. "You're talking five p.m. on a Sunday. This Thorpe guy runs his own business and he's a hustler. He's out here at that time. But the tank company is United Chemical and Gas. It's the biggest in the country. I called on their delivery hours. None at five p.m. And never on Sundays."

"But if not them . . ." I shrugged at her. "Who? At this hour?"

"You get off the highway there." Remy pointed west. "Inadvertently take the wrong exit. It could be anyone. This is the road you go down to get back on."

"Sure," I said. "But we gotta check it out, right? I mean—if not that—what's left?"

Remy agreed, and we called Abe, putting him onto the job of contacting United Chemical and Gas to see whose route this was and when the last delivery to Fultz's house was made.

Remy talked about Fultz's concern—about the rocks in the meadow.

"You get up near Dixon," my partner said. "By my grammy's place, there's billboards to get your land tested."

"Yeah, I've seen those," I said. "You're talking about fracking."

"But if someone set up a drill, deep in that canyon," Remy said. "We'd know, right?"

"I reckon."

I told Remy about a guy named Harmon Gale, who ran the renewable energy program at UGA. "If there's anyone who can give us a quick answer on this, it's him."

I called up Harmon, but just got his voicemail.

"How do you know this guy?" Remy asked after I left a message.

I explained how Harmon had dated my mom when I was a teenager. Back then he was in his late twenties or early thirties.

"How old was your mom?"

"Thirty-eight or thirty-nine," I said.

Remy smirked.

"You call my mom a MILF, we're gonna have problems," I said.

Remy put up her hands. Playing innocent.

My phone buzzed with a message from Abe. We had an appointment with United Chemical and Gas and needed to get on the road. A guy named Cass Thieland, who was president of sales. We got on the interstate and headed south.

27

The girl found her way to the third floor, in just her hospital robe and bare feet.

She hid in a tiny room with an angry vending machine. It made a loud whirring noise, and she knew no one would look for her there.

After a moment, she peeked out and saw a nurse.

Find Pop, the girl thought. Pop will know what to do.

When the nurse left her station, the girl ran over and clicked on the keyboard. It demanded a password.

She moved to the next keyboard over, which was unlocked.

Typing in her mother's name, she saw a room number and looked at a door nearby.

One floor down.

Within a minute she was down the stairwell and in Room 209. She saw her dad asleep, sitting in a chair by an empty bed.

"Where's Mother?" she said. The little girl liked calling Anna "mother."

He opened his eyes and looked at her. "What are you doing here, hon?"

The girl's eyes moved to the bed. It was empty.

"Your mother's in surgery," he said vaguely.

Her father turned away from her then.

But the girl put her hand on his cheek and moved it back.

"Pop," she said. "The man who hit us. I saw his face."

Her father squinted at her. "It was an accident," he said.

She noticed he had changed his clothes. He must've gone home and then driven back here.

"No," the girl said. "The man hit us on purpose, Pop. And he's in the hospital. The man came into my room. Looking to get me."

"Sit up on this bed, honey," her father said.

He hesitated, staring at her.

"He drove along the shoulder of the road," the girl said. "And then swerved back—hitting our car on the back right corner."

Her father's eyes lit up.

He knew how smart she was. He and Anna had talked about it. How the world was gonna be her oyster.

"Are you sure?" he asked.

"Pop," she said. "We should leave."

"You just wait here, sweetheart," he said. "I'm gonna get someone we can talk to."

"A police?" she asked.

They shared a look, because they both knew what had happened to her before. She'd told him and Anna about the man who had hurt her in the last place she'd lived. Who had done so after the police had come and heard her story. The police who didn't believe her until it happened a second time.

"A nurse to start," her father said. "Then to the police, but a good one."

He left then, and she found the same closet as in her room. Took a pillow in there and pulled her knees to her chest.

She waited.

Five minutes? Ten? When her father didn't come back, she opened the closet door.

No one was in the room.

Had her dad gone downstairs? Maybe to find that nurse?

She walked into the hallway and opened the stairwell.

And there he was.

His legs and arms tangled strangely at the bottom of the stairwell. Her father's neck, turned at an impossible angle.

28

By five p.m., Remy had pulled up outside the local head-quarters of United Chemical and Gas, about eight miles north of downtown Atlanta. The address Abe had texted landed us in a corporate park with three white prefab buildings, each with a blue *UC* logo at the top.

It was one thing if a United Chem driver had inadvertently delivered an incorrect tank to Ennis Fultz's house. It was something different if it was tied to some break-in and poisoning. Right now, that was all just speculation.

Instead of parking, I asked Remy to follow the road farther down, where other United Chem buildings stood. These were flatter and wider. One-story giants that looked like factory floors.

"It's a dead end." Remy pointed at the security gate ahead of us.

"I know," I said, looking in Remy's rearview mirror as a white delivery truck approached from behind. "Pull in there, will ya? Get boxed in on purpose."

Remy let the GMC truck follow us into a fenced area approaching the security booth. She parked about a half inch from the wooden bar gate.

A guard leaned out a window. He was black and in his twenties, about five-eight. He wore gray slacks and a white golf polo with the *UC* logo in blue.

Remy leaned out the window. Flashed her badge. "We have an appointment with Cass Thieland in Sales."

"Visitor parking is in the 500 building turnaround, Officer," he said. "This is for U-Chem vehicles only."

He took a step into the tiny space in between Remy's Alfa and his booth, realizing the truck behind us had blocked us in and would need to back up.

Remy placed her hand on the man's arm, her thumb resting on the inside of his elbow. "I can just pull in and turn around."

The man smiled. "Oh yeah, sure. That's fine."

He opened the gate, and we drove into the work yard.

A dozen white delivery trucks were backed into slots at the loading dock far to our left, while others were parked to our right. Out my window, I took pictures of the two kinds of trucks with my iPhone, in case we needed to show them to Thorpe, the grass seed guy.

One kind was a GMC Sierra heavy-duty pickup with rails built onto the bed liner, for hauling tall chemical containers. The second was a larger vehicle the shape of a UPS truck, with doors that slid open from right to left along each side.

Remy made a U-turn and headed back toward the gate to exit.

"You think we're gonna need some human intel?" my partner asked.

This was an expression I taught Remy when she was a rookie. For when we got shut down on official channels.

"Probably."

She pulled up at the gate, and the guard lifted the exit board. But Remy didn't gas it.

The guard walked over. "Everything okay?"

"I'm sorry," she said, the slightest lilt in her voice. "I just had to ask. Do I look familiar?"

Remy was wearing one of her go-to outfits—black slacks, a cream blouse, and a black blazer. She looked good, and she knew it.

"'Cause you look really familiar to me," she said.

"Man, I wish I could say I remember you." The guard smiled. "But . . . no."

"All right." Remy tapped at her temple. "It's gonna come to me while we're in our meeting."

Remy pulled past the gate, and I shook my head. In the side mirror, I could see the guard still staring at her. A truck going in the opposite direction beeped to be buzzed in.

"That's the appetizer," Remy said. "We'll see if we need more later."

We parked in the turnaround outside the glass building. Once inside, we flashed our badges and were chaperoned into an elevator and up to a large office on the fourth floor.

Cass Thieland headed up Sales and Operations for United Chem's south and southeast divisions.

"Thanks for seeing us on short notice," I said.

Thieland wore a suit, but he had slick black hair that he tied in a loose ponytail. He looked like the type of guy who water-skied on the weekends on Schaefer Lake and ate boiled peanuts out of a paper bag as he drove.

"Well, we don't get a lot of calls from the po-lice," he said. "'Specially homicide detectives."

We reminded him of what Abe had already discussed: that Ennis Fultz was a customer and had died. We held back anything about the tank or nitrogen playing a part in the crime.

"At this point, we're just looking to populate a timeline," I said. "Place moments onto it that help us figure out when Mr. Fultz was in his house and when he was gone."

"Sure," Thieland said. "I was a big *CSI* fan. I get it."

This used to drive me crazy, when people gave that reference, but lately I leaned into it.

"Great," I said. "It's exactly like that."

"Well, I looked up the customer after the other detective called," Thieland said. "I can tell you Mr. Fultz's last delivery was on Tuesday, April twenty-second. Signed for at 10:53 by Louise Randall."

He meant Ipsy, of course, but the date he mentioned was two weeks before the murder.

"And what about deliveries since then?" Remy asked. "Like on Sunday, May fifth?"

Thieland consulted his computer screen and shrugged. "Nope."

Maybe the delivery truck wasn't United Chem. I sat down in one of the two chairs in front of the desk and paged backward, to my notes from the Thorpe conversation.

"How does it work?" Remy asked, buying me some time. "You fill the canisters here or they come that way from some central location?"

"We fill 'em here," he said. "This location fulfills out to Alabama, southern Tennessee, and all of Georgia."

Thieland's office windows looked out toward 85 in one direction and the shipping yard in the other.

"And does each driver own a particular route?"

"Yes, ma'am," Thieland said.

"So the drivers get to know the customers?" Remy said. "Build relationships?"

Thieland ran his right hand along the edge of his hair. A gesture that made me think he didn't tie up those locks on the weekend. Party out back when the suit was off.

"We like to say that our drivers are the tip of the sword," he said.

I looked up from my notes.

United Chem was a large multinational, and my experience was that these companies typically clammed up and sent in lawyers when the police showed up with too many questions. Still, we needed to know more about the process by which a tank got into Fultz's house.

"So the guy who delivered to Ennis Fultz's place. Can we talk to him?"

Thieland leaned back in his chair. "The fella who called . . ."

"Detective Kaplan," Remy said.

"I asked him if you were bringing a subpoena or something." Thieland smiled. "This is a highly matrixed organization. Lotta layers. Lotta rules."

"We can get one, if we need to," I said. "We were just hoping for a casual conversation with your driver. More about what he thought of Ennis Fultz. We can ask him off-site, if that's easier."

Thieland crossed the room and closed the door to the hallway before returning to his seat. "So, there's where it gets a little . . . dicey," he said. "We haven't seen that employee since last Friday."

"They're missing?" Remy asked.

"We consider seventy-two hours as abandonment of job. Especially if you don't return a truck."

Remy and I exchanged a glance. "The driver still has the truck?" I said.

Thieland hesitated. "This particular person is not, uh—you know—a driver anymore, per se."

"You fired them?"

"Well, there's where it gets a little—uh . . ."

"Dicey?" I said.

"What's this employee's name?" Remy asked.

"See, the brass here are real sticklers for HR rules, Detective Morgan."

"Did you report the vehicle stolen?" I asked. "There's a steep penalty for the theft of a commercial—"

"I didn't report it," Thieland said, a nervous smile on his face. "We keep spare keys. Early this morning I had one of our managers drive over to the employee's apartment. Grab the truck."

"You stole it back?" Remy said.

"Does the *brass* know that?" I asked.

"No," Thieland said. Biting at his lip.

"Can we see the truck?" Remy asked.

Thieland ran a hand through his hair again. "I'm confused how this helps you populate a timeline, Detective Morgan."

I stared at Thieland. My college roommate was one of these

types. Slippery as an eel. He told me I lacked the "moral flexibility" to make it in life.

"You know what?" I said. "We'll come back with that subpoena."

Thieland stood up. "All right then."

"What's the timeline on a response from that?" I asked.

"I'll put the ask into corporate. Same with your request for the driver's name. Figure ten to fifteen working days."

"Sounds fair," I said.

Remy glanced at me. One of her eyebrows was raised above the other.

I shook Thieland's hand, and he opened the glass door to the hall. "Our district attorney will reach out in the meantime," I said. "On the other issue."

Thieland blinked first.

"What other issue?"

"You not reporting the stolen truck," I said. "She'll want to file charges—on your behalf, of course. So she'll need info on how you stole it back. Whether any private property was entered. And who authorized that."

"Whoa-whoa-whoa." Thieland motioned us back inside, closing the glass door behind us.

"Don't worry," I said. "She doesn't have to bother you. She can talk directly to your head of Legal."

Thieland used his hand to wipe sweat from the back of his neck. "Did you two just want to take a *quick look* at the truck? Is that all?" he asked. "'Cause maybe we do that and your DA doesn't need to be bothered."

"Sure, that'd be great," Remy said.

Thieland led us down a stairwell and through a series of hallways.

The factory floor opened up from there, a giant space with forklifts moving crates that contained tanks of three or four different sizes. The loading bays were to our right, and Thieland was checking the trucks backed into them—for a particular license plate.

"This is it." He pointed to a stall marked *17* in yellow numbers on the concrete.

Backed into the space was a white GMC Sierra with those safety stickers that Travis Thorpe had mentioned. From there we could see out into the yard, where we'd driven earlier.

One of the reasons I wanted to see the truck was to test the tanks. Maybe even protect others from potential nitrogen poisoning if there were other tanks still on the vehicle. But the truck was empty.

"Where's all its tanks?" I asked.

Thieland shrugged. "I was told he fulfilled all the orders. The truck was empty."

Remy took out her cell and held it up to her ear. I hadn't heard it buzz.

"I gotta take this," she said to Thieland, who nodded. She started walking out into the open asphalt area where she'd made her U-turn earlier.

"Listen," Thieland said to me quietly. "A lot of these drivers— they don't have the good sense that God gave a rock. So it's not like a high crime, us taking back our truck, right?"

I stared at him. Said nothing.

"There's things I'm not supposed to talk about." Thieland smiled. "You know? Employment rules and all."

"How about off the record?" I said.

This was a trick I'd learned from my old partner. Abe would do this "off the record" bullshit, and people would offer him the world, as if he were some reporter and there were rules for on and off the record. As if he wasn't gonna haul their ass into court to repeat the same information.

"Well, off the record," he said, "I suspect this particular guy had some drug problems. A couple weeks ago he had a shipment that got stolen off the truck while he was at a Waffle House in Smyrna eating lunch. I thought maybe he sold it to someone."

"When was this?"

"Last month," he said. "Twenty-second."

"You write him up for that?" I asked.

Thieland exhaled loudly through his nose. Shook his head. "No, 'cause he filed a police report on the theft. I just didn't believe it."

"And what was on the truck that got stolen?"

"The usual. Mostly compressed oxygen."

"Any nitrogen?"

"One container," he said. "This fella mostly delivers medical."

I blinked, not following him.

Thieland turned. Pointed at the factory floor. "We've been reorganizing the business by industry. So that guys who deliver to nursing homes aren't the same guys dropping stuff at factories and farms. This driver still did a bit of both."

This information was layered. One, the driver may have stolen the nitrogen off his own truck. Two, he worked with farmers.

Which made me think about a delivery out to the Sorrell brothers.

"This driver," I said. "Does he deliver out to any farms in Paradise Grove up north?"

"Maybe," he said. "I'd have to look it up."

"Do the drivers enter the home?"

"Oh sure," he said. "They hook up the equipment. Carry out the old tank. Most customers know how to do all that, but that service is one of the reasons they work with us, versus the new tech that compresses oxygen right out of the air in your home."

"So, you never put anything in writing to this employee," I said. "Now you suspect he's a drug addict who stole your stuff—and you can't have him hauling your product around."

"Pretty much," Thieland said.

"And this time maybe you figured you dodged a bullet in having to go through the process of writing him up? You grab your truck back. If he complains, you file grand theft auto against him."

"When you put it that way," he said, "we sound like the bad guys."

I noticed Remy had walked over to the booth and was chatting up the security guard. Same guy as before.

I grabbed on to the rail and pulled myself up into the pickup bed, so I could see my partner.

Remy was waving at us, and I had a guess at what was going on.

I turned to Thieland. "I think my partner's getting griefed by your security guard while she's trying to take a call."

Thieland glanced over at her.

"Give your guy a thumbs-up, will ya?"

Thieland waved at the guard. Then put his thumb in the air.

I asked Thieland about the protocol of how tanks get onto the truck. He explained how the orders came down from Sales and into Fulfillment. How the loaders put tanks into a crate and then a floor manager checked them after they were on the truck.

"So there's never issues of the wrong chemical getting on the truck?"

"I'm not saying it's never happened," Thieland said. "But it's rare. The tanks have stickers that are color-coded."

"Are they removable? The stickers?"

"I guess." He shrugged. "We remove and apply 'em here, so by definition, yeah."

Remy turned toward me and lifted her head just slightly. Smiled.

I thanked Thieland and told him that maybe we didn't need to come back with a subpoena or call the DA.

"I appreciate that."

"I'ma walk out this way," I said. "Grab Detective Morgan and walk back to our car."

"Sure."

I strolled over to where Remy was. When I got there, she was deep into it with the security guard she'd flirted with before.

"This is my partner, Detective Marsh," she said.

The guard shook my hand. "Willie Teague," he said.

"Willie was telling me some background on Thom Sile," Remy said.

Nice. The thumbs-up from Thieland had worked in getting

the guard to start talking about the driver. Starting with his name.

"You know this guy, Willie?" I asked.

"Thom-with-an-*h* is what we call him. 'Cause of how it's spelled," he said.

Remy flicked her eyebrows at me. "Willie's been thinking of applying for the academy next year."

"Well, we need good people," I said. "How're your observation skills?"

"Good."

"Your memory?"

He nodded.

"Do you remember if Thom's truck was empty or full when the manager drove it back here today?"

"It was dead empty, Detective. I'm sure of it."

"You talked to Thom before?"

"Small talk," Willie said. "On the way out. He's a 'Bama fan."

"Well, none of us are perfect," I said. "Where's he live?"

"Ferris. Was telling your partner that."

This was a town east of Mason Falls. A tiny place. If a good song came on the radio, you might pass Ferris by accident.

"There was a truck that he lost the load on, Willie," I said. "About two weeks ago. Sile said it got stolen while he was eating at a Waffle House. You believe that?"

"No."

"All right." I took out my card. "When it comes time for the academy, why don't you give us a call."

The guard beamed.

"Do me a favor." I turned back. "Keep our conversation quiet. Even from Mr. Thieland. You know—just in case he wants to be the man about all this. The guy who pulled the trigger. Got the truck back. Called the cops."

Willie put up his hands. "Hey, he's the boss."

We walked back to the 500 building and got in Remy's Alfa.

"So what are you thinking?" She turned to me.

"If you're Thom Sile and making these house calls," I said, "maybe you're in the same boat we thought Suzy was in?"

"You see cash sitting around," Remy said. "The old man gone."

"Walking the gorge two hours a day," I said.

"You're saying Thom Sile delivered the wrong tank on purpose. Then waited for it to take Fultz out and circled back."

I explained to Remy what Cass Thieland had told me about nitrogen being part of the missing chemicals at the Waffle House.

We drove to Ferris. The city had a police department of eight and relied on the county for other services. Abe worked up a search warrant for us, and we met with the sergeant at the station to coordinate a visit on Thom Sile's apartment complex.

"Two guys would be great," I said. The sergeant told me to give him an hour.

While we waited for the extra help and warrant, Remy drove me over to Fultz's to grab my truck, which we'd left there.

When we got back, we were introduced to Officers Cable and Stoops. Two six-footers, each white and built like S.E.C. football linemen.

Stoops was the senior guy, blond, and he met us at Remy's car. He held out a paper.

"Thom Sile's sheet," he said.

I looked it over. A DUI last year. A possession charge in '15 for marijuana. Nothing else.

Officer Cable came out and stood by his car. He was younger and had a beard that was an odd shade of blondish gray—the color of a pantry moth. He said he would accompany me, while his partner worked with Remy.

"Let's go," I said.

29

I parked my truck behind the patrol car driven by Stoops, which the officers left a block shy of the Tatham Arms Apartment Complex. The place where Thom Sile lived.

It was almost seven p.m., and the skies were an odd mix of grays and purples. Maybe it was pollution from Atlanta, or maybe rain was on its way. If the end of times comes to big cities first, folks'll probably just mistake Armageddon for a smog inversion layer.

We walked to the apartment complex, not wanting to spook Thom Sile with a couple patrol cars.

The Tatham Arms had an office that fed in from 2nd Avenue, and inside we met a guy named Brian in his thirties, who was the manager. We confirmed Thom Sile lived there, and asked if he was home.

Brian flicked a few buttons on his computer and pulled up a camera angle on an underground parking level. "Well, there's his car," he said. "That old black Jetta."

The manager clocked in around two bills. He wore a faded Braves T-shirt and his head was shaved on the sides.

Officer Stoops asked Brian what he thought of Sile.

"Keeps to himself," he said. "Venmos the rent. Never calls to fix nothin'."

In other words, a perfect tenant.

A window faced out onto the blacktop of the apartment's parking lot and driveway. There were four buildings, placed at angles to each other. Some green areas and a couple spots where barbecue grills were set up for residents. A good amount of parking.

"You been inside Sile's place recently?" I asked Brian.

"At quarterly roach check," he said. "It's in okay condition. Carpet's worn down."

"He park his work truck here?" Remy asked.

"That's part of why he moved here," Brian said. "We got an area for oversized vehicles. RVs mostly. He needed that. But—" Brian leaned his head toward the window. "It ain't here now."

Yeah, I thought. *United Chem stole it back already.*

We left the manager and walked across the parking lot to Building 3, where Thom Sile lived.

Officer Cable and I moved up the stairs to the second floor while Remy and Officer Stoops covered the parking lot.

I banged on number 203 and stepped sideways, standing near the jamb. Next to the door, yellowing vertical blinds covered a small window.

"Thom Sile," Officer Cable hollered.

After a minute, the door opened a touch, catching itself on the security chain.

The man inside was white and thin, and matched Sile's DMV picture. He wore sweats with no shirt, and his cheeks were sallow.

"Police, Mr. Sile," Cable said.

Thom Sile shoved the door closed, and we heard the dead bolt lock.

Cable banged on the door, and I heard a bumping noise inside. I looked down from the second floor at Remy, motioning for her to look around the side. The manager said there was only one way out, but I wanted to confirm.

Remy hustled around to her left, getting a wider view from farther out into the parking lot.

"We got a jumper," she yelled.

I hustled down the stairs and saw Sile had yanked the screen off his bedroom window and hopped about eight feet down, onto the roof of an adjacent building.

"Shit."

Remy climbed on top of an air-conditioning unit and pulled herself up onto the same roof.

I raced across the parking lot, following Sile, while keeping an eye on my partner.

"Police, stop," I heard Remy yell, but Sile kept going.

When he got to the end of the roof, he jumped off the one-story laundry building into the parking lot—about twenty feet in front of me.

He landed hard and collapsed in pain, holding his leg.

"Dipshit," I said under my breath.

I had my cuffs out. Locked them around his right wrist and pulled his other hand back.

"My leg," Sile yelled in pain. "Fuuuck!"

Sile was a hundred and thirty pounds soaking wet: the figure of a teenage model. Remy stood at the edge of the roof above me, and I encouraged her to go back the way she'd come.

Stoops and I helped Sile stretch out his leg.

"I tore my ACL." Sile groaned. "Last year."

"Well, good news is your knee looks fine," I said. "But your left leg." I touched it, and he screamed in pain.

The city of Ferris contracted with a local ambulance company as EMS, and Officer Stoops called them. Remy stayed with Sile while Cable and I got Brian, the manager, to open up his place.

Brian unlocked the dead bolt, but the chain was still on.

"Stand back," Cable said. "I can kick this in."

The manager put up his hand. "Hold your horses, cowboy. I'll have this open in thirty seconds."

The manager had brought a roll of duct tape with him. He wrapped a rubber band around the chain and then secured a strip of duct tape to the rubber band. He reached in through the crack and stuck the duct tape to the inside of the door. Then closed the door. When he reopened it a second later, the tape had pulled off the chain. Some kind of magic trick.

Cable and I cleared the apartment, seeing drug paraphernalia spread throughout the place, but no one else inside.

As we moved outside onto the balcony, a bus showed up in the parking lot, and Sile was loaded into it.

I walked down from the second floor and approached the back of the ambulance.

"Mr. Sile," I said. "I need to speak to you about Ennis Fultz. Your customer out by the gorge."

The ambulance tech gave Sile something for his pain, and he leaned forward, vomiting into a bag.

"Jesus," I said.

"That means it's working," the tech said.

"Great," I said, checking my shoes. "Look, Mr. Sile. Ennis Fultz. When's the last time you saw him?"

Sile squinted, holding the bag in his hand. He was rail thin, and the smell was horrible. "I ain't sayin' shit to you, pig."

The tip of the sword, I thought.

"Ennis is dead," I said. "But I bet you already knew that."

Sile turned his head, looking the other way.

"We need to go, Detective," the tech said.

He jumped in the back and closed the doors behind him. I walked over to the driver. "Give me the lay of the land on this clown," I said, motioning my head at the back of the ambulance.

"If he broke his tibia, which is what it looks like," the driver said, "he goes into surgery and they put a rod in it. You're not interviewing him 'til tomorrow."

I tapped at the hood of the bus and walked back upstairs, letting them take Sile away.

Inside the apartment, Remy was taking photographs with her phone.

"You find any delivery papers related to United Chem?"

"A clipboard." Remy motioned at the kitchen counter.

I picked the clipboard up. It was one of those metal numbers with a fastener at the top that kept your papers from blowing away. Also a letter-sized area an inch thick to store receipts inside. I unclasped the papers from the top and opened the receipts area.

Inside was a stack of seven or eight signed yellow carbons with the initials *P.O.D.* in big black letters at the top. Each listed a location and time where Thom Sile had dropped an oxygen tank. There were deliveries on Thursday and Friday. Even one on Saturday. I realized P.O.D. stood for "proof of delivery."

"Nothing on Sunday," I said. The day Thorpe had seen the truck out there.

"You expecting to find a receipt?" a voice snickered. "One tank dropped off. Man poisoned. Signed for at one p.m.?"

I smirked at Abe, who stood in the doorway. It was a different energy when he and I were partners. Sarcasm all the time.

"I heard you guys could use a hand."

"You heard right," I said. "You know any good detectives?"

Abe smiled at this, and I walked with him out onto the landing outside the front door.

"There's a manager's office." I pointed toward the street. "The guy working there was showing us Sile's underground parking spot. I watched him click through three or four screens," I said. "Must have ten cameras all over this place."

"You want me to go through 'em?"

"Yeah," I said. I walked Abe through what we'd learned at United Chem and reminded him of Ennis Fultz's time of death.

For Sile to be a legit suspect, we needed to know if he was out at Fultz's place. And find cash that tied him to the murder.

"I want to know when Sile came home," I said to Abe. "When he left. We need to calendar the shit out of him."

"On it," Abe said.

I returned to the apartment, and Remy and I split up the

place. I took the living room and bedroom, while my partner took the bathroom and kitchen.

The warrant allowed us to search the apartment for money that we could connect to serial numbers off Fultz's cash, as well as any property of United Chemical.

I stared at the room that Thom Sile probably spent most of his time in.

The living room had five pieces of furniture in it. A black futon was parked in the center. It faced a sixty-inch big screen, which was leaning, unmounted, against the far wall. A set of two giant speakers from the 2000s flanked the TV on each side. Near the futon, there was a shiny lacquered coffee table with a red bong and two pipes atop it.

I leaned the futon mattress against the wall, running my hands along the padding and eventually opening the zipper. No money or drugs were inside. I looked around the back of the TV and checked for any compartments in the coffee table. Nothing.

In the bedroom, I spent even more time, running my gloved hands across every shelf in Sile's closet and looking through every drawer.

In the bedroom closet I found a shovel. The blade was clean, but the grip had dirt stuck in it.

I moved into the bathroom, where Remy was working. Alvin Gerbin, our evidence tech, sat atop the commode. Clothed, I mean. He was helping Remy catalogue the prescription drugs inside Sile's medicine cabinet.

I held up the shovel. "Remember what Ipsy said about cash buried in the yard?"

Remy raised her eyebrows. "You find any cash?"

"Good point," I said, and turned. Kept looking.

Walking back into the living room, I placed the futon mattress back onto the frame. I sat down on it and looked at the bong and two pipes. Staring across at Sile's AV setup, I noticed there were no screws at the corners of each speaker's cover. Just four empty holes.

I stood up and walked over, popping off the black fabric screen from the right speaker.

"He-llo," I said, seeing a clear plastic tube about five inches long and three inches wide, hidden next to the subwoofer. The container was crammed with marijuana. Beside it was a pile of peach-colored pills in a quart-sized ziplock.

Gerbin heard me and came out, taking good pictures of the right speaker. I took one of the pills from the baggie and laid it on the table.

"You got your pharma guide with you?" I asked. Seeing the marking *dp* on the round pill.

"Don't need it," Gerbin said. "I know that one. It's Adderall. Thirty milligrams."

I held up the plastic tube with the weed in it. It looked to be around three ounces, which in Georgia is a felony. Five grand and a one-year minimum. Of course a good lawyer would get rid of that charge if we didn't find any cash nearby since that was the thrust of our warrant.

I popped off the other speaker cover. Six rolls of hundred dollar bills. At first blush, it looked like ten grand.

Alvin whistled, and I thought about how Abe had connected one of the bills Suzy had on her to the serial numbers on Fultz's cash. If we could do that here, Thom Sile wouldn't have the same way out as Suzy did. He wasn't lucky enough to be mentioned in Fultz's will.

My phone pulsed, and I looked down. Abe calling.

"We just hit a jackpot," I said as I answered.

"Yeah, I got something too. You should come down here."

I walked down the stairwell and found Abe with Brian, the apartment manager.

"What've you got?" I asked.

Abe switched chairs, and patted the one in front of the monitor for me to take a seat. A pile of DVDs sat to my right.

"We got three different time periods we're looking at," Abe said.

Brian put in a DVD and punched some keys to queue up a specific time.

"Most recent first," Abe said, pointing at the screen.

The camera angle was on the front gate at the Tatham Arms Apartment Complex—the gate that folks drove out when they left.

Outside—across the street—a man smoked a cigarette. The time code down the corner read *11:01 a.m.*

"So here's your shift manager from United Chem," Abe said. "Stealing his truck back."

"He waits for the gate to open," Brian said.

Suddenly, the gate began to roll back as a car drove out of the Tatham Arms. The man from United Chem walked past the car and was in.

A minute later the delivery truck followed another car out of the gate and onto the street.

"You need a clicker to get out of here, not just in?"

"Both ways." The manager nodded.

"Okay," I said. "So, we knew about the United Chem driver already."

"Sure." Abe smiled. "But I show you this for fidelity, Mr. Juror. My video is reputable, yes? The time and date line up with other evidence you have from United Chem?"

"Okay," I said. "You established your baseline, Detective. What's next?"

Brian ejected the DVD and placed another one in. He reversed the action to a specific point and paused it.

"This is Monday morning," Abe said. "Real early."

"What time?" I asked.

"This particular DVD covers five to ten a.m.," Abe said.

Ennis Fultz's original time of death was later than this range. Between ten a.m. and two p.m. Monday. But recently Remy and I had surmised that the tank could've been tampered with earlier.

Brian unpaused the video, and I stared at a nondescript figure moving across the parking lot. It was before dawn, so we didn't have the benefit of the sun to see the man, making him a shape of gray with no face.

I stared at the time code, running in the corner of the screen: *5:10 a.m.* The morning Ennis Fultz had been killed. Five hours before our initial T.O.D.

The figure came alongside the United Chem truck and adjusted something in the back. A shine flashed across the screen and we saw that there was a tank in the bed of the truck. The man's back was to us.

I leaned in closer. Our angle and resolution was for shit, but a moment later, the truck moved out of the apartment complex and onto the street. Made a right.

Five-thirteen a.m. on the Monday morning that Ennis would be killed.

"So we got Sile leaving here," Abe said.

"You mean you got a grayed-out six-foot-tall guy leaving here," I said.

"True that." Abe smiled.

"And the guy's own company stole the truck back the next day," I said. "So any good lawyer will argue that if United Chem could steal the truck—"

"Anyone could," Abe finished my sentence.

"Is there more?" I asked.

"He comes back fifty-three minutes later," Abe said. "At 6:06 a.m. Still can't see his face. But he drives back and parks in the same space."

Fifty-three minutes was enough time to drive over to Ennis Fultz's place while the old man was asleep and switch out a tank. Hours before Fultz would need it.

Abe showed me this other moment on tape, and I saw the truck pull back in. Again, the man avoided walking close enough for us to see his face.

"Do the tenants know where the cameras are?" I asked Brian.

"Some do," the manager said. "We had complaints from folks that their privacy was getting invaded, so we put up signs near each one. To inform them."

I pointed at the screen. "He avoids it for sure."

I was thinking about the rolls of hundreds we'd just found

upstairs. Had Sile seen the cash around Ennis's place? Was the old man an easier mark than I'd thought?

"What about other cameras?" I asked Brian. "Do we see him walking out his front door? Coming down from the second floor to his truck?"

"Been aiming to fix those," Brian said. "But they're broken."

"Did he drive his Jetta in and park?" I asked. "Then grab the truck? Was he somewhere else before?"

"His Jetta was here the whole time," Abe said. "Sile had to have come from upstairs."

"What about anyone else on camera?" I asked. Thinking this was a great way to canvass for witnesses.

"There's a guy who walks through the front gate right before six," Abe said. "Only traffic around that time."

I nodded. It was the sort of setup where you could follow another car in or out if you didn't have your clicker with you—and the gate stayed open for the next car too.

I wanted to nail Sile and only Sile for this.

"The guy who walked in off the street around six that morning wasn't Sile," Brian said. "He's taller and dressed nice. Good-looking guy. Not a tenant here."

"And how far back did you go?" I asked.

"So far," Abe said, "we went backward and forward three hours. Looked at every car going in and out."

"And nothing in that range or after?" I asked. "Between ten and two?"

"Not nothing." Abe looked down at his notebook. "I have three cars that followed someone out. And two that followed them in."

"Meaning they didn't have a clicker?"

"Doesn't mean that necessarily," Abe said. "If the gate's already opening, you don't click your clicker."

"Sure," I said. "Anyone not use the clicker both ways?" I asked Abe. "To get in and out?"

"One car."

Abe paged through his notes as Brian fast-forwarded the tape. "Here," Abe said. "Doesn't click out either way. What do you call those old beaters? Rednecks drove 'em when I was a kid."

"El Caminos," Brian said. A little too fast. Like maybe he was the sort of redneck Abe was referring to. I tried not to smile.

"Black with a gray pinstripe on the side." Brian pointed at the video, showing the El Camino waiting behind another car as the gate came to life. "That make's called a choo-choo."

I nodded. There wasn't much more to see.

Abe squinted at me. "Are you looking for it *not* to be Sile, P.T.? Because we got the truck leaving here for the right amount of time."

"No," I said. "I'm just running through each of the bases, partner. Trying to be a hundred percent."

I checked the time on my phone. It was past one a.m.

"Thorpe." I pointed at Abe. "The grass seed guy. He's the reason we got onto Sile in the first place. He said he saw the truck after he dropped off his seed bags."

"Sure, that's the night before," Abe said. "Sunday evening. Thorpe talked to Fultz around five p.m."

"Do we know if the truck was gone then?"

Abe tapped at a pile of DVDs. "We didn't get to Sunday yet," he said. "But it's possible Sile was doing recon when Thorpe saw him. You know—checking out Fultz's place."

"Sure."

"Or maybe he was gonna switch out the tanks on Sunday, but he saw Ennis Fultz and Thorpe together and bailed. Put it off 'til Fultz was asleep."

This was also sound logic.

I looked back at the pile of DVDs.

"So early Monday he leaves. Comes back fifty-three minutes later." I talked it through out loud. "So if the goal is robbery, we're saying Sile put the tank out there early that morning. Around dawn. Then he drove back Monday afternoon or evening after Ennis was dead and cleaned him out."

"Exactly." Abe nodded.

"What do we know about Sile's whereabouts late Monday?" I pointed at the DVDs. "Like Monday afternoon or night?"

"Monday's still to come too." Abe smiled. "It's an exciting job you've assigned me."

I grinned at my old partner.

Sile could've come back for Fultz's cash any time *after* Suzy left and *before* we got there Tuesday morning. A twenty-hour window.

"We'll go through the DVDs," Abe said. "Find out when Sile leaves here again."

"Good," I said. "Let's get it airtight."

"Ten-four, brother."

I turned and headed back up to the apartment. There were inventory control procedures we had to follow when we found over a thousand dollars in cash, and I wanted to sign off on them and package up the money myself.

Before three a.m. a taco truck parked across the way, and Remy and I walked down to the street. We ate ceviche on soft corn tortillas, and Remy motioned at the picture on the side of the truck. The ad read *Fresh Fish*.

"Where you think these guys fish?"

"Aisle eight," I said. "The frozen food section of Kroger."

Remy smiled. "But the green chiles on top." She took a bite. "Damn good."

As we ate, my partner flipped her hair back, which was looking different these days. Straighter maybe.

This triggered a memory of something my wife, Lena, had once said. "Never ask a black woman if she's got a weave, Paul," she told me. "Not unless you're ready for the answer, followed by her kicking your ass."

"What?" Remy said, noticing me staring.

"Nothing," I said.

The city of Ferris sent a fresh set of patrolmen to sit with us. Along with them came word that Thom Sile had gone into surgery. Apparently his tibia was fractured in two places.

"He's gonna be asleep 'til noon," Remy said. "And Abe has him on video, leaving in his Jetta around two p.m. Monday. Gone until nine."

Two p.m. Monday meant Thom Sile had seven hours to search Fultz's place. Remy and I wouldn't show up there until the next morning. This was enough time to dig for cash. Take out the bad tank. And go through every closet and hiding spot that Ipsy had shown us.

"Go home and get some sleep, Rem," I said. "We got this degenerate. I can friggin' taste it."

Remy stood up and patted her chest. "That may be the tacos coming back up. But I feel it too, boss. My guess—we close this by afternoon."

30

Remy took off, and I drove back to the precinct, checking the cash into evidence.

The case was on its last legs, and there was no better feeling.

As I counted the money for the old-timer that ran our evidence locker, I thought of Marvin and the conversation with Garva, the nurse, about Marvin's personal property.

I wondered if Marvin's phone was in one of his two cars, and I thought about what I'd have done back on patrol with a gas explosion like this.

If there had been cars in the mini-mall's parking lot, I would have cleared them to an impound yard immediately just in case there were further explosions. The last thing anyone wants near an open gas pipe are fifteen-gallon pods of gasoline, otherwise known as cars.

I pocketed Marvin's wallet and keys and drove over to his house.

When I got there, Marvin's old Chrysler 200 was gone, but his

1972 Dodge Charger was in the driveway. I clicked the fob to unlock it and looked inside.

Spotless. Like it was every time I was in it.

If my father-in-law was going to be in the hospital for a while, he'd want me to come by and start his Charger—at least to let the engine run.

My mind was going ninety miles an hour, and I needed to let it rest. Oftentimes, being in motion soothed me. I got in the Charger and let out the engine.

On SR-908, I headed northeast toward Centa. The night air was cool with the windows down, and a Chase Rice country song about hitting it big in Nashville played on the radio.

To my right, a ghostlike haze hung along the tops of the trees, and the ground was covered in a thousand short stumps that represented the failure of logging control.

Centa was a small town, and after about ten minutes of circling the four main downtown streets and not finding the police station, I pulled into a twenty-four-hour donut place and talked to a guy working the counter.

"City council disbanded the police three months ago," he said. "Same thing across half of Shonus County. A lot of cops became state policemen."

I motioned at the street in front of the donut shop. "So this is all GSP jurisdiction?"

The man nodded, and I walked back to the Charger. This meant Marvin's car might be at any number of Georgia State Patrol substations.

I had set up Marvin's iPhone myself, so I logged on to the

Find My iPhone microsite on my cell, watching as the last location of Marvin's iPhone pinged. A spot half a mile away.

I drove down Ball Street, turning at 1st. Two blocks away I moved out of the tiny downtown area and stopped at the corner of 1st and Fern.

Yellow police tape hung taut around the stoplight. I turned my wheel to illuminate the area to its right and saw the tape ran west, blocking off a small corner mini-mall with five or six units in it.

This was where the explosion had happened.

From the picture on my phone, Marvin's cell phone was somewhere in the center suite.

I parked the Charger and got out, grabbing a flashlight from the glove box.

I ducked under the tape and stopped, panning the light over the scene.

The mini-mall itself was a simple L-shaped building, tan with a red Spanish-style roof. It held one larger unit that contained a check-cashing place, and four smaller stores, some of which were unrecognizable now. The area of the blast looked to be the center store, since there was nothing left there. No ceiling, no walls. A pile of burnt debris lay in the center of the small parking lot nearby. Beside that, one of those Bobcat earth movers was parked, a scoop claw on the front for cleaning up the mess.

"Jesus," I said, wondering how Marvin was alive if he was in that center suite.

I stepped over a pile of trash and into the destroyed office space.

I decided to go the easiest path first, and called Marvin's

phone. The old man usually kept it charged, and with no apps sucking at its power, I wondered if the phone would still have juice a day later.

I heard a buzzing noise and crouched, scanning the area under the desk with my flashlight as I called the phone again.

In the corner, I saw a glimpse of something move and dug my hand through a pile of chalky white drywall dust until I found Marvin's phone.

I blew the dirt off it and saw the battery was still at ten percent.

I crouched and looked through his texts, seeing one from Lucas Royster, the P.I. It mentioned a time for him and Marvin to meet.

I moved to voicemails then, and saw the one I'd left two days earlier, before scrolling down to other names.

Exie, Lena's sister.

A woman whose Doberman Marvin walked once a week.

I checked missed calls and saw several from Lucas Royster.

Marvin and the P.I. were communicating regularly.

A light shined through the mess of debris, and I dropped the phone.

"Put your hands up," a voice said. It came through a bullhorn, and I turned my eyes, blinded for a second.

Knowing my body was half hidden in the rubble, I decided to make no sudden movements.

"I'm a cop," I said.

"Put—up—your hands!"

The voice sounded familiar, and I shook my head.

There was only one cop in Shonus County who I'd dealt with before. A cop who didn't like how things turned out for him.

If the voice was Andy Sugarman's, like I suspected, and he was now GSP, I was probably headed to jail.

"Sugarman?" I hollered. "That you?"

I didn't want him to see the phone.

"Stand up now!" the voice screamed.

I had installed a Google Drive backup feature on Marvin's phone, and I leaned over, hitting the button to activate it.

Then I left the phone there and stood up.

"Andy," I hollered. "It's P. T. Marsh."

I walked toward the light with my hands raised, struggling through the debris.

In his last job as sheriff of nearby Shonus, Andy Sugarman and I had some run-ins. At first they were positive, but then I'd failed to mention I was entering his jurisdiction in search of a murder suspect. By the end of that case, thanks to me, Sugarman looked like a small-town chump.

"What in God's green earth are you doing here, Marsh?" he said as I got closer.

"The explosion," I said.

"Gas leak," he corrected me.

"My father-in-law, Marvin, was one of the victims," I said. "He's in an induced coma, and I'm trying to help him out."

"By investigating?" Sugarman squinted at me. "There's nothing suspicious here, P.T. No evil men doing bad things in a mini-mall."

This was a smart-ass reference to our last work together. Which told me his bitterness was alive and well.

"Andy, I'm sorry."

"What the hell you looking for?" He scanned the rubble with his light.

I glanced over at where I'd left Marvin's phone. If I mentioned it to Sugarman, he'd probably seize the thing. Put it into evidence.

"His wallet," I said. "It was stupid. I should've called you guys."

"Yeah, but that's not your strong suit, is it?"

Sugarman turned. "Wait right there." He pointed. When he walked, his body stayed upright, like someone had stuck a broomstick up his ass and left it there.

I put on a friendly voice. "How's the new gig?" I hollered as he headed to his cruiser.

"It's awesome," he said. "I used to be in charge, and now I light up speeders on the highway. Thanks to you."

Sugarman made a call. Took some notes in his pad.

"I'm reporting this, Marsh. You shouldn't have come here."

I thought of the Fultz case. We finally had momentum. Had found our guy—and then I came here. Derailed myself.

"C'mon, man," I pleaded. "It's my father-in-law. I was just walking through a pile of trash."

"Is that your car?" He pointed at the Charger. "Why don't you move over there? Wait by your vehicle."

I walked over to Marvin's car and stood there. Five minutes later another GSP cruiser came by. An hour later, I was still there. Sugarman told me his boss was on the line with my new boss, Chief Senza. The guy I'd just met. Who told me I was no hero.

An older officer arrived finally, and he told me I could go. "Your chief said to come see him tomorrow. Sounds like fun."

"Yeah, appreciate the brotherhood," I said.

"Stay the hell out of our jurisdiction."

I walked over to Marvin's car and drove back to Mason Falls.

When I got home, Purvis had been indoors a full day, and I leashed him up.

We got to a grass area with a duck pond that Purvis liked, and I thought about walks I took here with Jonas. We'd bring a ziplock full of bread, and my son would toss it at the mallards. Last year's rains had overflowed the three ponds in the neighborhood. When the water level settled, it threw off the chemical balance, causing a bad smell that drove away the wildlife.

I let go of Purvis's leash, and he walked on his own, sniffing at the grass.

What exactly is going on? he said to me. *You avoid Sarah. You drive off to surrounding cities. You're tilting at windmills, P.T.*

"I'm working the case," I said.

My bulldog huffed.

You know where this leads. To the bottle.

"You don't understand," I said.

But Purvis just turned and headed home. He was tired of being bullshitted.

31

By nine a.m., Remy had moved all the case evidence we'd collected to the conference room, and she and Abe were pinning it up on the cork wall at the south end.

When detectives talk about their records, you hear numbers like 56 and 2. Or 30 and 1. It's those one or two losses in court, though, that drive us mad. The non-convictions that keep us up at night. I didn't want that to happen with Thom Sile, and I told myself I was done sneaking around at night.

"Let's run through Sile's whereabouts," I said. "Sunday to Monday?"

Abe laid a portable whiteboard on the conference room table. "A mile ahead of you," he said.

My old partner had recently switched from a porkpie hat to a fedora, and he looked good in it, a tan linen suit against his light brown skin.

The whiteboard contained a simple horizontal line, across which Abe had marked six points.

Saturday, May 4, 2 p.m. The last delivery Sile made for
United Chem, per the receipts in the clipboard

Sunday, May 5, 5:30 p.m. Sile potentially spotted by
Thorpe out near Fultz's house

Monday, May 6, 5:13 a.m. Sile drove United Chem
truck out of apartment complex

Monday, May 6, 6:06 a.m. Sile returned home in the
U-Chem truck, 53 mins later

Monday, May 6, 2 p.m.–9 p.m. Sile was gone from the
apartment complex, his whereabouts unknown;
potentially looting Fultz's house

Wednesday, May 8, 11 a.m. United Chem employee
repossesses the truck

The theory on Thom Sile murdering Ennis Fultz went like
this: Sile regularly entered the Fultz home and saw the cash Ennis kept around. The deliveryman also had access to nitrogen
tanks from his job at United Chemical, and may have stolen one
two weeks earlier.

A truck like Sile's with a flammable sticker was seen by
Thorpe, our grass seed guy, the day before the murder, perhaps
as Sile was casing Fultz's home.

The following morning, while Ennis Fultz was sleeping, Sile
woke up at five a.m. He snuck out to his truck, loaded the nitrogen canister onto it that he had from the Waffle House theft, and
drove out to Fultz's place.

There he broke in and delivered the nitrogen tank. He knew
the lay of the land since he not only delivered to Fultz's house,
but hooked up tanks for a living.

Later that day, Sile went back to Fultz's after the old man was dead, put back the oxygen tank, and raided the place of cash. Which he hid inside the speaker in his apartment.

We still had to compare the bills found in Sile's apartment with the serial numbers on Ennis Fultz's withdrawals. And we had to talk to Sile himself.

"When does Mr. Sile come up for air from his surgery?" I asked.

"I swung by the hospital on the way in," Abe said. "They say noon-ish."

My cell buzzed with a text, and I saw it was from Harmon Gale. The geologist friend my mom once dated, who ran the UGA Renewable Energy Program.

I'd left him a message after Thorpe told us Fultz's theory about those rocks in the meadow below his house.

"I pulled Sile's cell records," Remy said. "He's on the phone all night long. Calls at two, three, four a.m."

Aside from the Adderall and marijuana, we'd boxed up three cartons of various drug paraphernalia from Sile's place. Everything from needles and roach clips to syringes.

"So he's a dealer?" I confirmed.

"For sure," Remy said.

"How much money did you guys recover?" Abe asked.

"Nine thousand three hundred bucks," I said.

With Suzy Kang, we'd tagged one of the serial numbers from Fultz's cash withdrawals to what Suzy had exchanged at the airport. We were in the process of trying to do the same here, but it took time.

"And Johnny Tobin's going through those hundreds?" Abe asked, referring to our resident financial guru.

"Bill by bill," Remy said.

I turned to her. "You said the calls are 24/7. Any of them overlap with Ennis Fultz's time of death? Or a time we suspect Sile is out by the gorge?"

Remy nodded, knowing where I was going with this. "Yeah, there's a call at 5:26," she said. "You want me to triangulate his location?"

"Exactly," I said. "Sile lives twenty miles from Fultz. And Fultz lives in the middle of nowhere. If we can find a call from Sile's cell that pinged off a cell tower out by the gorge . . . between that and the cash, we nail this guy."

"Copy that," Remy said.

I stepped out for a minute to have a cigarette and check my voicemail.

On it, I heard Harmon Gale's voice. He mentioned that the area Fultz lived in was close to one of Georgia's biggest potential shale deposits.

"Don't know that it means something, but just in case," Harmon said in the message.

As I stood there, I saw Chief Senza moving out to the parking lot. He had on glasses this time. Looked more like a budget consultant than a cop.

"You never came and saw me, Marsh," he hollered. "I assume it's 'cause you're chasing an arrest in this Fultz case."

"You assume right," I said.

"Well, I'm going to help patrol with the motorcade," he said. "But let's talk tomorrow."

"Ten-four."

We had the U.S. president driving through the area on the

way to the Chattahoochee. Some sort of goodwill tour of the National Forest System. So everyone not named P.T. and Remy was being assigned to help with patrol.

"No stone unturned, Marsh," Senza yelled as he got into a white Audi SUV. "No hookers or rednecks unless we got 'em dead to rights."

I turned to walk back inside, and Sarah was heading out with a colleague. She motioned she'd catch up—and we met each other, twenty feet from the front door.

"Hey," she said.

I nodded. Stared at her without saying anything.

Sarah usually had her hair tied back at work, but it lay lazily, past her shoulders.

"We should probably talk, huh?" she said.

By the look on her face, she must've put together what some of my babbling meant the other night when I was beating at that worktable in the garage. That my comment that "it's never gonna be fixed" wasn't about Marvin. It was about me continuing to live in the past—about me still thinking about Lena.

She walked closer until we were inches away.

"I don't want to lose you," I said.

There was a sad smile on her beautiful face. "I know."

She stopped talking then, and my phone buzzed.

A text from Harmon Gale came in, and I glanced down.

You good to chat now?

"Why don't we talk later," Sarah said. "Amy's waiting for me."

"Sure," I said, and she walked off.

Harmon sent a second text—saying he was entertaining some

out-of-town folks at a bar, and I wondered if it meant something—that shale being in the ground and those rocks that Fultz fixated on.

At ten a.m.? I typed. **Where?**

Harmon told me he was at a place about twenty miles away. Hosting a few researchers in town from California for a conference. They wanted to see a "real Southern bar."

I walked back into the conference room. Turned to Abe. "Do me a favor and go down to Tobin. Sit on him, will ya. We need to match *one* serial number in those hundreds to Fultz's cash before our boy wakes up in the hospital."

"Got it," Abe said. His eyes trailed down to my keys. "Where are you going?"

"To meet an old friend," I said. "I need to close off on a theory. Make sure we're not missing something."

Abe squinted at me. "We're running hot, and you're walking out the door?"

"Sile is our guy," I said. "Stay on him. I just got one box to check. I'll be back in an hour."

Across the room Remy was standing by a particular picture on the wall. It was of Nesbit Sorrell, the brother of Greer out at the farm. Patrol hadn't found him at that trailer park.

"Is this peckerwood still in play?" she asked.

I smiled. "Peckerwood" was not a Remy word.

"Not for this murder," I said. "But Nesbit Sorrell destroyed Fultz's Beemer in a rage, so he's still going to jail. Let's put the word out on all the airwaves. With patrol. In the jails. That we got a witness who saw Nesbit beating the hell out of Fultz's BMW. See if the dirtbag gets nervous."

32

MotorMouth was a biker bar set on a strip of gravel off State Route 902, just inside the Mason Falls jurisdiction.

I stepped inside and recalled the place immediately. Remembered coming here once to get Marvin.

A ceiling light bathed patrons' faces in blue, and an old Harley Panhead hung suspended from the ceiling.

"Subdivisions" from Rush's *Signals* album played overhead, a song I hadn't heard since I was a kid. And even then, the song was an oldie.

My eyes scanned the crowd of leather-jacket-wearing bikers. I heard my name and turned, seeing Harmon. He was slender and dressed in a white-and-blue-checkered flannel and jeans.

"Paul," he yelled.

There's a small fraternity of people who call me by the name on my social security card. This included folks from Lena's family, as well as anyone who knew my mother well.

Harmon pulled me into a hug. He was nearabout fifty, and his gray hair was pulled back in a ponytail.

"Been too long," I said.

He introduced me to his crew of four guys who fit in here even less than him. They wore collared shirts with different check patterns. Looked like guys who wrote tax code for a living.

I pointed around the place. "So, environmental researchers know how to party, huh?"

"We can mix it up," one of the Californians said.

After a few minutes of small talk, I leaned into Harmon. "Think we can step outside where it's quiet?"

"Sure."

We threaded through a crowd of leather to a door that exited onto the back parking lot. The asphalt gave way to a dirt lot where trucks and bikes were parked under large live oaks. An old Dodge Magnum wagon was covered in so much dirt you could barely read the license plate.

I gave Harmon a rundown of what we'd seen in the grassy meadow below Ennis Fultz's house and the old man's theory about someone drilling down in the gorge.

"To be honest, we're onto a different lead now, and it just looked like a pile of rocks to me," I said. "But I'm not myself lately, and I got a new boss. I need to check all the boxes."

Harmon lit up a Marlboro Light and began to explain about the oil industry in Georgia. Or the lack thereof. Apparently, there was big interest in fracking for oil throughout north and northwest Georgia.

Harmon defined fracking more simply than I'd heard before—simply as shooting liquid at high pressure into the ground to open up pockets of oil.

"But overall," Harmon said, "there's a lot of splashing and not much water, if you forgive the pun."

"Meaning what?" I said. "There's no actual drilling?"

"Everyone talks about it as this giant future industry," Harmon said. "And it is. But not more than a couple counties in the state have issued an actual license to frack."

Harmon sucked on his cigarette.

"Why not?" I said.

"Environmental concerns," he said. "Safety concerns. But all that shit usually goes out the window in favor of the almighty dollar once it's profitable."

"So it's not profitable?"

"It's dependent on a lot of variables," he said, using his hands as he spoke. "The price of crude for one. The rule of thumb used to be that once crude hit over sixty bucks a barrel, fracking's good to go. It makes money."

"How much is crude now?"

"Seventy-five bucks a barrel," Harmon said.

"But it's still not going in Georgia?"

"It's complicated," he said. "There's politics. Labor shortage in Texas. Yemen warlords overseas. Point is—it's still sitting down there, this reserve."

"In this area?" I asked.

Harmon walked over to a spot of dirt with no cars or bikes. Overhead, a string of lightbulbs hung between the trees. He took the edge of his Converse high-top and drew a rough shape of the state of Georgia in the soft dirt.

"The Condesale Shale," he said, making a circle with his foot that moved past the shape of the state. "It runs from the Alabama border heading east into Georgia. Up into Tennessee. It's estimated—five hundred trillion cubic feet of natural gas."

I had no context on this. "That sounds like a lot."

Harmon smiled. "Yeah, there's an industry term for it. A fuck-ton."

"And Condesale Shale, as in the Condesale Gorge?" I asked. This was the name of the gorge behind Fultz's house.

"Of the same family," he said. "Condesale River. Condesale Canyon. And it extends to this area you're talking about."

"You see these ads," I said. "Billboards to get your land tested."

"Sure." Harmon raised his eyebrows. "See, folks can test without going through any long permit process, as long as the company shuts off the well after. And there's other ways of testing—before you test."

"Meaning what?" I asked.

"Technology, 3-D scans."

"So people are prospecting?" I said. "Looking for the best spots?"

"Now you're cooking," Harmon said. "You mentioned the gorge. That's where your victim lived?"

"Yeah."

"I haven't heard anyone testing in there," Harmon said. "And I think I would've. We track every site within a hundred miles of the university."

I described what we'd found in the field, and Harmon mentioned that an explosion as part of a seismic test could send rock rubble to the surrounding areas.

"But it's pretty preliminary in the drilling process, Paul. Ahead of test drills. And your guy would have to sign up for it. Land lease. Contracts."

I nodded, understanding the sequence of events a little better, but still not totally clear on what the hell it meant to Ennis Fultz's murder investigation.

I thanked Harmon. "It's good to see you."

He told me to come by the university sometime. He'd walk me through more on drilling, if it amounted to anything.

"Paul," he said after I'd walked about twenty feet away. "Your mom was the best woman I ever knew. I never told you that, but I should've."

"I feel the same way," I said.

Harmon had an odd look on his face. "I always felt bad. How you were left alone. Your mom and dad splitting up."

I squinted, confused. "Did you know her way back then?"

"Yeah," he said. "I was her first teaching assistant."

I never knew this.

"Listen, Harmon," I said. "I'm kinda in the weeds right now."

"On this case?"

"In a lot of ways," I said. "The lesson was great." I pointed over to where he'd drawn in the dirt. "But do you think if I sent you the address, you could swing by? There's a walkway behind the house. Heads right down into the gorge."

He pointed at the bar. "I'll do you one better. I'll bring the guys."

I smiled at the thought of this.

"'Cause you know what trumps a good Southern bar for a few California environmentalists?"

"A Southern murder involving intrigue and gas?"

He grinned. "Bingo."

I thanked Harmon and got in Marvin's car. Headed back to help nail Thom Sile.

33

Once I was on the road, my cell buzzed. Remy told me she was at Mercy Hospital.

"Sile's awake already?"

"Not yet. I'm here for something different, P.T. I went through Sile's cell records. There's a number he called four times early on the Monday morning Ennis was killed. It goes right up to—and past—the time he's driving that truck from the apartment complex—out to Fultz's house at the gorge."

"A phone number in the hospital?"

"In Critical Care," Remy said. "A nurse's station."

We had Sile on camera early that morning, 5:13 a.m. Leaving in his truck to head out to Ennis Fultz's house with the bad tank.

"Wait," I said. "That's good. What time were these calls?"

"Between five a.m. and six," Remy said.

"Did you triangulate the phone's location?"

"I did," she said. "But get this—his phone doesn't move, P.T. It's in his apartment the whole time."

I got off the highway and started heading in Remy's direction.

"Wait—what?" I said.

This didn't make sense. If Sile was driving the truck and made a call, it should've pinged off a tower out by the gorge. By Fultz's house.

"So Sile never took his phone with him when he drove out to Fultz's place?"

"Well, if he didn't take his phone," Remy said, "who the hell made these calls from Sile's phone? I asked around. Sile's got no girlfriend. No roommate."

This suddenly threw our theory about Sile driving out to the gorge in doubt. And it gave Thom Sile a great defense.

"Wait a sec," I said. "You said the calls were to a nurse's station?"

"And since it's the night shift, I already found out which nurse was on," Remy said. "His name is Bodie Dunne."

"Does he have a record?"

"DUI ten years ago," Remy said. "Nothing since. He's coming on in fifteen minutes."

"Be right there." I hung up and put my foot down on the Charger's gas pedal.

Fifteen minutes later, I found Remy. She was sitting like a patient, reading a magazine in the waiting room.

We didn't know what Bodie Dunne's connection to Thom Sile was, but if you worked in a hospital and you consorted with a drug dealer, it usually didn't mean something good.

I sat next to Remy. "Is he here?"

"Got here early and took everyone's coffee orders. Went out to Starbucks across the way."

"What's this guy look like?"

"From the employee of the month sign in the lobby?" Remy raised her eyebrows. "Not what you're thinking."

The elevator dinged, and a man in his thirties headed out. He walked to the check-in desk at Family Practice, juggling four drinks in a cardboard holder. He wore a conservative pink-and-purple-striped dress shirt and black slacks.

Remy was right. I'd pictured someone who looked like Thom Sile. Sallow face. Thin frame. The usual signs of drug abuse.

The man approached the three women at the desk. "Iced carmel macchiato for you. Chai tea latte for you." He winked at a third woman. "And you didn't ask for it, but I know you're a cold-brew fanatic. I've seen you with it."

"Thank you, Oprah," one of the women said in a way that made me think this was part of a recurring schtick.

"He's charming," I said.

"Good-looking too," Remy added. "If he asked you for the keys to the pharma cabinet after a couple free macchiatos . . ."

We crossed the open area to intercept Bodie Dunne, and caught him as he got back on the elevator. He was a nurse at the hospital who had taken calls from a suspect. Officially, we had nothing to hold him on, but like anyone else, he was subject to questioning.

"How you doin'?" I asked as we got on.

"Good," he said. Bodie was holding the last drink—a red fruity iced tea of some sort.

As the door closed, Remy pulled up the edge of her jacket, revealing her badge, clipped at her waist.

"We need to speak to you about Thom Sile," she said.

Bodie's neck tensed up, but other than that, he held a poker face.

"I don't know any Tom," he said. "I think you're mistaking me with someone else."

"Sile called here four times between five a.m. and six a.m. on Monday," Remy said. "If we pull records and you're calling him back, you might have some trouble keeping your job here."

Bodie stepped off at the first floor, and took two steps before stopping.

"We're not here to jam you up," I said. "But we need to chat."

"Is there somewhere private we can talk?" Remy asked.

Bodie stared at us. He was doing the calculations. Could he give us some information and walk away clean?

"Over here," he said.

Bodie led us to a training room full of posters. One wall listed the F.A.S.T. method of spotting a stroke, while the other bore pictures of CPR training dummies.

We sat down at a small circular table.

"This past Monday, real early," I said, "Sile called you. Why?"

"He was sick," Bodie said.

"Sick how?" Remy asked.

Bodie ran his hands through his hair. "Said he'd been vomiting. Some bad heroin, I figured."

"Did he mention he was driving when he called you?" Remy asked.

"No," Bodie said. "And I don't think he was."

"What makes you say that?"

"He was in bad shape. Wanted Narcan."

Naloxone was a drug that had been around since the 1960s for overdose situations with heroin or pain meds. Narcan was the brand name of the nasal spray version of the drug. It reversed the effects of opioids and restored normal breathing. There was discussion last year whether we'd start carrying a couple doses in our squad cars like paramedics did.

"How do you know?" I asked. "Did you bring it to him?"

"It's not a controlled substance," Bodie said.

"Did you bring it to him?" Remy repeated my question.

"I think I should talk to a lawyer."

"Listen." I leaned in. "You can do that. But we didn't come here to arrest you. So, if you make the first move, you're forcing us to make the countermove."

Bodie swallowed. "I drove over to Thom's on my morning break."

"Which was when?" Remy asked.

"I got to his place in Ferris a little before six."

"A.m.?" I clarified. "On Monday?"

Bodie nodded. Which made no sense if you believed Sile was on the road to Ennis Fultz's house at that time. He'd arrived back at the apartment complex at 6:06 a.m.

"Was Sile there when you arrived?"

"Yeah."

As Bodie talked, I thought about the conversation with Abe last night in the manager's office. There had been a man who walked into the complex through an open gate a few minutes before six. Not a tenant, the manager had said. And well-dressed. Could it have been Bodie?

"So Sile buzzed you in?" I said, testing him.

"No, I parked on the street," Bodie said. "The gate was opening for some car so I just walked in."

Remy and I exchanged a glance. "So you walked in and Sile was there?" my partner asked. "Or maybe he drove up *after* you?"

"No, he was there when I arrived."

"And what was Thom Sile's condition?" Remy asked.

"He was sweating," Bodie said. "Crashing hard. Had thrown up a couple times."

My head was swimming. If this was true, someone *not named Thom Sile* was on camera taking the United Chemical truck.

"You understand that if you lie to us," I said, "we're gonna bring a world of hurt on you."

Bodie nodded. We got up and told him not to talk to anyone about this.

Outside, Remy paced the sidewalk.

"What the hell?" my partner said. "Who the hell's in the U-Chem truck if it's not Sile?"

"Beware of rabbit holes."

"Frig." She pointed at me. "Don't tell me you knew."

"Hell no," I said. "But this matches with the cell triangulation. Someone else was in that truck."

"Who?"

I shrugged, unsure.

"And not just that, Rem," I said. "Someone *took* that vehicle— to set up Sile."

Which meant there was a bad actor in play, and we had no idea who it was.

I looked at my phone. I'd felt a pulse while we were inside, but hadn't checked it.

Two missed calls from Harmon Gale.

I rang him back, putting him on speaker. "What's up, Harmon?"

"P.T.," he said, "I'm out at the gorge."

"Yeah?"

"I sent the guys from California back to their hotel in an Uber. You should make it out here. I think I can put some of this together for you."

"Give me the one-liner," I said. "We're in a bit of a spin cycle today."

"There's oil here," Harmon said. "And judging by how much has been mapped, the old guy might've been sitting on the mother lode. I'm no homicide detective, but it could be enough to kill over."

"Be there in twenty," I said.

I turned to Remy. "Let's talk as we drive." I motioned at Marvin's Charger parked out front.

"Hold on a sec," Remy said.

My partner hustled over to her Alfa, grabbing a black box from the back seat. She'd been volunteering with Animal Services after hours, and the box contained her tranquilizer gun.

In Georgia, a police officer leaving this in their car was tantamount to leaving any weapon sitting around.

As she put the case in Marvin's trunk, I thought of yesterday, out at the gorge. Remy came at me, thinking I was drinking. Today, I saw how seriously she was taking this work for Animal Services. I wondered if a transfer request was coming soon.

I hit the ignition on the Charger.

"So this entire line of thinking on Sile?" my partner asked. "It's dead?"

"I dunno," I said. "I need a second to think."

As we buzzed out of the hospital parking lot, Remy pointed at the main tower. "You see Marvin today?"

"I'll check on him later."

I could feel Remy's eyes on me. "Is Marvin all right?"

The case was in shambles, and we were scrambling from one desperate lead to the next.

The last thing I wanted to do was talk about my father-in-law.

"Marvin's in a coma, Rem," I said. "He's not all right."

"So it's the same?"

"Yeah," I said.

But this was a lie.

I'd gotten a call at eight a.m. from Dr. Burke. A call, preparing me that things had gotten worse. That Marvin might not wake up.

34

The little girl had been pushing at her father's body for minutes, but he wasn't moving.

She thought of Anna. Mother.

She yelled for her, but with the injury to her throat, all that came out was a noise that sounded like a bullfrog.

She stared at the sign ahead of her. EMERGENCY EXIT *pulsing in red.*

Survival.

She grabbed her father's keys and cell phone from his pocket, and took the stairs to the bottom. Ran out into the parking lot as an alarm began whooping behind her.

She would go home. Hide in her room.

Wait until Mother was out of surgery.

Home was safe. And the man didn't know where she lived.

She opened her father's Uber app to order a car, but a message popped up. His credit card had expired.

"No," she said, frustrated.

She saw her father's Camry sedan in the parking lot and stared down at the keys.

She'd driven their ATV all over the property, but a car was bigger. Harder.

She remembered a day, a month ago. She'd sat on her father's lap and steered the Hyundai around the vacant land beyond their house. Pushed the gas while he handled the brakes.

"For shits and giggles," he'd said later when Mother was angry. He'd pointed around at the desolate land. "Who's gonna see us, hon? Way out here?"

The girl looked in the passenger seat of the car. She needed something to boost her up in the seat.

In the trunk she found a pile of bricks for one of the planters they were building. She dragged four of them to the front and climbed on top.

She hit the button that read Start, and the car came to life.

Pulling the handle to take off the brake, she put the car in D and leaned to one side to get her foot to touch the right pedal.

The car shot forward, and she dinged a car next to her.

The girl started crying then. She steered harder and scraped her way free of the car.

Looked out at the road ahead.

Which way was home?

She hit the talk button on her father's cell phone.

"Go home."

"Directions to home," the voice repeated, and a map appeared.

The girl sat back. A piece of the moon hung over the night sky. No one was around. A perfect time to escape.

She wiped the tears from her cheeks.

"You can do this," she said out loud. And she hit the gas again, surging forward out of the parking lot.

35

When we got to Ennis Fultz's house, Harmon's old Chevy Blazer was parked in the gravel area outside.

Remy and I were spinning on the case.

We walked around the back of the place, passing the bags of grass seed and finding our way down the line of tiered flagstones to the meadow that sat just above the gorge.

Harmon was farther down, another fifty feet below us, crouching beside a pile of rocks at the bottom.

We scaled the rocky steps, and I introduced Harmon to Remy.

"Okay," I said. "Lay it on us."

"You know anything about seismic testing for shale?"

"Zero," I said.

"Well, let me give you the layman's version. Shale here's probably eight thousand feet down. As a point of reference, the water supply's around five hundred feet."

"Okay," I said.

"I told you before about the Condesale Shale, right?"

"Big-ass strip of oil," I said. "Lots of money, but nobody knows the perfect place to drill."

"Right," Harmon said. "So if you're prospecting, how you do lay the odds in your favor? These days, you use seismic testing. You send vibrations down into the earth, and the echo that comes back makes you a 3-D picture. Not perfect, but good enough."

I blinked. "How do you send vibrations?"

"The easiest is what you call a thumper truck. Looks like a garbage truck on the front. The middle or back's got a drop hammer that sends the vibration."

I looked around. "You'd never get a truck down here. We can hardly get down here."

"Which brings up the other way. Explosive charges."

"You toss dynamite?" Remy asked.

Harmon turned to her. "You build what's called a shot hole. And it's not out of the question to use dynamite or other explosives just like it. Explosions cause gas to expand. Which forces pressure to the surrounding areas in the form of seismic waves."

I looked up at the grassy bluff where we'd met with Thorpe.

"And that's what sent those big rocks up there?" I asked.

Harmon nodded, and Remy pointed at an area where he'd been digging as we came down the flagstone path.

"What were you looking at when we got here?" she said.

"A piece of metal rebar," he said. "When you do this work, you usually make a grid. Someone's done a good job of covering the rebar with stones and rubble, but they're all here. And they cover the whole gorge. A job like this? Six digits in cost. And you don't keep going wider—unless the pictures you're making show massive deposits."

I looked around. "Why go through all the trouble to hide it?"

"Prospecting is prospecting, P.T. If you don't own an area, you hide your trail 'cause you're afraid someone else might get there first. One place looks like scrub brush. The next space over is worth gold."

"Hiding from whom?" Remy asked.

"Whoever might own the land and not know its value," he said.

Harmon used his Converse sneakers to motion at the ground. "And you can tell by the way the ground is cratering which direction they were betting on."

"Back up," Remy said. "You're not drilling down like conventional oil?"

Harmon shook his head. He explained how in fracking, once you go deep enough, you start drilling sideways.

"And this gorge is great cover," he said. "Because folks hate fracking. Doesn't matter if they understand it or not. But these cliff walls—they're great for privacy. Once you're down here and set up the well, you switch out the drilling rig for a completion rig—it's even lower than the gorge walls. No one can see you're down here."

"Privacy from whom?" Remy asked.

"Pesky environmentalists," he said. "Liberals."

"People like you?"

"People exactly like me." He grinned. "Only one problem, guys. You gotta get your product out of this canyon. And geographically speaking—the only way in and out is through Fultz's property. So if he wasn't on board—"

"How much money are we talking about?" Remy asked.

"If you could control all this property and the exit route," Harmon said. "A hundred million bucks."

Remy whistled, and I thought of Fultz's will.

We still hadn't sorted through the out-of-state partnerships that held Fultz's house and any other land he may have owned down into the gorge. All that was the property of the Lyman family. Eventually it went to Cameron.

"We've been looking at this murder as a crime of opportunity," I said to my partner. "As something done by a lowlife."

"Maybe Fultz realized the profit down here," Remy said. "Abandoned his love of the place—"

I was pacing now. "Went back to his center? Making money off real estate?"

Remy nodded.

"Then why build all those trails?" I asked. "Why a public garden if you're just gonna throw down a bunch of oil derricks?"

"Or—maybe he *always* knew what was down here," Remy said. "Remember what our real estate guy Quentin Reed said. Fultz was the type of guy who'd wait years for an opportunity to pay off. Every family, every situation—he knew where the bodies were buried."

Harmon started talking then. Some detail about drilling depth.

I was caught back on the expression that Remy had used.

"The bodies are buried?" I repeated.

"Not real bodies," Remy said.

I turned and looked up at the house.

"You have your laptop with you?"

"Yeah," Remy said.

I climbed up the angled rocks to the meadow, and Remy followed me.

"What is it, P.T.?"

I didn't slow down, hustling up the flagstones with her and Harmon in tow.

"Maybe nothing," I said.

We entered Fultz's house, and I flipped open Remy's laptop. I asked her to find the interview we'd had with Suzy Kang.

Remy started it from the beginning, with Suzy telling us Fultz was already dead when she got there.

I reached over and moved the slider about three minutes forward. Hit *Play* again.

"Why would I touch the tank?" Suzy said on the video. "He loved that thing."

"He loved his tank?" Remy asked Suzy.

"He talked to that damn fish all day," Suzy said. She imitated Ennis Fultz, "'Let's see if old Sally agrees,' he'd say. 'When no one's around, I tell Sally everything. She knows where the bodies are buried. She watches my treasure.'"

I stopped the video.

Looked across the room at the fish tank that ran from floor to ceiling.

A decorative box sat at the bottom of the tank.

"You think there's something in there?" Remy said to me. "Bullshit."

"What if he told her on purpose?" I said. "Repeated it. Over and over. The little girl—Lyman's daughter?—said he did magic. It's a classic magician's trick."

Harmon walked over, squinting through the thick glass of the tank.

"He *did* will Suzy the tank." Remy shrugged.

I moved a chair in front of the fish tank and rolled back the long sleeves of my shirt. The tank had to be sixteen feet wide, from left to right. There was no way Suzy could take it to some apartment. It was custom-built for this place.

I grabbed the screened scooper tool from off a nearby shelf.

Reaching in, I found the treasure chest, sitting beside a conch on the floor of the giant tank. It wasn't the plastic kind you use for fish tanks. Fifteen dollars at the local Petco. Instead it was a real miniature metal box, which was starting to rust in the water.

I pulled the box off the floor of the fish tank, disrupting the water and sending algae and pebbles scattering.

I held the box above the tank, letting the water drain from it.

The treasure box was maybe five inches by three inches. I grabbed it with my other hand, carrying it over to the granite countertop nearby.

Remy undid the metal latch and opened it.

Inside was a heavy-duty plastic bag, folded carefully with some paper in it. Remy gloved up and took the paper out. It was a computer printout of a list of numbers.

> *PN 096 324*
> *PN 096 325*
> *PN 096 326*
> *PN 096 327*
> *PN 096 843*

PN 096 844

PN 096 845

We stared at the list, not clear what it was, but realizing that Fultz had tipped Suzy over and over to tell someone about his "treasure," without her even knowing it.

"They're nearly all sequential," Remy said. "What do you think the *PN* stands for?"

"Fultz was a real estate guy," I said. "Parcel number."

"There's a website every county has," Harmon said. "You can look up these properties."

Remy pulled up the website on her laptop and entered the first number. A listing came up with a ton of information, from the address of the parcel to sewer, electric, and gas access.

"Click on the map," I said.

She did, and we saw that the property was located on the opposite bluff from Ennis Fultz's home. The other side of the gorge.

"What about the next one?"

Remy clicked, one by one, until we had a picture of what Ennis Fultz had done. Between July and August of last year, he'd bought up all the properties that ran along the entire gorge, from north to south. East to west.

"So your victim's the prospector?" Harmon asked. "I thought you two said he didn't know about the drilling."

I thought about what Thorpe, the grass seed guy, had told us. About Fultz coming back from the hospital and seeing the rocks in that meadow.

"While he was in the hospital, someone prospected the bottom of the canyon." I turned to Remy.

"What do you wanna bet this list is the rest of the properties in those tax shelters?"

Remy squinted at me. "I don't understand, P.T. Is he pro-drilling? Or is he building a public garden?"

"I dunno."

I was thinking about what Quentin Reed, the real estate expert, had told us. How Ennis Fultz spent every waking moment researching property records down at the county office.

"We can't wait on this like we did with the will," I said. "Let's go to the Assessor's. It's off 909, not far from here."

Remy and I thanked Harmon and hopped in Marvin's Charger.

A few minutes later we were down in the basement at County, introducing ourselves to a clerk named Jim.

The man was in his fifties and wore a lime-green button-down and tan slacks.

"I knew Ennis well," Jim said. "Never came in here without bringing me fresh fruit. Studied properties like some folks study the Bible."

Remy showed Jim the list of properties on the paper. We mentioned how they were all adjacent to Ennis Fultz's house. And we believed they were owned by Fultz, but weren't sure.

"Well, there's a process to look at detailed records out here. Ennis of all people knew about that."

"So you keep some notes? When someone investigates a property?" Remy asked.

"If they want the full abstract," Jim said, "then yes. Online you can only see so much. Nothing historical in terms of who owned it last. Or before that."

We gave Jim the list on paper, and he left the front office for a few minutes.

While we waited, Abe rang us up.

"I just talked to Thom Sile post-surgery," he said. "His story's the same as Bodie's. He never left the apartment until Monday afternoon. Sick as a dog."

"Was he alone?" Remy asked. The implication being, why the hell would we trust Sile?

"If you believe him, yeah. But get this. Said he made a sale at five forty-five a.m. When he would've been out at the gorge if he was driving that truck."

"A drug sale?" Remy snorted. "That's his alibi?"

"Guys, he says it was to a cop. Twenty pills of Oxy."

I groaned.

"He gave me the first name and a description of a guy in traffic," Abe said. "I know the kid. Went down hard on his bike last year. Maybe he's having pain still."

Jesus, I thought. *Not a cop.*

"What about the cash we found in Sile's speaker?" I asked. "Does it match to anything Fultz withdrew?"

"Nope," Abe said.

Which meant Sile didn't steal the money from Fultz. And it didn't look like he drove the truck out there either.

Jim came back out, a couple three-ringed binders in hand.

We told Abe to stay on the trail and hung up.

Jim held up one of the binders. "Ennis was kinda famous in the real estate community for his research."

Famous. That's not the way Quentin Reed had framed it.

"So these." Jim held up the binders. "They cover the history on most of those properties. And if you look inside—I make this note on the inside cover, real small, when someone checks a binder out."

I stared at the notation—and Remy and I exchanged a glance.

We saw the name "Fultz" three times, but the initial before it wasn't *E* every time.

"C. Fultz," Remy said. She looked to Jim. "Is that his wife, Connie?"

Jim hesitated. "Well, I guess it's okay to say now, but that's the son, Cameron."

I exchanged a look with Remy.

"The boy didn't want his dad knowing," Jim continued. "I think he was trying to impress his old man. You know, boning up on his knowledge of the family portfolio. Ennis was hard on him."

I paged through the binders, looking at the history of each of the properties. Since 1960, they had been owned by the same company, Farming Collective LLC.

"Who is that?" I pointed.

"Big investor of a lotta scrub brush on the outskirts of town. Some doctors and dentists. Long-term passive investors. Especially if it's gorge property."

"Meaning what?" Remy asked.

"Well, the state dammed up that river when I was a kid," Jim said. "The gorge ain't worth much without the river going through it."

Unless the river is made of oil, I thought.

I flipped to the next binder.

> *C. Fultz. 4/2018*
> *E. Fultz 7/2018*
> *C. Fultz 4/2019*

"Same as the other," Remy said.

"If this is right," I said. "Then *Cameron* was the one looking at this record first. Not his dad. And when he did, it was still owned by these doctors and dentists."

The clerk rechecked his notes and nodded.

"So he wasn't boning up on his *dad's* portfolio," I said to Jim, "because his dad didn't own these parcels. Not until recently."

Jim swiveled the binders around so they faced him. "Well, I guess you're right. This one Cam checked out in April of last year. Then Ennis came back a couple months later." Jim flipped to a different area that listed transfers of ownership. "And *then* Ennis bought it. Cam probably recommended the purchase to his dad."

I took a step back, trying to form a timeline in my head.

Were Cameron and Ennis partners? Father and son working together?

"So Cameron began researching the ownership of the seven properties at the bottom of the gorge a year ago, April," I said. "He saw that these doctors or dentists owned them."

"Check," Jim said.

"Then in June, while Fultz was in the hospital, someone prospected that canyon for shale exploration."

"They did?" Jim asked.

I ignored the guy since, really, I was talking to Remy.

"In July," Remy continued, "Ennis is out of the hospital. He saw the rocks in the meadow and figured out what was going on. He came in here. Saw it was his *own son* who'd done the research. Seven months later, he bought up all the properties."

"So they're working together?" Jim asked.

"If they're working together," I said, "why does Cameron come back looking in April? He'd already know who owned it. Him and his dad."

"More likely, Cameron had an investor," Remy said. "*Cam* did the prospecting on the land. While his dad was laid up. Figured out it was worth a hundred million."

Jim's eyes went big at the number.

"Then in April, Cam came back," I said. "Realized his dad grabbed all that land from under him."

I turned to Jim. "Do you remember any of these visits from the Fultzes?"

"Funny thing," Jim said. "I remember the last one last month. Cameron was at this small desk we have in the back and I was in the bathroom. And boy, I never heard a Christian use words like *those*."

"He was cursing?"

"I thought he was on the phone, and when I came in, there was another man with him. The guy must've come in while I was in the back."

Remy faced me. "Cameron saw the name of his dad's company on the deed, P.T. He knew his dad figured out what he was doing."

"Who was the guy?" I asked Jim. "The one with Cameron."

"Husky guy." Jim shrugged. "Leather jacket. Olive complexion. I never saw him before."

I thanked Jim and asked him if he could give us some space to talk this through.

When he left, I turned to Remy.

"Cameron," I said. Just one word.

"Hey, the son had a solid alibi." Remy held up her hands defensively. "He was in Jacksonville all weekend."

I nodded, pacing. Not disputing the fact.

"You told me the other day Cameron's house had a construction lien against it. He was mortgaged to the eyeballs. You remember how much?"

"Ninety-five grand."

Roughly the same amount that Harmon said it would cost to 3-D-test the gorge for shale.

I grabbed a chair and turned it backward, staring at the list of parcels. "You met Cameron at his house?" I asked.

"Yeah," Remy said.

"Did it look like it had been renovated? Inside? Out? Anywhere?"

"No," Remy said. "Why? What are you thinking?"

"When I worked in burglary, we arrested this guy. He tried to trade everything he knew to get out of jail."

"Okay. So?"

"He told us about these guys down in Grove Park in Atlanta. Loan sharks, basically. But they owned construction companies too."

"You're talking organized crime?"

"Yeah, but when they lent you the money—just in case you ran off—they'd lien your property. A legit-looking construction lien."

"You're saying Cameron's lien has nothing to do with his house. It's a personal loan against cash he borrowed to test down in the gorge."

"He wouldn't be the first guy to get in with a bad element," I said. "Problem is that if he used the hundred grand to test, he'd need even more to buy the properties."

"So let's say *Cam's* the one who had the place mapped while his dad's in the hospital," Remy theorized, getting us closer. "He finds proof that the area's shale-rich, but needs more money."

"From someone not named Dad," I said.

"Most likely person is whoever he borrowed the money from the first time."

I pointed at Remy. "Except if you go back to a loan shark a second time, they either break your legs—or become your partner."

"Ennis gets out of the hospital," Remy said. "He sees the rocks in that meadow and figures things out. He's got cash. He starts gobbling up all the land. What's his game?"

"Maybe he doesn't appreciate his son sneaking onto his land. He's trying to force his son to admit it. To come to him."

"Or maybe these are two guys going in opposite directions," Remy said. "The dad, trying to turn over a new leaf. He buys the land to attach to his garden—to *prevent* the drilling that'll ruin the area. The son, trying to get rich and away from his old man."

"So let's play this forward," I said. "Cam lines up the money to buy the parcels. He reaches out to the doctors and dentists, but they tell him they already sold it. He comes down here with his new partner and sees it's his own dad who bought it."

"He goes by in person," Remy said. "To chat Ennis up. Sees the old man is getting off his meds. Losing weight. He's gonna live forever."

"Well, he's got *something* to live for all of a sudden." I grinned. "Maybe the escort."

"But Cameron's partner doesn't want to wait," Remy said.

"And if they're in organized crime, there's ways to speed up the inheritance process. Murder, for one."

"P.T.," Remy said, "I talked to Cameron's girlfriend the first day. She said that her and Cam had a couple drinks Sunday night in Jacksonville, and she passed out early. Like eight p.m. You think Cam could've waited until she was asleep and then drove back from Jacksonville to here?"

I thought about the shadowy figure driving the truck out of Thom Sile's apartment complex. A trip from Jacksonville at night would take five to six hours.

"That's a long hike," I said. "Back and forth. But he could've grabbed the United Chem truck. Put the bad nitrogen tank in his dad's place and then turned back around. Drove back to Florida before his eleven-thirty a.m. tee time."

"Maybe that's why no money was stolen," Remy said. "It wasn't about a few grand in cash hidden in some closet. It's the big score when the old man dies."

I suddenly felt played. "Suzy, the escort." I shook my head. "Sile, the druggie delivery guy—"

"You thinking the son lined our plates with the usual suspects? Set these folks up for us to grab?"

My fingers balled into a fist. Pissed.

"If he did, he's a sociopath and we missed it."

"Then let's get over to his place," Remy said, "nail the son of a bitch."

36

We pulled up outside of Cameron Fultz's ranch-style home where Remy had interviewed him just three days ago.

We hustled out of the car. But as we got close to the house, we saw the front door was open and the screen door hung ajar.

Remy and I pulled our weapons, and my partner used the radio clipped to her belt to call in our location.

Blinds covered the windows beside the front door, and I approached from the left, planting my body by the door, waiting for my partner.

Remy stuck a flashlight in her back pocket.

I grabbed the edge of the ajar screen door and swung it toward us. It banged against the outside.

Over my shoulder, Remy pointed her flashlight with her left hand and held her Glock 42 with her right.

"Cameron Fultz?" I hollered. "Police."

I trained my gun on the far wall inside and moved left, just inside the door, while Remy moved against the doorjamb.

Inside, the lights in the house were off. A kitchen area was to our right and a slender hall lay to our left.

My partner and I knew how to divide a space up better than anyone in the department. How to "pie the pizza," as SWAT calls it. Divide one space into many. Avoid the vertical coffins that hallways become and shelter each other as we moved from concealment to cover.

Visually clearing the living room and the kitchen, I moved down the hall.

Smack. The front door shut and left us in darkness.

Remy's flashlight found the dark area in front of me and lit it before I moved there.

I looked in the bathroom, and a smell like rotten eggs moved under my nose. Some word or picture was smeared on the mirror, but the space was empty.

I moved into the bedroom and the smell got worse.

The air reeked like a mixture of old cabbage and feces, and a handful of black flies sailed past me.

Remy's flashlight found a leg, and then a body. We flicked on a light and saw him.

Cameron Fultz was laid out across the floor.

His head was facedown, but I could see a hole the size of a peach pit through it, below his right temple. Blood was pooled around him, but it hadn't yet turned black.

"This is a couple hours old," I said.

"He must've known we were close."

We cleared the rest of the house and came back to the room.

"Boss," Remy said, motioning at Cameron's side.

A .45 was tucked under his right hand, his body crumpled atop it.

I bent my knees, avoiding the blood that flowed around him.

When you die on your feet, you don't fly backward. Opposite forces attract, which makes you fall forward—with quick and deliberate energy. In Cameron's case, the fall caused his nose to break, which produced a second pool of blood, moving out in a different direction.

"There was something in that bathroom," I said.

I took four or five steps backward to the washroom. On the mirror above the sink, written in toothpaste were two words:

Sorry Dad

I stared at the messy letters, the toothpaste dripping down on the two *r*'s in "sorry."

"Jesus," I said. I'd never seen a suicide note written this way.

"Guilt," Remy echoed from behind me.

My partner took a shot of it with her phone, and we walked back into the bedroom, examining the body again.

The house must not have been on even ground, because the blood had left Cameron Fultz's head and followed the course of gravity, moving downward along his side and then pooling where his left thigh was up against the south wall of the room.

The human body begins the decomp process immediately after death, and biologicals tend to seep into carpet and tile pretty quick. It's one of the details you notice when you roll a body over and look underneath. That and the gases that are released from bacteria growing in the intestinal tract.

Remy moved outside to call the M.E. and grabbed her iPad to take notes in.

I crouched by Cameron's body and looked at the burns around the wound on the right side of his head—the upward angle of entry.

There were some basic procedures to establish C.O.D. in a suicide.

The first was establishing the three basic investigatory considerations around suicide. Was there a weapon present? Did the victim appear to have produced the wound that killed him? And did he have intent in doing so?

Cameron had powder residue from unburned carbon on the fleshy area above his thumb, the gun was just under his body, and the suicide note was on the bathroom mirror.

Three check marks.

I thought about having to notify Connie Fultz, Cameron's mom. She'd lost her husband less than a week ago and now would find out her son had killed himself after murdering his dad.

I'd made a lot of tough calls in my time, but that one felt impossible.

Outside I heard backup arriving. Remy gave instructions to set up a perimeter and get the medical examiner here.

In Cameron's home office, I looked through a file cabinet. A few drawers in, I found a map listing eleven shot holes where Cameron had used explosives to test for shale down in the gorge. Just like Harmon had guessed.

There was also a signed construction lien to Enfatigo Capital for $95,000.

Enfatigo was a name well known by the police in Atlanta.

Vincent Enfatigo was the reason why. A crime boss who'd been put in prison down south in Valdosta, he had once overseen everything from drug trafficking to extortion to heavy weapons.

When the Atlanta PD and the FBI finally caught him five years ago, it was hailed as a victory. But while Vincent was in the can, his family operation had only gotten larger. The mobster's son and daughter took over, and the official story was that they went legit. But when you saw liens like this one with Cameron, it just smelled like a new brand of dirty.

Remy walked into the office, and I showed her the paperwork. This case had thrown us in more circles than most.

"What we still don't know is why," I said to Remy. "Why hadn't Cameron just told his dad what he'd found down in the gorge?"

It didn't matter. Ennis Fultz figured out Cameron's plans. And the father bared those teeth that he'd sharpened all his life— buying up every piece of land around his boy's discovery, forcing Cam to come to him. And Cam came to him, all right. With a deadly tank of nitrogen.

Remy shrugged. "He was a shitty father, the wife said."

"And I guess the apple fell right beside the tree."

"Check this out," Remy said, holding up Ennis Fultz's will. "I found a copy on Cameron's kitchen table." The document was folded open to the part about the trust.

"Cameron knew he wasn't getting that land for a while," I said.

We heard the noise of the coroner's van, and out the window I saw Alvin Gerbin from our crime scene team walking with Sarah past the crime tape that patrol had set up.

Sarah wore white capris and a black blouse, but she went to

the back of the van and began pulling on a one-piece cover-up over her outfit.

"Hey," she said as she walked into the house.

Like earlier outside the precinct, her face didn't light up when she saw me.

"You okay?" I asked.

"Absolutely," Sarah said.

The smell had absorbed into the carpet of the place, and Remy and I took breaks for fresh air while Alvin and Sarah inspected the body.

It was an odd end to the case—but in a way, it was the usual ending. Money. Jealousy. Revenge. Some combination of the three were in every murder I'd ever solved.

Sarah examined the body, telling us that the time of death was between three and five p.m. A few hours ago.

Gerbin took pictures of the mirror, as well as Cam's body, a close-up of the gun under him, and other details throughout the home. Remy and I took our time, going through every drawer in the house, tagging evidence and boxing up paperwork that might be relevant to the case.

A couple hours later, we had twenty-eight items bagged for evidence, and five file boxes filled.

Gerbin lifted up a 3-wood from a handful of Cameron Fultz's golf clubs leaning against the far corner of the main room, near Cam's leg. "I can move these, right?" he asked.

"Of course," I said, helping him. I had learned to play golf from my dad when I was eleven and played the sport in high school, even though the old man had disappeared by then.

The case was drawing to an end, and Cameron's death was an

unfortunate postscript to his father's murder. It was a strange legacy that Ennis Fultz had left behind, a man who befriended escorts but screwed over farmers and real estate developers.

But as it turned out, when it came to vengeance, he'd taught his son well.

I regrouped with my partner outside, but my mind was suddenly on my own father. On the need I felt to find him. I had always known I had resources to locate my old man; I had chosen not to look.

"How about I drop you at your place?" I said to Remy. "I'll do the paperwork and you can head home."

"It's midnight, P.T.," Remy said.

"I got energy," I answered.

"The last time you said that, you didn't go home at all," Remy said. "How about we haul this crap back to the office and we both crash. We can dot our i's and cross our t's tomorrow?"

"Deal," I said.

A fresh shift at patrol pulled up to sit sentinel while Gerbin and Sarah finished their work. It always amazed me to see how long we spent at crime scenes, going through evidence.

"We got our guy," Remy said, standing on the front lawn.

"Yup," I said. Even though, to me, some things were still off.

My phone buzzed, and it was Abe. I put it on speaker.

"I'm here with Johnny Tobin," Abe said. "We spent the last hour unraveling all those partnerships and tax shelters. There's one that holds nearly all the property."

"Great," I said.

We'd need all that financial information—to put a bow on the case.

"That trust is joint and several, P.T."

"That's not unusual," I said. It was the same way with my personal home. When Lena died, no paperwork was needed for it to pass to me.

"Bill Lyman, Anna Lyman, and Alita Kang Lyman."

"Alita Kang Lyman?" I repeated.

Alita was the little girl. Lyman's adopted daughter.

But "Kang"—that was Suzy's last name.

"As in?"

"We looked up her birth records," Abe said. "Unknown father. Mother Suzy Kang. Had a drug problem and gave up the baby."

"No," Remy said.

"The girl bumped around from foster home to foster home until last summer."

"In June," I said to Abe. "After he got out of the hospital."

"Yup," Abe said.

I looked to Remy. "Fultz found out. The girl's his daughter, Rem."

Suddenly something that had made no sense was clear: why Fultz had left the land to the Lymans. He'd arranged for them to adopt his illegitimate daughter.

And Suzy's relationship with Fultz. Because she worked at a sex club and Fultz was paying her, we assumed she was an escort. But she was the mother of his daughter. For all we knew, they were in love.

I suddenly realized what this meant for Cameron. If the tenancy was joint and several, Cameron would have to wait until the little girl grew up and passed away before he got those oil-rich parcels.

Which under normal circumstances would've been long after Cam was dead.

Remy pointed at me. "You think Cameron found out Alita was his half sister?" she asked.

"If Cam knew his father's estate wasn't going to him—"

My eyes got big. Thinking through this.

"What?" Remy asked.

"The Enfatigo family," I said. "If Cameron was involved with them, they might've been the ones to knock off his dad, with or without his blessing."

"Yeah, we already assumed that," my partner said.

I was still stuck on something.

"Rem, when did Fultz's will become public?"

"Yesterday," she said.

"So if I'm Cam's business partner at Enfatigo," I said, "and I find out about this last night, before Cam killed himself . . ."

"And you're in the mob and accustomed to violence and crime . . ." Remy said.

"Then there's a solution to the problem," I said. "Take out the Lyman family."

Remy's eyes got big. "Then Cameron gets the property," she said. "And you're his partner. So you're back in business."

"Abe," I said. "Send patrol to the gorge. Couple cars. These people may be in danger."

"P.T.," he said, "everyone is up north. The motorcade thing . . . they decided to make camp for the night up in the national forest. Some sort of publicity stunt. The president staying in a yurt."

"What are you saying?" I asked.

"We got two patrol cars covering everything in town."

"We'll go ourselves then. But while we're en route, see if you can get ahold of these Lyman people. The wife works nights at some vet. The husband should be home."

"And tell them what?" Abe asked.

"Get out of their house," I said. "Right now. Get somewhere safe."

37

When the girl got to her house, she ran inside.

She never wanted to drive again.

She yanked off the hospital smock. Grabbed a pair of leggings and a sweater.

But after a few minutes, she heard a noise outside and ran to the window.

The white Toyota truck. Parked outside.

She locked the front door and ran to the slider out back. Locked it. Checked that the wooden dowel was in place like her dad had showed her.

She grabbed the phone to call 911, but there was no noise. The phone wasn't working.

She'd left her dad's cell in the car, and she opened the front door again, but immediately shrieked.

A fire covered the wood of the door, and smoke poured in.

She threw the door closed and ran to the laundry room.

The man. He was trying to get to her, like he had with Pop.

She climbed on top of the dryer and pulled the ladder down. It led to the roof, and from there, her dad had left a hanging ladder, for emergencies.

38

We jumped in the Charger and raced toward the gorge. It was a twenty-minute drive for us from the north side of town if we kept it above seventy.

Abe called us ten minutes in.

"I put a BOLO out on their car," he said. "There was a bad accident near the bridge at I-32, P.T. The Lymans' Hyundai hit the bridge."

I took my foot off the accelerator. "Are they okay?"

"They got rushed to County," Abe said. "Four or five hours ago."

"Go there and sit on 'em, will you? We'll be right behind you."

"Gattling was near the hospital," Abe said, referring to a patrolman we both came up with. He must've been two of the cops still in town. "Alita's not in her room at the hospital," Abe said. "And her dad—they found his body in a stairwell. He's dead, P.T."

"The mom?" Remy asked.

"In surgery, but the girl's MIA. So is her dad's car."

"Jesus," Remy said.

"He also talked to a nurse," Abe said. "There might've been a guy there impersonating a doctor. And he was in Alita's room."

"Did he take the girl?"

"The nurse said Alita was already gone. It looked like she unscrewed her IV and took off."

I stared at Remy. Thinking of the moment when we'd first met the girl.

"She asked her dad if she could take the ATV home," I said to Remy. "It was odd, right?"

"You think she can drive a car?" Remy said. "She's tiny."

"She's a survivor," I said.

I took the exit at Four Bridges Road, heading toward the gorge.

"We're gonna keep going to Fultz's place," I hollered at Abe. "Go to the hospital. And get patrol to lock that place down."

39

When we came over the hill, we saw it.

A bright orange flash, lighting up the night sky.

A structure was on fire, about a mile in front of us.

My partner got on her waist walkie and called the fire department. In the middle of nowhere, at one a.m., a house could burn to the ground before anyone noticed a plume of smoke in the air.

I pressed down on the Charger's accelerator, and the speedometer passed eighty. Then ninety.

I saw the turn onto Fultz's property and hit the brakes, swerving onto the gravel road we'd gone up that first day.

"Over there." Remy pointed, and I turned left. Followed a bumpy dirt road.

In front of us, a house—maybe a thousand square feet in size—was engulfed in flames.

I parked far enough away to be safe and jumped out.

In front of the house a dinged-up Camry was parked. As was a Toyota truck.

Remy and I pulled our weapons.

"Go that way." I motioned. "I'll meet you around back."

Black smoke billowed out of the house, and I headed north while Remy went south. As I came around my side of the place, the far wall crumbled under the flames, and a burst of ash spit up into the sky.

"Alita!" I hollered.

I ran around the back side of the place, where I saw my partner through the haze. The smoke funneled up into the sky, blocking out the little moonlight coming down on us.

"Rem," I screamed. "If the girl's inside, she's dead already. But she knows these paths as well as anyone."

I took a few steps south. With the brightness of the fire, I could see the two cars out front. If some man was chasing Alita, I didn't want him to have an easy route out of the place.

I pulled my knife from my boot. Ran over and flattened the two front tires of each car.

"P.T." My partner came over. "Look."

She motioned through the smoke unfurling from the house. The brush heading out toward the gorge was burning. Almost in a straight line, as if someone were moving through one of those maze-like pathways with a torch in hand.

"I think he's chasing her," Remy screamed.

We took off in that direction, moving through flames and smoke.

The visibility dropped, and I felt ash in my throat. I followed Remy, running through the corridors of arborvitae that Bill Lyman had cut. Half the paths that he'd carefully trimmed were on fire or gone.

The girl.

I saw a flash of color and turned to get Remy's attention.

But my partner must've taken a different path through the maze of bushes, and we lost each other.

I looked ahead again. "Alita!" I yelled.

Heavy smoke swelled up from the ground, and I ducked, closing my eyes.

Opening them again a moment later, I could see Fultz's home off to my right, ahead of me, a few lights left on. It helped me place where the gravel road was. I followed a trail in that direction, and came out onto the road.

A hundred feet in front of me I made out the shape of the girl. "Alita," I said.

She turned, and her eyes lit up. Recognizing me. I ran to her.

"There's a man," she said.

"I know."

I looked around, but Remy was gone.

"He was on the road," Alita said. "Then at the hospital."

I crouched beside her. "You did good," I said.

"He went that way." She pointed—back where I'd come from. "Toward the equipment shed."

I glanced ahead, to where Fultz's house was. The fire was nowhere near it. "Do you know how to get into Mr. Fultz's house?"

"He hides a key," she said. "Our secret."

"Good. Go inside. And lock the door. Don't let anyone in, except me and my partner."

I watched then as Alita ran up to the house.

The area was dark without the flames lighting it. But the girl found something in the dirt outside and went in. And I headed back in the direction she told me. Where the fire was still raging.

As I got closer, I heard a buzzing sound, and glanced around. I couldn't tell where it was coming from, but ran faster. Cutting across bushes that were burnt down to just strips of red, six inches off the ground.

I heard a popping noise. A gun firing.

Out of a line of smoke about a hundred feet away, an ATV came.

A man was at the helm.

He was six-two maybe. White with a reddish-brown beard and a bald head. Two hundred thirty pounds, if not more.

He was driving toward something, but through the flames I couldn't see what.

Remy rose up in front of the ATV, and the driver let go of the accelerator. He put his hand out to clothesline my partner, but she threw herself at him—hard—right into his chest.

The two collided.

Remy went down, struck in the head. And the man was thrown backward.

I ran toward them. In a flash of a red and black sky, I saw tires spinning. The ATV, upside down seventy or eighty feet ahead.

Remy disappeared in a haze of ash, and my lungs burned as I ran.

Thirty yards away.

Twenty.

I pulled my weapon and came through a slice of visibility.

The man had Remy by the throat and yanked her to his chest with one hand. Made a fist with the other.

My partner's head was bleeding.

"Police," I yelled.

He pulled my partner closer, and I clicked off the safety.

"Let her go—and on your knees," I screamed.

Remy wriggled free, and I had a moment.

I tapped once on my gun. Then a second time.

The man winced. But nothing hit.

He grasped Remy by the throat again, pulled her in front of him. I moved two steps at a time, closer to them.

"You're not gonna kill an unarmed man, are ya?"

"Shoot him," Remy said as she squirmed to one side.

I fired again. Aiming for his leg.

Pop.

When I ran forward, Remy was on the ground, but the man was gone.

I'd missed him. Three times.

All along the ground around us, little wisps of bushes were on fire. I lifted my partner up.

Remy was coughing. Drowning in the smoke.

I lifted her over my shoulders and hustled back toward the house. I saw Alita in the window and waved for her to open the front door.

Inside, I lay Remy down on the couch.

My partner was coughing and spitting. "What the fuck was that?" she yelled.

Remy looked mad enough to chew splinters. She walked over to the kitchen and wiped at her face, which was covered in soot. Alita backed up onto the stairwell and glared at us.

My partner's hair was singed, and her face was bleeding.

"Why didn't you kill that guy?"

"I missed the shot, Rem."

"Yeah, I saw that. You missed *three shots*, partner. Three easy ones, and I could've died. Last time I put my life in *your* hands."

She turned and headed toward the nearby bathroom.

"Plus, you should've left me there and chased him. What the fuck, P.T."

40

wenty minutes later, Fultz's property was covered with vehicles. Two ambulances were parked on the grounds, and
three fire crews kept a line between the scrub brush and Ennis
Fultz's house.

Plumes of smoke blanketed the black-purple sky with gray
smears, and visibility was low as the fire went out and the sky
became black again.

The hit man who'd come after Alita and her dad was gone.
Disappeared into the ether. But we had a solid description of
him from Remy, myself, and the girl. All three of us had seen his
face and build.

Inside Fultz's house, Remy and I got inspected by EMS, who
asked us to come with them to County.

"Pass," I said to the EMT who put me on oxygen for five minutes. "I'll roll down the windows. Get some country air in my
lungs and I'm good."

Remy's face was cut in places, and a different EMT placed

Steri-Strips on her chin, to tape together two pieces of bloody skin.

"I'm tired," Remy said to me after he was done. "I'm gonna get a ride home with patrol."

"*I'll* take you," I said.

In Marvin's car, my partner was quiet. Pissed still.

I dropped her at her place and drove to the precinct after.

In my office, I pulled the blinds down and settled into the couch, putting my feet up on the coffee table. Sarah had come by once and found me like this. Had asked why I slept in here some nights, instead of going home. I didn't have a good answer.

My office phone rang, and I picked it up. Someone had a package for me at the front desk.

Exhausted from being up most of the night, I lumbered down the stairwell and popped out onto the first floor. A man in his twenties wearing a hoodie held a manila envelope.

"You Marsh?" he said.

I nodded.

"You're a tough guy to find. Been coming back every two hours."

"What do you need?" I asked.

"You've been served." He handed me the envelope, and then snapped a photo of me with his phone, holding it. Turned and left.

Inside was a civil complaint, suing me for the wrongful death of Donnie Meadows.

I paged forward and saw the amount on the complaint. Two million dollars. More than anything I owned was worth. Unless you *really* liked Purvis. Then again, he wasn't for sale.

I dropped into an armchair in the front lobby, staring at the far wall.

"You okay, Detective?" Ginger at the front desk asked.

I nodded vaguely, but the bile inside me was rising.

My face got warm, and all the anger I'd been holding in rose to the surface.

Merle—Abe's partner—came down the stairwell from the second floor, heading out the door.

I blinked. I hadn't seen Merle work this late in a decade.

"What are *you* doing here still?" I asked.

"The new boss had me helping Robbery out with a case," he grumbled. "Then after I'm up most of the night, I just checked my voicemail and saw a call regarding these Sorrell boys. I got an attorney turning in Nesbit Sorrell."

Merle had taken over the follow-up on Nesbit, the younger brother who'd trashed Ennis Fultz's BMW.

"Why you leaving then?" I asked.

"A lawyer's bringing him down later," Merle said. "Turning himself in for that property damage."

I blinked. "What do you mean later?"

"Around lunch," Merle said. "The lawyer reached out and suggested noon. I said yes."

This is how suspects skip town, I thought.

"Send a patrol car now," I said.

"C'mon, P.T.," Merle said. "We didn't have a lead on this guy 'til the attorney reached out."

"So what?" I said. "Why should Nesbit get to stay in his bed a couple more hours? Get laid with his girl?"

Merle stared at me.

The reason Merle Berry wasn't the senior detective in Mason Falls, even though he had eight years on me, was because of shit like this. I'd be unsurprised if he has calluses on his ass, from sitting around so much.

"Do you know where this Nesbit fella is?"

"P.T.," he said, "the lawyer's got bail lined up. Nesbit's gonna be home as soon as we book him."

I knew I was carrying anger from the lawsuit into this. Exhaustion from the fire and Cameron's suicide. But I didn't care. There was justice. And there was everything else.

I pointed at the station around us. "What the hell does this look like, Merle?" I said. "Some backwater? We're not running a country club."

"I gave the lawyer my word," Merle said.

"Well, you shouldn't have. Pick the fucker up and charge him. If he wants to post, he'll post. Do your job or get out of the way and I'll do it."

Merle turned toward the stairwell, heading back to his desk. He cursed at me under his breath.

My head was a mess, and I knew it. I walked out the front door and found Marvin's car in the parking lot. I felt like driving fast. I sped onto 5th Street and put my foot to the floor.

By the time I looked up, I was doing ninety on the interstate.

I let my foot off the pedal and coasted.

The 20th Avenue exit was a mile away. The exit I took to my father-in-law's house. And maybe it was better if I wasn't driving Marvin's car right now. If I wasn't a cop with nothing to lose—driving a Charger that could top off at one sixty on the highway.

I slowed at the exit and exhaled, maybe for the first time in twenty-four hours.

41

Ten minutes later I had parked outside of Marvin's house. My hands were still shaking. Seeing my truck outside, I pulled Marvin's car down his long driveway and into his garage.

I let myself into the house and sat in the living room, wondering if my father-in-law would ever come back here. Or whether this would become where *I* lived—if I lost my house in the Meadows lawsuit.

I picked up the phone and called the night nurse at the hospital. There was no new news on Marvin. And no signs he was waking up anytime soon.

"Mr. Marsh," she said. "You gotta have faith for the two of you. Y'understand?"

"Sure," I said.

Except I wasn't good at faith. I was good at proof.

"I got a suggestion," she said. "Get a couple things from his house. Some things that make his room less sterile. A couple picture frames. Maybe his favorite blanket."

"Yeah," I said. "That's a great idea."

I walked around Marvin's place, looking at the pictures of Lena and Exie on the wall in Marvin's living room. My wife had the most beautiful eyes I'd ever seen. Her skin was mocha and the curls in her hair went on forever. On our first date, I couldn't keep my eyes off of her.

The pictures reminded me of Marvin and his phone. I'd sent the files to back up when I'd visited the site of the gas leak, but with how busy the case had gotten, I'd never logged in to see if the backup had worked.

I fished through the kitchen drawers and found an old smartphone that Marvin used before his current one. Then I read a quick blog on how to blank the phone. I began the process of taking Marvin's info and downloading it to the old phone.

While the backup worked, I took a hot shower.

I changed into a T-shirt and shorts I found in my father-in-law's closet. When I came out to his living room, the download was complete.

I looked through Marvin's texts, but there was nothing unexpected. A couple from myself, telling him I'd come by to see him, even though I hadn't.

I looked through the emails from Lucas Royster, the P.I.

> Marvin,
> I think that picture could be it. Call me.
> Lucas

Switching over to Marvin's photo app, I paged backward.

A few images in, I stopped, staring at two pictures of the front of a sedan.

The first was a manufacturer's photo of a 1983 Dodge Aries K-car. The sedan was blue with tires with the whites facing out. The car's logo and the year were printed in the upper right. It was a PR photo from the manufacturer.

The second image was the same make and model, but this picture was of someone's actual car. A used white Dodge Aries K-car. Busted up a little. A photo of the car from the front.

I squinted, confused.

I had worked hard in the last five months to forget the past, but lately it had been creeping back in. The old questions and suspicions. The guilt.

My wife and son had been stranded at the roadside seventeen months ago, thanks to our family Jeep having a recurring battery problem. I was busy at work on some $30 robbery, and asked my wife to call her father, instead of coming to help.

What happened next was a subject of some disagreement.

If you believed Marvin, he found Lena stranded off I-32 and was talking to her, leaning against the driver's-side window with her inside. A car came along and slammed into the back of Marvin's Chrysler 200, pushing his car into Lena's Jeep.

Before Marvin could do a thing, the Jeep slid down the hill and was dumped into the Tullumy River, where my wife and son drowned within minutes.

For twelve months after the fatal car accident, I had a different theory. About a father-in-law who had been drunk since his own wife had passed. Who tried to push his daughter's car with his own, but was loaded and misjudged the distance—misjudged the force of his own vehicle. He drove his daughter and his grandson off the road, down the hill, and to their deaths.

But in the last few months I realized that I'd been blaming Marvin mostly because I didn't want to take responsibility for not showing up to help Lena myself.

And I'd come to a simple conclusion that helped me sleep at night: Of the big mysteries of life, maybe none are ever solved.

But now I was looking at a picture of a white sedan, and Marvin's words repeated in my head. That he'd recognize the front grille of the car that hit his—if he ever saw it again.

Had Lucas Royster helped Marvin identify the make and model he'd been searching for?

Was this what Marvin came by to talk to me about?

I wanted to talk to Marvin. To know what he knew. But I wasn't sure if he'd ever wake up again. Worse, the P.I. was dead and his office destroyed.

I fired up Marvin's desktop computer, my heart racing with the possibility that my father-in-law had located the cowardly son of a bitch who'd killed my wife and son.

I started punching into Google every variable I could—to learn more about the Dodge Aries. My eyes scanned through pictures. I found car clubs where collectors restored "the car that saved Chrysler."

After an hour, I knew I'd make more progress at work and grabbed my keys. I drove to the precinct and asked the desk officer to give me a list of early '80s Dodge Aries K-cars that were registered in the area.

The printout listed forty-two owners, and I scanned through the DMV addresses. Nineteen of the cars were white or tan. I could tell I'd have to go door-to-door to investigate each one. Asking them their whereabouts seventeen months ago—and doing so on my own time.

It was five a.m., and the adrenaline had subsided.

I emailed Abe for help with the list, but didn't want to tell Remy, especially after the night we'd had.

I was crashing hard and got in my truck. I needed an hour away from the K-cars and would come back with new ideas on how to narrow the list down.

I drove home.

But as I got off the interstate, I realized Sarah was going to be there, getting ready for work. She'd probably caught a few hours of sleep after leaving Cam's house and now had to head in. Get to work on Cameron's autopsy.

I didn't want to talk to her about today. About this list. About getting served in a lawsuit. Or how I'd let a man go free because I couldn't shoot straight. Lately I just felt like telling Sarah something else: that I was never gonna be free of the past. Never gonna be a blank slate for her and I to build upon.

I pulled over a few houses down and grabbed the list of VIN numbers. Folded it in my back pocket so I didn't look like I was still searching the past for answers. A madman, obsessed with his wife's death.

I wanted a drink. One shot of Thirteenth Colony, just to quiet my mind and help me sleep.

But as I looked up, I saw the same Mustang that I'd seen before, parked in front of my house.

And something was wrong.

I'd seen the Ford at least two times before. Once when I came back from sitting with Purvis by Tullumy River on Lena's birthday. And a second time after Marvin had been in the hospital.

It was an older Mustang, in primary blue, with dark stripes across the front hood. It wasn't a neighbor's car.

The Mustang's engine was off, but the dome light on. Something glassy was up on the dash, a tiny reflection shining off of it.

I crossed the street quietly under the live oaks that lined the sidewalks and walked closer to the car.

The men inside didn't see me, but I saw a glint of light shift. As I got closer, I confirmed they were holding binoculars.

My eyes moved to the face of the man in the driver's seat. Then to the other man in the passenger seat next to him. Even sitting down, I could tell the men were huge. Nearly seven feet, with the same skin and features that I'd seen in their cousin Donnie Meadows.

The man holding the binoculars was pointing at my house.

In the bedroom, Sarah had the shades up and was sitting on the bed in short shorts and a tank top. She'd probably been up since she came from Cameron Fultz's place. Maybe gotten an hour or two of shut-eye and just showered, ready to head in for Cameron's autopsy. Or maybe she was about to crash, and just waiting for me. Worrying.

As she rubbed moisturizer on her legs, the men took their turns with the binocs—staring at her.

And something rose inside me.

I thought of Donnie Meadows in that cave, trying to drown me. I thought of his sister, trying to steal this house from me.

And now her cousins had been stalking us? Staring in at Sarah when I wasn't home? Coming here over and over?

Something behind my eyes tore, and I heard a noise in my head like a cat biting through steak fat.

I walked to the back of my truck. Found the spare tire, and below it, the tire iron.

I began walking down the middle of the street, the attention of the two men still turned on my house.

The rage inside me was a hurricane, and every hair stood on end.

The men didn't see me until the tire iron was over my head.

I brought it down on the front windshield of the Mustang, and I heard the glass crack under the pressure.

"Get," I screamed.

A second hit, and a chunk of the glass broke apart onto the dash.

"The fuck," I continued, moving around to the front of the car and smashing the front headlights.

"Away from my house."

Inside, the men were scrambling. Screaming at each other.

I moved to the passenger side and hit the glass again, the windshield dislodging atop the two men.

I heard the ignition fire. The Mustang flew into reverse— straight into the intersection without looking to see if cars were coming.

The car screeched off then, and I stood there, covered in sweat.

I heard dogs barking in nearby houses, and turned.

Sarah stood on the front lawn, in her Victoria's Secret shorts and a tank top.

Her face: it was twisted with fear.

"What the hell?" she said. "Do you know those guys?"

"They were peeping," I said.

"P.T., this is a public street. They're allowed to park here."

"What am I supposed to do?" I asked. "Hand these fucking Meadows people my life?"

My hands were shaking, and I looked down. Dropped the tire iron.

"I've got nothing left," I said. "My mom and dad."

Sarah stared at me.

"Lena. Jonas. Marvin. What the fuck."

"You have me," she said. "Come inside."

"I don't want to."

"Why not?" she demanded, her voice a tremor.

"Jesus, Sarah, can't you see? I can't be the one you rely on. We're building on friggin' quicksand."

"You're scaring me, Paul," she said.

"The person who killed her is still out there."

"Killed who?"

I shook my head, not wanting to say it. To say Lena's name.

I pulled out the list. "Someone who drives a Dodge K-car."

Sarah looked at the paper. I'd folded it and unfolded it ten times in the last hour, and I knew I sounded like I had only one oar in the water.

"I mean, for all we know, it's them," I yelled. Pointing at the empty space where the Mustang had just been. "Who killed my Lena and Jonas."

"They had a horrible accident—"

"You don't know that," I said.

Sarah stared at me. A face-off on the lawn.

"This is my fault," Sarah said after a minute. "You were never ready. I pushed you."

She walked back into the house, and I stood there.

Since my wife had died, Sarah was the only person I wanted to be with. But she was right. I didn't want it enough to stop holding on to the past.

Sarah came back out with her pocketbook. "Find someone you can talk to, Paul," she said. "Before it's too late."

She walked off then, and behind me, I heard her Acura fire up.

I didn't want to turn to see her leave.

And I couldn't stop her.

I just stood there.

Eventually I walked inside. But the weight of the place was too much, so I passed through the house and out into the backyard.

There was an old swing set that I got when Jonas was four. I lowered myself onto one of the two swings.

I heard the plastic flap on the doggie door, and Purvis walked over, finding a place on the grass to my left.

Crabgrass had begun to encircle the rusted legs of the swings, and Purvis bit at the longer strands.

I swung back and forth, staring at the ground.

You were gone as much with her as you were with Lena, Purvis chirped.

"You have no idea what you're talking about, dog," I said.

I walked inside and went to the kitchen. Got out the bottle of rum and started drinking. A half hour later, the bottle was empty.

I got in my truck and made my way to a package store about a mile away. The place had just opened, and I bought a fifth of gin and took it to the register.

Up at the counter were small clear jars with baby quail eggs, soaking in a solution of sliced garlic and spices.

I tossed two of them into my bag along with the liquor and shot home.

42

Three hours later, I woke up in a pool of drool on the living room floor. My back felt as thick as a board, and the sun filled the room.

I showered, fed Purvis, and opened the fridge. Almost nothing inside.

I made some toast and smothered both pieces with muscadine jelly. When I no longer felt like I was walking on a slant, I got in the car and drove to County Hospital, where Alita had been brought last night to be with her mother.

A strong police presence was at the hospital, with two squad cars parked at angles to the front door. Inside more cops were posted.

In the fourth-floor lobby, I saw a woman named Iris from Child Services, who I'd worked with before.

"Hey," I said. "How are things?"

"Mom's out of surgery, and doing well," she said. "Alita's taking a nap."

Iris motioned at a door about twenty feet away, and I saw another blue-suiter, sitting in a chair outside the room. Abe or Remy must've bulked up protection.

"Anna Lyman's sister just got here. To help out. Also a place for Alita to go at night 'til her mom's better."

"That's good," I said.

"The little girl's not talking much," Iris said. "But she found her dad's body two floors down from here. This place doesn't have good memories."

I explained to Iris how the girl had driven to the house. Leaving a trail of cars with dings in them. And how Remy and I had faced off with the hit man out to kill her.

"Jesus," Iris said. "She's so tiny."

"But tough."

I walked into Anna Lyman's room and introduced myself, since we hadn't met in person.

Anna was a tall woman. Slender, a mix of Native American and white. Her hair was in a messy bob that curled around her cheeks.

"I heard what you and your partner did for Alita," Anna said.

I glanced over at her adopted daughter, who was asleep nearby, her legs strung over the side of the chair and a blanket thrown over her small body.

"I wish we could've figured it out sooner," I said.

I grabbed a chair and placed it on the side of the bed farthest from Alita. Lowered my voice. "So you knew Ennis was Alita's birth father?"

"Not at first." She shook her head. "We just knew we couldn't have kids of our own."

"You'd been trying?"

"Eight years," she said. "We'd met with an adoption agency last spring. And finally Bill told Ennis how we were thinking of moving because of it."

I squinted, not following her.

"Bill was handy, and we'd fixed up the house real nice. But we looked like squatters. The place wasn't up to code, and we didn't pay rent or own the land."

"Not good for adopting?"

"Our housing situation made no sense to the agency."

"So Ennis pulled some strings?"

"Not at that time," she said. "But a couple months later, after he got out of the hospital, he told Bill he'd like to help. He'd use his influence, and we'd get a little girl."

"Just like that?"

"Isn't that how the world works?"

I nodded. There was pain in her face, along with something concrete and tough. "When did you figure out it was his birth daughter?"

Anna looked over at Alita.

"The day before we signed the papers. Ennis went for a walk with Bill and told him. Said we should know before we signed. We could back out."

Anna took a moment to gather herself. Wiped at her red cheeks.

"I was furious," she said. "But my husband said, 'You're getting what you wanted. And he doesn't want anything out of it except a good home. What's the problem?' Bill was methodical that way. And he was right. I mean—you've spent time with Alita, right?"

"She's remarkable," I said.

Anna stared over at her sleeping daughter.

"What about Suzy Kang?" I asked.

"Her name was in Alita's file. So we figured, given Fultz was the birth father, she'd come around sometime. We knew she had no legal rights. A month later, she started coming every week."

"On Mondays?" I asked, and she nodded.

"Ennis and her kept their distance. Watched from his house. He asked Alita up for dinner once when Suzy was there, but all three of us showed up. Make sure everyone got the message."

I pointed at her daughter, and my voice dropped to a whisper. "Does Alita know?"

Anna shook her head. "Ennis didn't want her to. A month ago, he told us that when he passed, Alita would be taken care of for life. We didn't ask for more details."

We talked for a minute more. About Alita taking walks with Ennis Fultz.

"He wanted to play the part of the friendly neighbor," she said. "So I guess Bill was right. I got what I wanted. Until all this happened."

Anna put her head in her hands and started sobbing.

When she was able to speak again, she asked me what prompted the hit man to hunt them down. I tried to explain that like most crimes it came down to jealousy and greed.

Before leaving, I gave her a hug. Got in the truck and headed into the precinct.

I found Remy sitting in my office, looking through the coroner's report on Cameron Fultz. I counted myself lucky to have avoided that meeting with Sarah and listened as Remy went over what we already suspected. A self-inflicted gunshot wound was the official cause of Cameron's death, making the manner of death officially suicide.

"The entry wound was thirteen millimeters in diameter," Remy said. "Hard contact—sort of a mix of a stellate and muzzle imprint."

Remy handed me the photograph of the bullet entry in Cameron's head. In a hard contact wound, the head of the weapon is pushed against the skin and can almost indent it, because the skin envelopes the muzzle of the weapon.

"There's two ways the end went down for Cameron," Remy theorized. "One, Cam needed that land and the only way to get it was to kill his dad. Eventually afterward, the remorse overtook him, and he couldn't stand to be alive."

I thought about this. The only tweak I'd make to that theory was about that decision to kill Ennis. Maybe Cameron made the call, or maybe his business partners made it for him. Enfatigo Capital, who held the paper on that lien on Cameron Fultz's home, was not to be messed with.

"And the second way the suicide happened?" I asked.

"The second way starts the same. Cam killed his dad or had him whacked. He feels bad, but he's getting the land."

"Then Cam sees the will," I said.

"Right." Remy pointed. "He realizes he's got a half sister and she's next to get killed. If she and her adopted parents die, the land is Cam's. Which is to say, the land is Enfatigo's."

"So he kills himself," I said. "Once he's dead, it doesn't do anyone any good to touch Alita. If Cam's dead and you take out the Lymans—the land goes to the environmental group. And for sure, no one's ever gonna drill there."

"Exactly," Remy said.

I thought of Ennis Fultz. He'd screwed over half the people in real estate, including partners like the Sorrells and his ex-wife. Even bought the property his son was trying to buy.

But then there was Alita and Suzy. There he tried to do one good deed. Fix a mistake he made with Suzy and make good for his illegitimate daughter. Ultimately, that propelled his own death.

"Enfatigo Capital," Remy said. Thinking of the mob-connected company that had the most to gain from all these deaths. "So we go after them?" she asked. "Presuming they hired the hit man?"

"I doubt we'll be able to touch them," I said. While Vincent Enfatigo had been in prison, his kin had not only doubled the size of their business empire, but had tripled the size of their legal staff. "The only way to them is to find that hit man. With how this went south, you can bet one of their own people is coming after that guy. Trying to take him out."

"So we don't even try?" Remy asked.

"You and I should make a house call," I said. "Drive down to Atlanta and meet with Enfatigo. Make sure they know Cam's dead. His house'll be sold, so they'll get the principal on their loan back. But touching Alita or Anna Lyman isn't gonna do shit for them. Their play is over."

"They're gonna hear us out?" Remy asked.

"They'll listen," I said. "Just don't expect them to acknowledge what we're talking about."

"And what of the hired gun?" Remy asked.

Early this morning, Remy had sent a sketch artist to the hospital, and we had a good drawing on the hit man. The guy who'd run the Lymans off the road. Who I'd somehow missed out at the gorge, even though I'd emptied half a clip.

How multiple shots had not hit the assassin was a mystery to me. But my gut told me I probably needed a break from killing unarmed suspects in big cases, no matter how guilty the sons of bitches were. No more Vonte Delgados and Donnie Meadows in my life for a spell.

"That guy's sketch is in every patrol vehicle from here to Macon," Remy said. "Surrounding states. And all over social media."

"And the white Toyota truck?"

"It was stolen," Remy said. "Two days ago from the parking lot of a Moe's Taco Shop, south of Braselton."

I ran my hands through my hair. Wondering if we'd catch a lucky break on finding the hit man.

"Chief Senza came by for you," my partner said. "In person. He seemed a little tense."

"Was he asking about the case?" I pointed around at the evidence.

"No," Remy said. "He seemed pleased about this."

I thought about the incident with the Meadows cousins outside of my house last night. For all I knew, some neighbor recorded it on their damn cell phone.

There was also the episode with the state police in Centa at the site of the explosion the night before. I hadn't yet talked to Senza since that had happened either.

"He said to stop by." Remy furrowed her brow. "'Mandatory' is the word he used."

Abe stood just inside the doorway to my office.

"Will do," I said to Remy.

"You got a sec, P.T.?" Abe asked.

I got up and followed him out.

"I got that list of Dodge Aries K-cars," he said. "You emailed me—middle of the night."

"Yeah," I said.

"There's one car," Abe said. "It's got an interesting history."

"Interesting how?"

Abe pulled up the record at his desk, pointing at his computer screen, which listed the vehicle's DMV history. "The car was stolen two days before your wife's accident, a year ago December," he said. "Never recovered."

"Okay?"

"Then it pops up a month ago as salvage—with a back date to a week after Lena's death."

I wasn't following Abe. "What do you mean 'a back date'?" I asked. "What's backdated?"

"Yeah," Abe said. "So I called up this salvage place and talked to a kid there. He said they've been cleaning up old records. Cars that fell off the grid."

"Wait," I said. "If a car's in DMV records, we must know who the owner was."

"This car was stolen, P.T.," Abe said. "We know who owned the car *before* it was stolen. Old lady in her seventies. Reported it gone a week before Christmas a year ago. We had a BOLO out on it ourselves."

I was still hungover and putting facts together slowly.

"So someone stole some old lady's ride," I said.

"Check," Abe said. "The thief goes for a joyride—maybe he hits Marvin's car. Into Lena's car. Wakes up the next day and checks the news."

I nodded.

"He hears what happened," I said. "Freaks out and dumps the car at some 'no-questions-asked' salvage yard?"

"A lot of assumptions, I realize," Abe said. "But those old cars, P.T. They weighed twenty-three hundred pounds. If someone was okay leaving with no cash, these salvage houses would pick up a pretty penny for all that scrap metal and might look the other way. Not check if it was stolen or where it came from."

My heart started racing.

There was a part of me that had never believed Marvin's story about the hit-and-run. And a part of me that did.

Now I might have a chance to hunt down the cowardly son of a bitch who killed my wife and son in a hit-and-run.

"I was gonna chat up the old lady," Abe said. "You want to go check out the salvage yard?"

I was grateful for what Abe was doing. Treating this like it was a real case.

"Yeah," I said. "Thanks, buddy. I appreciate the discretion too."

Abe patted me on the shoulder, and I turned, staring across the squad room toward my office, where Remy was.

Whatever the chief wanted, it wasn't good.

Tusila Meadows had sued me. And in response, I'd attacked her cousins. When cops take the law into their own hands these days, bad things usually happened.

I wondered if I should talk to the Meadows cousins myself. Try to reason with them.

I slid a chair over to the nearest terminal and put in the name Meadows, along with a description of the Mustang from last night.

A name came up.

Daoto Meadows

And an address at Grant and 23rd in the numbered streets. I exhaled. Considered how I might apologize. And then changed my mind.

Screw them. Finding the truth on what happened to Lena and Jonas was more important than politics. I turned and walked out the door. Pointed my truck east toward Counsa County, where the salvage yard was located.

I was at my best when I was hot on a lead, and this one was personal. Who knows? When I found where this path went— maybe what I did to the Meadows cousins might be the least of my problems. And maybe I didn't care what happened next.

43

I pulled off the state highway onto a side road that I hadn't driven down before.

Rural broiler farms dotted the landscape, selling chickens by the thousands. The area smelled like shrimp had been left out in the sun, and I pushed hard on the truck's accelerator, the scent becoming laden with ammonia before the farms disappeared.

A half hour had passed since I left the precinct, and the land gave way to vacant space, with weedy scuppernong filling dirt pastures and trumpet vine choking fence posts stuck into old Georgia dirt.

Faded hand-painted signs at the roadside advertised boiled peanuts by the bag and fresh apples, but the places that once sold them were long gone.

In another minute I saw a flash of color dotting the hillside in the distance, a piece of a rusted yellow school bus protruding up into the sky over a barren hill.

As I came around the bend, the junkyard appeared in full,

with stacks of smashed cars, along with an area full of tractors and work trucks. The vehicles were piled atop each other into a pattern of beauty that appeared in repetition, like a watercolor, done in three coats, each smeared atop the one below it.

My phone buzzed with a text, and I glanced down.

A message from Abe.

He'd met with Grazia Lauroyan, the old lady whose Dodge Aries was stolen two Christmases ago. She was seventy and retired a month ago from a business she ran in Burna, Georgia, a thirty-minute drive from Mason Falls. She had no clue who would want the old car, and never saw the theft coming.

Another dead end.

There was a gap in a corrugated metal fence with the word SALVAGE and an arrow spray-painted on it, and I turned in at the arrow's tip.

I steered around a handful of older cars that weren't crushed and pulled my truck by a white trailer. Got out and looked around. Not a soul manning the machinery. Not a noise in the place. I walked up the steps and into the trailer.

Inside sat a man in his late forties with olive skin. He had jet-black hair and wore a short-sleeve linen shirt and jeans. His desk was the kind you bought used, in a school auction, and the rest of the place was bare-bones. Two white melamine card tables were stacked high with paperwork.

"What can I help you with, boss?" he said in a thick New York accent.

"I'm looking for Trevor Bogota," I said.

Trevor was the kid Abe had spoken to by phone. The one

who'd registered the VIN number tied to the '83 Dodge Aries I was looking for.

"That's my boy." The man put out his hand. "I'm Tommy Bogota."

"P. T. Marsh," I said, shaking first and then badging him after. "Your son talked to a detective on my squad about a car you guys had here."

"Sure thing, boss," he said. "Hold on."

The man grabbed a walkie and pressed it three times. Some signal to his son.

Had these two interacted with the man who killed Jonas? Purvis asked. Purvis in my head.

"I'm in the middle of something," a voice squawked on the walkie. Younger. The same accent.

Do they run a dirty business? Purvis persisted. My bulldog's voice was angry. Jonas had been his favorite person in the world.

Calm down, dog.

"There's a cop here," the man said.

"Okay," the kid answered. "Coming in."

"Have a seat." The father pointed to a single chair in the office. It was a captain's chair that had been removed from a minivan and placed against the trailer wall beside a water jug and a pile of those pointy white paper cups.

"Where are you from?" I asked.

A swamp cooler pumped away in the corner, but it wasn't making much progress against the heat.

"The Bronx," the man said. "Logan Avenue. Why? I don't sound like youse?"

"No, you sound just like us," I said.

I wanted to smile. To joke with him. But I was unable to.

"I inherited this business six months ago," the man said. "My wife's from down here. Her brother died."

I relaxed my attitude toward the man and his son. "Sorry to hear that."

The door swung open, and a kid came in. Twenty-one or twenty-two years old. Taller than his dad. A similar look but less gut and more muscles.

I introduced myself, and he remembered the phone conversation with Abe.

"I didn't know you were driving over." The kid wiped grease from his hands onto a white towel that hung off his hip. "I kinda told everything I know to the other cop. We had an '83 Aries in here about a year ago. Got crushed and sold for weight."

"My son's been setting up our records," the father said proudly. "QuickBooks for accounting. Transfers of title for the DMV in Excel. My brother-in-law wasn't exactly a stickler for paperwork."

"Sure," I said. "That's good, right? Family business?"

The kid gave a sideways look. Like maybe he wasn't a hundred percent on board with the job yet.

"I don't know if Detective Kaplan told you," I said. "That Dodge is part of a case we're looking into. It was stolen a couple days before it was brought here."

The father sat up straighter. "Lotta stuff happened before we owned the place, Detective. Legally we inherited just the assets."

I put up both hands, palms out, telegraphing that I wasn't coming after them. "I'm not concerned about some old car theft."

The swamp cooler made a hissing noise, the compressor whining hard to cool even a tiny space. It was the kind of day where two trees fought each other over a well-hydrated dog.

"This is personal," I continued. "My wife may have been hit and killed by that car."

"Jesus Christ," the dad said.

"I need to find some information," I said. "And I'd consider it a personal favor if we took a second look together."

"Of course," the dad said. "Trev, why don't you walk Detective Marsh out to where you've been working."

"C'mon," the kid said.

I thanked the old man and followed the kid out of the trailer.

In much of the junkyard, the cars weren't actually crushed, in the way you think of it, Jetsons-style, down to a cube. Instead, each was slightly smashed down and piled atop one another. The dead cars formed tall structures, each atop the one underneath, like giant hallways big enough for the tow yard's Caterpillars to get down. Or for us to walk through.

We arrived at a different trailer, this one with a blue stripe down the side. Trevor walked up the two steps and flicked on the lights and the window AC.

Inside the air smelled like a wet dog, and the place was crammed with boxes. Three or four hundred of them.

"This was my uncle Bob's system," he said. "I was going to SUNY for finance in Albany, so I've been trying to clean stuff up. Digitize old records."

I looked around. The place was a shithole.

"We had to meet with Motor Vehicles," Trevor said. "They actually sent a guy out here, and I showed him what we inherited. He agreed to take a spreadsheet every month."

"A spreadsheet of what?" I asked.

"I put in plates if I got 'em. If not, VIN numbers. A lot of this stuff wasn't ever registered with the State of Georgia as salvage."

I took the top off a nearby box. Inside was a stack of maybe a hundred pages, each of them on eleven-by-seventeen ledger-style graph paper.

"And these ledgers have the VIN numbers?"

The kid nodded. "Your Dodge Aries." He pointed. "The original paper's somewhere in here, but I can't promise there's a lot of detail with it. But that's where the DMV got the info."

I looked around at the mess. "What I need is who brought the car in."

"Yeah, that's where it might get a little murky," the kid said. "We can look, but if I had the info, I'd have already passed it on to the DMV."

Trevor had a PC on one of the tables, and flicked it on, showing me an Excel spreadsheet with columns listing each car's VIN number, make, model, and other info.

"I enter about fifty records every morning before it gets hot. Then move on to other work."

The kid did a quick "find" in Excel for the word "Aries" and showed me the line item that he'd turned in to the DMV.

From left to right, it listed the make and model, along with the VIN number. Under "seller," the column was blank.

"What does that mean?" I pointed.

"It either wasn't on the paper I found, or I couldn't read it. Sun-faded, blank, or illegible."

"So where is the original paper you found?" I said. "That you got the VIN number off of."

The kid pointed to the left side of the trailer. "The boxes on those two tables. That's what I've gone through in the last month. It's somewhere in there."

I stared at the boxes.

"Here," Trevor said. "Let me get a couple chairs. It's ten or so boxes, but maybe we get lucky. Find it in the first few."

I took the folding chair and we divided up the boxes, the kid taking a couple and me the rest.

He showed me where to look on the ledger, and what the first so many digits of the VIN number was, to help scan through each page more quickly. We worked quietly for the first half hour, and once I could do it in my sleep, we started talking.

Trevor's mother had passed away from cancer when he was in high school, and then his uncle caught the cancer last year. His dad decided to pull him out of school his junior year at SUNY. Give them both a fresh start in a new location.

"My mom passed when I was a few years out of college myself," I said. "Breast cancer."

Trevor looked up. "So it was just you and your dad too?"

"My dad had already split before high school."

"Geez," the kid said.

"I got mad at the world," I said. "Got into some trouble. Along the way, I met this cop who was good to me. A little bit later I met my wife, and soon after that, I was in the academy."

Trevor began talking about the business here. His mom was from Macon and had gone to Mercer. His dad was born in the Bronx and worked fifteen years in a mechanic's shop.

"So you know cars?" I asked.

"I've been helping my dad since I was eight, and he's been in it his whole life. But the junk business is different than doing repairs."

"Of course."

"We obviously don't sound like we're from here, but everyone's been pretty nice."

"So walk me through the process," I said. "I drive in here with a car. What do you do?"

"Now or back in the day—Uncle Bob style?"

"Let's start Uncle Bob style," I said. "I assume nowadays you're doing things right."

"Okay, well, most yards pay a hundred and fifty bucks a ton if the car runs. So people drive some old beater in here. We take a look at the condition. Usually, three hundred bucks a vehicle."

"Regardless of the make?" I asked.

"Some cars have parts that are in more demand. We might go two hundred a ton."

"So four hundred for the car?"

"Exactly," he said.

"But a Dodge Aries from the '80s," I said. "Traded in late 2017 . . ."

"The hundred fifty bucks category," the kid said. "'Cause at that point you're just recycling for steel."

"What about a valid title?" I asked. "You don't need that?"

"With us, of course. You gotta prove you're the owner."

"But not with Uncle Bob?"

"Between us and the wall, Bob had this thing going," the kid said. "He'd have people sign a certificate that they were the owner, and then he'd take a picture of their driver's license. Since

Bob was a notary, they'd sign a statement that everything's legit and be on their way."

"And he'd make money off the notary fee."

"Fifty bucks," the kid said.

I thought about this. It was good news. If we could find the person who traded the stolen car in, they'd have shown their driver's license, paid the fifty bucks, and I'd have them.

"So back up," I said, the two of us still going through the ledger papers as we talked. I thought about the Dodge Aries hitting Marvin's car the December before last. And Marvin's car hitting Lena's into the river. The Aries must've had a smashed-in front bumper.

"So they drive in," I said. "Do you inspect the car? Are you looking to see if it's been in an accident?"

"Nah, we don't care about dings on old cars, because we're salvaging engine parts and selling the exterior metal," Trevor said. "First thing we do—we make a classification. Is the car what we call an 'EOL car'? Which are ninety-five percent of what we crush."

"What's that mean?" I looked up from my ledger paper. "EOL?"

"End of life," he said.

"And if it is?"

"We know we're gonna sell the car for scrap primarily."

"So you buy the old car," I said. "Maybe Bob does his notary scam. Maybe he's got a title and doesn't need to. What next?"

"We remove chemicals and state-regulated materials. Car batteries. Antifreeze. Oil. Power-steering fluid. There's a whole process for what to do with those."

"Then?"

"Then we scavenge for parts. From alternators to infotainment centers. When we're done, we put the car aside. Once a quarter we sell everything by weight to a scrap-metal place."

"And are most cars driven in?" I asked. "People come themselves? Or do tow trucks come here?"

The kid didn't answer so I looked over. He was staring closely at a specific page of ledger paper.

"You got it?" I stood up.

He nodded, and I walked over. Staring at the line item, written on the yellowing paper.

Under the "title" column, it read *no* and had an asterisk next to it. But under notary, it had a fee listed. But it wasn't the usual $50. It read *$200*.

"How come the notary fee is so high?" I asked.

"I saw another one like this last week," the kid said. "Showed it to my dad. He thinks it meant there was something squirrelly with the car. Because Bob's accurate with some stuff. He doesn't hide income, if you know what I mean."

"No," I said. "Sorry, I don't follow."

"Bob might've pulled a lot of weird shit. But he also got audited by the IRS pretty regularly."

"The auditors don't care if you run a sketchy business?"

"Hell no." The kid shook his head. "As long as you declare all your income on your taxes. So we think sometimes Bob charged a little extra if a guy didn't want to show him his ID."

I bit at my lip. So Bob took any car, regardless of ID. It just meant the person paid him more. Which meant there might be no way to trace who'd dumped the Aries here.

I looked off to the right on Uncle Bob's chart, where the fee paid for the Aries was listed. It read *$0*—along with the notation *(NSC $500)*.

"Why zero?" I pointed. "Isn't that where Bob would've put what he paid for the car?"

"Yeah," Trevor said. "So Dad and I—we think that means he didn't pay anything. He just gave them a car. NSC means non-salvaged car."

My head was pounding from drinking the night before. "What's a non-salvaged car?"

"Did you see the cars by the front entrance? Where you drove in."

"I almost hit one of them," I said.

"Well, people come in here with cars that are drivable. They're old, but nothing too wrong with them. Sometimes, instead of getting paid in cash they take one of those old beaters."

I had been sweating since I got into the place, and my shirt was sticking to my chest.

"Wait," I said. This wasn't bad for me. "Someone drives off in those cars?"

"Yeah, remember I said the EOL's are like ninety-five percent of the cars. There's a dozen cars usually that we keep on hand and don't crush. That's the other five percent. Instead of taking money, they can take one of those."

"Had that been going on before you guys? Like in Bob's time?"

"For two decades," he said.

"So, the guy I'm looking for could've come in here—dropped a car off—and instead of getting cash, he drove a different car out?"

The kid nodded.

"How many of those are there per year?"

"Five maybe," he said.

On five single days each year, one of these cars went out. That wasn't a needle in a haystack at all. "Did Bob keep records on the non-salvaged cars?"

"Yeah, well there's only a few a year. So he had one ledger just for that. For the whole twenty years he ran the place."

"Can I see it?"

Trevor walked over to a file cabinet against the far wall. "I don't want to get your hopes up, Detective," he said. "If Bob got a little extra to not put a name down on the trade-in, he might not have one on the car that left here."

"Sure," I said. "But maybe I don't need a name, Trevor. 'Cause if they drove that car around, they had to register it themselves. Which means I can find out their name."

Trevor opened the ledger, finding one entry in December of '17. The same day the '83 Dodge Aries was brought in.

A 1987 El Camino.

I scanned over to a column describing the vehicle. *CC*, it read. *Gray with black stripes.*

I blinked.

I'd seen a car like this recently.

It doesn't mean anything, Purvis said.

"What is that again?" I pointed. "CC?"

"It was a special make of the car," the kid said. "Made in Tennessee. The CC stood for 'choo-choo.' It's good for you. That make and model. 'Cause you know, it's already a thirty-year-old car. So there's even less of them on the road. Add to that fact it's a choo-choo, even rarer."

Brian, Purvis said. *The apartment manager. He'd said choo-choo also.*

"That's the VIN number?" I asked, pointing at the numbers to the right of the entry.

The kid nodded. "See, '87 was the last year of production, so you gotta think there's only a handful of these cars still on the road. A lot of people think they're ugly."

I hadn't breathed in a half a minute.

"Yeah," I said flatly, repeating the words Abe had said two days ago. "Rednecks drove 'em when I was a kid."

Trevor laughed. "I didn't want to say that, but yeah." He looked up and saw my face. "Are you okay, Detective?"

I had come to the junkyard to find the car that had hit my father-in-law's Chrysler into my wife's Jeep. To put a name with the cowardly bastard who was guilty in the hit-and-run death of my wife and son.

But now the world had shifted upside down.

The bastard who hit my wife had gotten himself a rare El Camino.

When Abe had gone through the security video at Thom Sile's apartment complex, there was a late '80s El Camino on it. Also gray with black stripes. Also a choo-choo. It was one of two cars that didn't use a remote to access the apartment's gate and instead followed a car in.

The only car that hadn't used a clicker in both directions, in and out.

Trevor stared at me. "Detective Marsh?"

"I'm fine," I said.

But I was lying. I was five counties from fine.

I took a picture of the VIN number with my phone and turned, staggering out the door of the trailer.

The humidity outside was like a blanket, and suddenly nothing made sense.

Marvin had said a car hit his Chrysler—accidentally—pushing it into Lena's Jeep, which slid down into the Tullumy River.

An accident, he'd said.

"I gotta go," I told Trevor, who was standing behind me by the trailer. Staring at me as if I were a ghost.

I got to my truck and pulled out of the junkyard, barely holding the wheel straight.

A mile down, I yanked the steering wheel to the edge of the road and got out.

The smell of ammonia was strong in the air, and I threw up in the ditch by the roadside.

I spat at the ground, going over it again in my head. The car that Abe had seen in the Tatham Arms Apartment Complex had been an El Camino. Same color and stripes.

I thought of Ennis and Cameron Fultz.

Our primary theory was still that Cameron had left the golf resort in Jacksonville and drove back to Georgia. Stole Thom Sile's U-Chem truck to set the driver up.

But what if he hadn't?

What if instead Cameron had hired someone to kill his father? Or Enfatigo had? And that someone drove an El Camino. The one we'd seen go in and out of the apartment complex.

Someone who had experience making death look like an accident.

The bile rose up again, and I vomited. The toast and jam. The gin from the night before.

I pictured Lena and Jonas, driving along I-32.

How many paid killers are living quietly in a town the size of Mason Falls?

I grabbed my notebook out of the truck's cab and stared at it, flapping pages until I found where I'd written something down. The location where the Lymans' car had been hit.

The bridge at I-32.

The same place Lena and Jonas had been hit.

"No, no, no," I said to myself.

Not the same guy.

I pulled at my hair, wandering in circles.

A car beeped, and I realized I was in the middle of the highway.

I bent over, my hands on my knees.

I'd had a gun trained on the man who killed my wife and son, and I'd missed the shot.

My phone was ringing, and I stumbled back to the truck. Remy calling.

"Hey, where'd you go?" she said.

"I had him, Rem."

"Had who?" she asked.

"I had a gun on him and let him go."

"It's okay," she said. "I'm fine, and we don't need to rehash it. We'll get the guy."

I started to feel sick again and headed over to the gutter at the roadside.

"P.T.," Remy said. "You left without talking to Chief Senza."

"Don't worry," I said. "I'll be talking to him soon. 'Cause he wanted to close this case up, but I got news for everyone. This thing is getting bigger, not smaller."

"So you're coming back here?" she asked.

"Not until he's dead."

Remy didn't say anything, and I leaned over. Threw up again. Pieces of spicy quail eggs littered the road.

"P.T.," Remy said, "I've been asked to bring you in. Are you hearing me? This thing with the Meadows cousins. You wrecking their car."

I suddenly realized Remy was trying to tell me something. Something I wasn't hearing.

"They say you're done, P.T.," my partner said. "I don't know if it's permanent or temporary. But we'll figure it out together. Where are you?"

"I'm sorry you got pulled into this, Rem," I said.

"P.T.," she said. "Listen—"

I interrupted her. "Rem, all these murders are tied together. Fultz. The El Camino. Lena. Cameron."

As I said this, a pit formed in the bottom of my stomach.

The weight of this discovery.

If the same hired gun took down Fultz and Lena, then my wife's death was no accident. Hired killers didn't work for free.

"P.T.," Remy said, "the DA had to settle with the Meadows people an hour ago for four hundred grand. I've been told to come get your badge and gun."

My mouth stopped working, and I felt numb. Someone was paid to kill Lena.

"I'm not coming in," I said.

"I can follow this information up," Remy said. "I don't know what it's got to do with Lena, but you know me. I'm not gonna leave any stone unturned."

I got back in the truck. Moving like a robot. No longer listening to my partner.

"Tell me where you are, P.T.," she said. "They have a BOLO out on your truck. I don't want you getting pulled over by some overzealous blue-suiter with a hyperactive trigger finger."

I said nothing to Remy.

"Are you at a junkyard?" she asked. "I know Abe was helping you with something to do with a junkyard."

I was thinking of the past. Of Lena, driving home with Jonas and her car battery dying. *Why hadn't we traded in that old Jeep? Why hadn't I come out to help my wife?*

"P.T.," Remy said, "let me help you."

I hit *End* on the phone and sat there in the truck, the hot sun no longer bothering me.

I was worn down, but at the same time, I had a purpose. Seventeen months of suspicions, all focused on one data point. The VIN number.

I called up my friend Shaina, who worked at the precinct in Admin.

"Hey," I said, trying to focus. To not sound like I was missing too many shingles off my roof. "I need help with a VIN number on a car."

"Gimme the number," Shaina said, cheery. She didn't know I was being hunted yet, but would soon find out.

I told her, and Shaina read me back the name and address of the car's owner.

Kian Tarticoft. Age 47.

2673 Forman Road. Burna, Georgia.

She checked his driver's license and the same address came back.

I hung up and stared at the information.

"Marvin," I said aloud. "I should've believed you."

But it didn't matter anymore. Because finally I'd found the son of a bitch.

The one who'd ruined my life.

And he had no idea I was coming for him.

44

The address I'd gotten from Shaina was in a town about halfway back from the junkyard toward Mason Falls.

I was about to race there, but my partner's words echoed in my head. About some patrolman cornering me.

I drove back to the junkyard, taking the turn-in by the arrow at a decent clip, dust forming around my back tires as I stopped.

I was halfway to the trailer when Trevor Bogota poked his head out.

"I need a favor," I said. "Those beater cars you sell off. I need one."

"There's a Chevy Malibu," he said. "Runs pretty good."

I pulled out my wallet. "I have three hundred bucks," I said. "Consider it a rental? I'll bring it back tomorrow."

Trevor's dad appeared behind him.

"Just borrow it," he said. "We won't report it stolen for seventy-two hours. If it's back by then, it's back. Give him the keys, Trev."

"Thanks," I said. I grabbed my supply box from the back of my truck. "Can you guys stow my pickup, somewhere out of sight?"

"Sure," the dad said.

I got the keys and shook each of their hands.

"You're a good kid," I said to Trevor. "Look after your dad."

I clicked the button on the key fob and two lights flashed on a green Malibu near the exit. I threw my supply box into the trunk of the old beater.

As I drove, I stared at the scrap of paper where I'd written the information from Shaina at the precinct.

Kian Tarticoft. Age 47.

2673 Forman Road. Burna, Georgia.

I passed the broiler farms and then rolled down the windows. The bad smell dissipated, and a hint of lilac and hyacinth spread over the countryside.

I got to Burna about twenty minutes later, carefully driving by the address and then circling down the alley behind it a second time. It was a custom parts machine shop, and it was clear from the street that the place was abandoned.

"Shit," I said aloud.

I parked the Malibu on the opposite side of the street. The machine shop had a large storefront window, and the blinds had been pulled up, probably to show potential vandals that there was nothing to take.

I walked down the street, approaching a bakery called Sweets&, two doors down. Inside was a black woman, decorating the top of what looked like a coconut layer cake. She was dressed all in white, except for a bright yellow headband.

"Now, there's a guy who could use a cookie," she said as I came in, her head over a piping bag. "What's your name?"

"P.T."

"That's not a name. Those are initials."

Under different circumstances, this would've made me smile. My mom once told me that if she'd wanted folks to call me P.T., she would've put periods on my birth certificate.

"Paul," I said. Flashing her my badge. "Paul Thomas Marsh. Mason Falls Police."

She put down the piping bag.

"You definitely need a cookie." She put up her hand. "And don't say no."

I obeyed, saying nothing.

"Autumn Fligger," she introduced herself. "What can I help you with?"

"The machine shop two doors down, Autumn," I said. "How long's it been vacant?"

"Couple, three days."

She used a pair of tongs to place what looked like a praline macaroon into a bag. Put the bag on the counter for me.

"You know any of the people who worked there?"

"Person," she said. "One guy. Oddball. Been there forever. Packed up and left Tuesday."

"Kian Tarticoft?"

She nodded. "What'd he do?"

I was used to deflecting this question when people asked it. Which literally every witness you interviewed did. But what would I say now?

I found myself choked up and pulled Marvin's wallet from my pocket.

Showed her the pictures.

"This was my wife and son," I said. "He took 'em away from me."

I choked back tears, and Autumn placed her hand on mine.

"They're dead," I said. "And I need to know everything you know about him."

The woman hesitated, but then nodded.

"Well, we'd get his mail once in a while," she said. "But he wasn't the talkative sort. He'd take it back and walk away. Not even a thank-you."

I confirmed what Tarticoft looked like, from the previous night at the gorge.

"Beard like a mountain man," she said. "Brick-red. Big dome of a head. Taller than you."

"You know the kind of car he drove?" I asked.

"I don't know the name," she said. "But it's like a car up front and a pickup in the back. He'd park it right out there."

I pulled up the picture of the El Camino, and she nodded, telling me it was the same color.

"You know why he closed the shop?"

"It wasn't for lack of business." She shrugged. "That drilling machine went all day long. It used to bother us, but the last couple days, it's quiet. You almost miss it."

"He live here in Burna?" I asked.

"Couldn't tell you."

"I need to find this guy," I said. "The car registration comes back to here. His driver's license—here. What can you tell me about him? Anything?"

"One of the girls said they saw a mountain lion in there. Some coyotes too."

"What?"

"Not alive, mind you. He was putting one of them fake eyes in 'em."

"He was a taxidermist?"

"Isn't that the darnedest thing?" she said. "Stuffing a lion inside a machine shop? Maybe that's why he used that car."

I thought about how handy an El Camino would be for carrying taxidermied animals.

We spoke for another minute, but I'd gotten all I could from Autumn.

"And the mail?" I said. "You don't have any of it still?"

She stared at me. "Let me look."

While Autumn hunted around the back of her shop, I did some basic Web searches on my phone for Tarticoft. Nothing came up. He was a ghost.

She came back with an official-looking envelope. From the State of Georgia. "I put this aside because it looked important," she said. "And then I forgot to give it to him."

I took the envelope and thanked Autumn. Even took the cookie she gave me.

"One more question," I said, grabbing my phone and looking at the name of the woman whose car had been stolen. The one who Abe had chatted up. I'd just realized she was from Burna too, just like Autumn and Harticoft.

"Grazia Lauroyan," I said. "Does the name mean anything to you?"

"'Course it does," she said. "The empty shop in between mine

and Mr. El Camino—that was Grazia's. She did custom uphol-
stery. Anything you wanted sewn—that woman was the best."

"Right next door?" I confirmed.

"Uh-huh."

"How did she get on with Mr. El Camino?"

"Hated him actually. They were in a legal dispute for years.
Suddenly, a month apart, they're both gone and the street looks
deserted."

"All right. Thanks."

Out in the car, I tore open the envelope that Autumn gave me
and saw it was an audit notice from the Counsa County Board of
Equalization. Inside was a reference to a business called HTM Inc.

Is this the name of Harticoft's business?

I searched the Web for the company, but couldn't find a damn
thing online. I punched at the Malibu's steering wheel. If I went
back to Mason Falls, I'd be off the case. No badge. No gun. No
ability to legally find out what happened to Lena and Jonas.

There was also the possibility that I could be arrested. De-
struction of private property. Assault on those Meadows boys.

I grabbed my phone, knowing what had to be done.

I paged down through my contacts. Punched in a number and
waited three rings until a deep voice answered.

"Detective Marsh," the voice that belonged to Georgia governor Toby Monroe said.

The governor and I had former dealings, and we'd agreed five
months ago never to speak to each other again.

"I'm surprised you're calling me," he said.

"I need a favor."

"I thought we were out of the business of trading favors."

"I don't have anywhere else to turn," I said. "So I'm gonna owe you one. Anything."

There was a long pause, and then Monroe asked if I was in trouble in my own department.

I told him I was.

"I know you got people," I said. "IRS. The GBI. Private."

"What do you want?" he asked.

"I need to find someone quietly and fast," I said.

"You got a name?" Monroe asked, and I ran down the few details I had on Kian Tarticoft. Including the business name.

"If I help you," Monroe said, "I'm gonna hold this chip until I got something you don't want to do."

"I kinda figured that," I said.

I took out an old burner phone that I'd bought last December. Not used much.

I gave Monroe that number, but he asked for a physical address too. "The guy I use, Marsh—he's old-school. Doesn't like to leave an electronic trail. He'll meet you somewhere and then you'll never see him again."

I thought about my home address. If Remy was right, a cruiser might be posted outside my house.

I gave Governor Monroe the address of Ennis Fultz's home. The house was empty and the land burnt to shreds and deserted. I knew I could break in through the back door like Tarticoft had done.

I switched off my cell then, killing any GPS signal that Remy could use to find to me.

As I drove the twenty miles toward the gorge, I thought about Tarticoft and the exchange of the Aries for the El Camino.

I'd been wondering how Marvin and his P.I., Lucas Royster, had attracted the animus of Tarticoft.

Which I assumed had led to the gas explosion.

If the P.I. had followed the same trail I did from the Aries over to the junkyard, I would've heard about it from Trevor Bogota or his dad when I got there. I hadn't.

Which meant Lucas Royster must've gone another route to get to Tarticoft.

I imagined his first stop was the same as Abe's—to chat up the old lady. And just maybe he'd even done it at her work, unlike Abe, who'd contacted her at home during her retirement. If Lucas Royster had met with her in Burna, he would've asked if she had any enemies or folks who'd want to do her harm.

This could've easily led to a conversation with Tarticoft himself.

At that point, all the P.I. had to do was say one word about a stolen Dodge Aries, and he'd be on Tarticoft's radar.

A dangerous radar to be on.

It was still late afternoon, but out the Malibu's window the sky grew a little darker. The winds whistled a story I didn't want to hear, and the live oaks shuddered, their green leaves fluttering in fear against the oncoming night.

As I passed the bridge where my wife and son had gone into the water, the anger inside me swelled.

And then there was that big unanswered question.

Paid killers worked for money. Who paid Kian Tarticoft to kill my Lena and Jonas?

My head was a mess, and I needed a drink. Before getting to Fultz's house, I veered out into the farm country south of the area.

I turned into an open driveway and slid the Chevy Malibu to a stop outside a roadside restaurant.

I found a booth inside the diner, needing a place to think.

The place looked like a Denny's had a lovechild with an outhouse. Knotty pine on the walls. Bad linoleum on the floors. Pressboard tables.

I slid into a booth near the door and asked the waitress for a shot of Bulleit.

"Nothing straight-up here, hon," she said. "We got Sweet-Water 420 and Bud on tap. White wine by the glass."

An old man in a cowboy hat was staring at me, and I looked back at the waitress. Her name tag read *Darby*.

One of the things you learn in AA is that alcoholics don't see that line in the sand that others see. They don't recognize the border between social drinking and excess.

I felt like I could eat a horse, hooves and all.

"No drink," I said. "What's your special?"

"Paradise Grove gizzards and onions," she said.

"I'll take a plate."

The waitress hurried off. Looking around, I locked eyes with the old cowboy again. I was sunburnt and sweaty. Did I look desperate? Crazy?

My mind was running through a half-dozen possibilities.

Had Tarticoft been hired to hit Marvin a year and a half ago at the roadside, but killed Lena instead? And if so, what for?

Did Marvin and the P.I. get too close to Tarticoft? Did Tarticoft start the gas leak that killed the P.I. and put Marvin into a coma?

I jumped backward in time to Lena.

Was there some case I was on—years ago—and Tarticoft was trying to throw me off course by killing my wife?

I wanted to strangle Kian Tarticoft, but first I needed him to answer these questions.

The gizzards came, and I ate up, waiting to hear back from Governor Monroe's guy.

If Tarticoft was hiding somewhere, I'd prefer to go there at night. Surprise the bastard.

I bought a pack of cigarettes from a machine near the restroom and popped outside for a moment, the Georgia sun dropping out of the sky.

The burner buzzed, and I picked it up.

"Is this Marsh?" The accent sounded like it was from Louisiana.

"Yeah," I said.

"I got a package for you. Half an hour. The address you gave."

I moved inside and looked around. There had been a shift change, and the restaurant was empty. No waitress. Few customers. I left a fifty on the table and headed out to the Chevy Malibu.

But when I got outside, I saw the old cowboy, across the parking lot. He had the hood of an F-150 open and was waving me over.

The back of his truck was tucked behind the restaurant, and I walked closer.

"You got some engine trouble?" I asked.

As I turned the corner, there were two men there, standing at angles to the truck. One was thin and rangy, in a pair of mechanics overalls, and the other had on a Bulldogs tee and white Dickies with dirt on them.

"What's up, fellas?" I said. Looking from face to face. All unfamiliar.

A noise came from behind me, and I felt the hit before I could turn. A stinger that cracked me across my upper back and neck.

I opened my eyes.

I was on my hands and knees on the ground, and a different guy was standing over me, a baseball bat in his left hand.

The hit had knocked the wind out of me.

I reached for my Glock, but it was gone. Maybe I'd been out a half minute. A minute. Or maybe it was more.

"I got no beef with you guys."

"What if we got a beef with you?" the old man in the hat said.

I stared at the guy with the bat in his hand. There was something familiar about his face.

"I'm a cop," I said.

"Yeah, we're aware," said the man in the Dickies.

"You hit a cop . . ." I looked around. "You inherit a world of hurt."

The guy with the bat started laughing then, and I placed why he looked so familiar. He was Nesbit Sorrell. The brother of Greer.

I remembered telling Merle to bust him at his house, even though his attorney had set up a time to bring him in. And now he was out on bail. And pissed.

"We got a police radio in the barn," the old man in the hat said. "You got an APB out on you, son. So odds are—you just *think* you're still a cop."

I looked to the old man. He was a dad or uncle to the Sorrell clan and held a long, sharp knife, maybe ten inches long, by his side. My daddy used to call that an Arkansas toothpick. When I pulled off south of Ennis Fultz's place, I must have driven right into Paradise Grove, the Sorrells' stomping grounds.

I got up off the ground, moving in a circle to keep my eyes on all of them. "Nesbit, right?" I said.

"Now the little hamster's running in that head of yours," Nesbit said. "Burning off some dust bunnies."

"What do you want?" I asked.

"Who ratted me out? With the old man?"

I squinted, not following him.

The big guy in the Dickies pushed me from behind, and Nesbit pushed me back the other way with the end of the bat—into my chest.

"Ennis Fultz," Nesbit said.

I put my hands on my knees, staring at the asphalt. The governor's guy was headed to meet me at Ennis Fultz's. To give me information on Lena's killer.

I had to make it there.

"If I hit you with the bat again, Marsh," Nesbit said, "you ain't getting up. So I'ma ask you one last time. Who saw me trash the old man's car? After this, I'm gonna take the same question up with that pretty black partner of yours. And not so gentle like."

I almost smiled.

The peckerhead believed the line we'd put out in the jails and to snitches. That we had a witness who saw him trash Fultz's BMW.

I needed out of here to find Tarticoft. And these guys just wanted to kick my ass and get a name from me.

Any name.

"All right, I'll tell you," I said. "But you gotta let me go after."

"Sure." Nesbit smiled. Lying probably.

"Guy who saw you." I bit at my lip. "He's a big dude."

"We don't look big to you?" the guy in the Dickies said, pushing me again from behind. "Wait 'til we pick up Vernal, along the way."

"Name," Nesbit demanded. Holding the bat up.

"There's two of them. Big Samoan guy and his brother. They live in an apartment at Grant and 23rd."

Nesbit motioned at the kid in the overalls, and he tossed Nesbit a pen.

"Name," he said, ready to write it on his forearm.

"Meadows," I said. "Daoto Meadows. His brother—I don't remember his name."

Nesbit tossed the pen back at his buddy, and the old man put the hood down on the F-150. Nesbit threw the bat to the big guy in the white Dickies.

"Kick the shit out of him." Nesbit pointed at me. "Then drop him at the po po. They'll throw him in with all the fuckers he's arrested. Get a taste of his own medicine."

Nesbit hopped in the truck and took off.

I came up swinging at the big guy, but the one in mechanic overalls jumped me from behind and landed a kidney punch that took my breath away. Then a second.

In a minute I was back on the ground, with the thin guy kicking me in the stomach.

I wrestled the bat away from the guy in the Dickies.

My face was bleeding from a bad cut, but I got up and waved the bat around, daring the men to come at me.

"I'll wrap this around your neck," I said. "C'mon. Who wants it?"

An older lady in a waitress uniform hustled out of the restaurant. "I already called the cops, so you boys best scram if you know what's good."

As she turned back into the restaurant, the two farm boys took off across the parking lot.

I dropped the bat. Steadied my body against a brick wall. I was torn up a bit, and my service weapon was gone, but something wild inside me was laughing, and I felt crazier than a shithouse rat.

Let the forces come at me.

Tonight I get to the truth.

Tonight I bring this son of a bitch Tarticoft to his knees.

And I don't care if it kills me.

I got to the Malibu before the police arrived. Fired up the engine and blasted out of there.

45

By the time I got to Ennis Fultz's house, I was exhausted. The early evening was cool, and the smell of burnt arborvitae still hung in the air.

A Maserati SUV was parked in the gravel turnaround by the house, and I saw a glow from a cigarette through smoked glass.

I walked over, and the window slid down. A guy in a black dress shirt and gray pants was inside. Dark hair slicked back with product.

"Sorry I got delayed," I said.

He stared at the cuts on my face. Handed me a manila envelope.

"Good luck, Marsh," he said. Turned on his car and flew down the gravel driveway, leaving a cloud of dust in his wake.

I took the envelope and walked over to Fultz's garage. Found a screwdriver.

Walking up the back stairwell, I used the tool and a credit

card to pop open the trashed back lock, not worrying about the mess I was making.

I put the envelope down and walked into the bathroom, washing the dirt and blood off my face and into the sink.

I found my way back to Fultz's desk and unclasped the manila packet.

Inside was a series of documents. Copies of incorporation papers, tracing HTM Inc. to another company. Then another.

There was a copy of a tax return, and at the top of one page it listed a business called HT Taxco, which made $33,400 in the previous year. Under business expenses it listed "taxidermy supplies."

The next page was a form declaring expenses for "Business Use of a Home." An address in a rural area thirty minutes away was circled in black Sharpie.

20977 West SR-905, Three Barrels, GA

On the next two pages were Kian Tarticoft's military records, which showed he was an artillery specialist with the 201st and had done two tours in Iraq.

I'd kill him.

But your gun. Purvis sighed.

Purvis in my head, all the time lately.

I knew what my bulldog meant—that I'd sent Nesbit Sorrell over to the Meadows place with my Glock. And then there was the second part to that. *What am I supposed to use against Tarticoft, a hired gun? A knife from Fultz's kitchen drawer?*

I walked out to the Malibu and looked inside.

Nothing. I grabbed the cookie that Autumn had given me

and ate it quickly, needing some sugar in my system to help me think.

I remembered Remy had left her animal tranquilizer rifle in Marvin's car—the day I'd driven the Charger to the hospital to meet Bodie Dunne, the nurse who'd given Narcan to Thom Sile.

I could use that to subdue Tarticoft.

And maybe it was better I didn't have lethal force.

I headed back to Mason Falls, knowing I'd have to be on the lookout for police.

As I got near the intersection by Marvin's house, I saw a cruiser, parked three doors down. Instead of continuing forward, I made a left, circling back and parking the Malibu one street over.

The area was a starter neighborhood that had never been upgraded, nearly all the homes still fourteen-hundred-square-foot bungalows with deep driveways and garages toward the backs of the properties.

Nice and easy, Purvis huffed in my head. *Quiet in. Quiet out.*

The house behind Marvin's had been for sale for over a year, and I parked in front of it, crossing the lawn quickly and vaulting over the fence into their backyard.

From there, I lifted myself over the neighbor's back stucco wall and onto Marvin's side.

My father-in-law gardened his back lawn meticulously, but the last few days in the hospital had caused the grass to get thicker than usual. I made my way across the lawn, using my key to open the garage.

Closing the garage door behind me, I popped the trunk and

took out the kit Remy had been issued as part of her project working with K-9 and Animal Services.

Gun case in hand, I scaled the wall back to the neighbor's house and moved out to the Malibu.

I sat there in the dark, breathing.

Step one: *Get some protection so you're not going after Tarticoft blind.*

Step two: *Grab the son of a bitch before he disappears. Or before Enfatigo sends someone to kill him.*

I looked at the packet with the address in Three Barrels and got onto the road.

The twenty-minute drive gave me time to think, but mostly what went through my head was an image of my wife heading into the water. The explosion that nearly killed my father-in-law. My son. Tarticoft had single-handedly taken apart my family.

As I headed farther south, the pines on the side of the highway turned from green to brown. The thickness of the wood got smaller and the volume of bark got larger until it appeared as if a thousand brittle twigs were closing in on me from all sides.

I leaned over to the passenger's seat and flipped open Remy's case.

There were two CO_2-based firearms, one a slender rifle with a twenty-five-inch barrel, and the other a small handgun. They each took five-millimeter darts, and the kit contained three darts, each loaded with a combination of animal tranquilizers. Along the side of each was written *BAM* in Sharpie, which was an acronym for the mix of three different drugs in the vials.

A crazed psych patient in County was taken down last year

with a CO_2-based dart. The medication worked intramuscularly, and took three or four minutes, from what I heard.

It wasn't perfect, but what other choice did I have.

And maybe it was better. After all, I was just trying to take him down, right? Not kill him?

At least that was what I told myself.

46

The night grew darker and the trees bordering the interstate grew so thick that the road looked like it might disappear. The moon cast a light on the sides of the red maples that lit them in pink. I put my hand out the window, testing how steady I was.

My fingers trembled in the night air.

Could I beat Tarticoft to death? Find out why he'd gone after my family—and then bury him alive in the forest?

Another quarter mile down and I killed the lights, driving the Malibu in the dark.

The last house I passed had been a quarter mile behind me. When I saw the road ahead was ending, I flipped off the ignition, and the old beater drifted to a stop.

A coal-colored mailbox was set atop a short stump of dilapidated pine. The classic red plastic flag that signaled outgoing mail hung lazily downward, almost broken off. The numbers on the side were in reflective silver tape:

20977 West SR-905

Kian Tarticoft's secret address.

All around, the ground was decorated with pointed sticks made from branches, each topped with the skull of a chipmunk.

I grabbed my flashlight and raked the edge of the road with light, seeing a *No Trespassing* sign crimped onto a sagging barbed-wire fence.

I loaded a single dart into the rifle and put the handgun and the other two darts into my pocket. Then I grabbed my Kevlar vest from the supply box I'd tossed into the trunk of the Malibu. I took my time, strapping it over my shoulders and tightening the area around my stomach and chest.

I passed the mailbox, and in fifty yards saw a dirt road that led through the property. I followed it for a minute, but to the east, I recognized the aroma of redwood burning. It smelled like manure, lit afire.

I flicked off the flashlight and left the gravel path, progressing through a forest full of ironwood and black walnut. Something dark and ominous seemed to move through the place, and I slowed. I took out my binocs and scanned the horizon from behind the trees.

The house in the distance looked like it had been made from reclaimed lumber, with each slice attached at a slight angle, overlapping the one above it.

The pine siding had been left unpainted. And with moss and debris atop the boards, the place nearly disappeared into the forest around it.

Bing.

A pine cone hit the top of the tin roof and rattled downward.

I took advantage of the noise and moved, hustling in a crouched position to my right, now within fifty yards of the place.

When I was ten, my dad and I drove up to northeast Georgia to a ranch where kids could learn to hunt deer and shoot squirrel or turkey. It was the kind of place where men dropped off their sons for three days, while some stranger made a man of them. But for my dad, the trip was more about getting away from Mom and being quiet with nature. It was where I first learned the names of trees and how to walk quietly in the woods. And how to kill something with a gun.

I slowed behind a large cedar a hundred feet from the house and heard something tick. I looked around and saw a burst of light to my right. A fire that lit quickly and went out about four seconds later.

"Shit," I said softly.

A trip wire, made with a AA battery. I'd constructed these as a kid in the woods behind our house. All you needed was a clothespin, a AA, and thirty yards of electric wire.

I held up the tranquilizer rifle. The sun was gone from the sky, and I felt my bones shudder in the cold.

Stay focused, P.T.

Any squirrel could've tripped the metal cord, so I stayed silent behind the thick red cedar, my left hand against the top of the rifle and my right near the trigger.

I slowly moved the scope across so it faced the house.

A figure came out on the porch. Six feet tall or so. Husky. Dark pants and a camouflage parka.

Tarticoft.

He stared out into the night, his eyes searching in my direction.

I looked through the rifle's scope. I couldn't see his face with the parka's hood pulled taut, but I felt him looking right through me.

I scanned his body, looking for a weapon and thinking of the best place to hit him.

I knew the heart was protected by the ribs and sternum. So even if I had a tranquilizer needle in hand-to-hand combat, it'd be tough to penetrate into a heart chamber.

Then there was the thickness of the parka.

I focused on the fleshy area of the neck, right below the jaw, and aimed.

Pop.

A mittened hand moved to where I'd made contact. A gasp.

I loaded the second cartridge in. *Pop.* Hit him in the neck again. Opposite side.

Tarticoft went down hard, crumbling onto the porch with a thud.

The forest went silent then, and I waited, counting the three minutes 'til the medication got deep into the muscles. I crouched, laying the rifle down. I still had the tranquilizer handgun, with one more shot in it. I took it from my pocket. Crossed toward the cabin.

I thought about Jonas and Lena.

Is this it? This son of a bitch had stolen my family from me, and I'd taken him down with an injection designed for a rabid animal?

I looked in the window of the cabin as I got closer. It was a two-room place off the grid with a large fireplace, flanked on each side by mounted heads of deer. No one else was inside. I leaned over to flip the body, and pulled back the parka.

Something struck me, and I felt hot steel against my neck. Birdshot. Six or eight pellets.

I turned, and saw that under the parka was an old woman. Seventy years, if not eighty, and unconscious.

I heard the pump of a shotgun and ducked.

Bam. Another six or eight pieces hit my shoulder. I took off, racing away from the sound.

I hustled through vertical lines of cedar, knowing I had only one shot in the handgun.

Birdshot smashed around me, throwing pieces of bark into my hair, and I heard a shotgun drop to the ground.

Tarticoft. He was switching to another weapon.

I ducked into a thicket of trees. Pulled to a stop behind a large ironwood, the forest becoming silent as he stopped too.

I turned quickly, my finger on the trigger of the handgun tranq. He was eight feet in front of me, an AR-15 in hand. I wasn't sure if he had a vest on, or if the tranq dart would knock him out, so I aimed at his face and pulled the trigger, just as he let off a round that took me off my feet.

47

When I awoke, I was inside Tarticoft's cabin.

My right eye felt swollen, and I ran my tongue over my lip. Tasted blood.

Tiny fragments of metal birdshot burned against my neck and stuck in my hairline, and dried blood caked below my ear.

I tried to wipe at it, but my hands were tied behind my back with some metal cord. It cut into my wrists.

The woman who I'd shot with the dart was across the room from me.

"He's up," she said. A woozy voice. She'd taken off her coat and was nursing a wound on her shoulder from my second shot. I'd hit the woman below the neck, by her collarbone.

Tarticoft grabbed me by the arms into a sitting position. Up close, I saw he was bigger than I realized at the gorge. Six-five, and probably two hundred and seventy pounds. All muscle.

"How the fuck did you find me?" He spoke in an accent that

was midwestern. Ohio maybe. Beady brown eyes under a pale hairless pate.

The Kevlar I wore must've stopped the bullet from the AR-15, but something cut at me. I inhaled and pain radiated across my chest.

Tarticoft had a swollen red stinger across his head, where the tranquilizer dart must have caromed off of him, into the night air.

I wanted to beat him to death.

"You hear me?" he said, kicking at my side. Why had I come here with inadequate weapons? Why was I thinking of hunting with my dad, who'd left me and Mom in junior high, rather than looking for forest trip wires?

Beep, beep, beep.

A little machine squawked at Tarticoft. Some alarm. The woman got up and looked at a monitor in the tiny kitchen. A sensor was up by the road. That was how Tarticoft had gotten behind me.

"You call for backup?" he asked.

"Go to hell," I said.

Tarticoft grabbed me by the wire that held my hands behind my back. Brought me to my feet. I pushed against him hard, and he hit me, square in the neck. I could feel the blood drip from my ear.

"Get the door, will ya, Mom?" he said to the old woman. "Close it behind us and flick on the light."

I passed a mirror on the wall and saw that my right eye was black. After I'd been knocked out, Tarticoft must've pulverized me with his fists.

We stepped outside, and Tarticoft held me in front of his body.

"Whoever the fuck is out there . . ." He pulled a .45 from his pocket, hollering. "You gotta go through him—to get to me."

A flashlight came on, about sixty feet away.

Remy stood there in a black running suit. In her other hand was a Glock 42.

"Mason Falls PD," she said. "Lower your weapon."

"Damn it," I said, exasperated that Remy had come here and put herself in harm's way.

On my feet, I could speak. It was a piece of the broken vest that had jammed into my ribs when I was on the ground.

"How'd you find this place?" Tarticoft yelled.

"I just found *him*," Remy hollered. "Now put down the gun before I put you down."

My head dropped. Remy must have put one of those GPS tracker things she used to find her keys into the case with the tranquilizer guns.

Tarticoft pulled me close, his back pushed up against the door. "How about you give up?" Tarticoft yelled into the night. "I've already seen how *he* shoots. You think I'm scared of you?"

Remy had been moving closer in the darkness and was now forty feet from me, under the light that Tarticoft had turned on outside his door.

My partner had her right foot placed back and her right arm supported with a bent elbow. The Weaver stance.

"That man's a police officer," she said. "And you're about to die."

Tarticoft pressed the gun against my cheek.

For all the shit that had gone on in my life in the last seventeen months, Remy was the constant. The calm. My best friend.

"This is a death penalty state," Remy said. "So if you do that, you will die by lethal injection. If I have to," Remy said, "I'll shoot through him. Take you both down."

Tarticoft snorted. "He's wearing a vest, missy."

"Maybe there's another way," I yelled. "A plan B." I swallowed. "Something a little more . . . simpatico."

"Simpatico?" Remy repeated.

She eyed me, and I couldn't tell if she remembered the conversation we'd had when she got mad at me, out at the Sorrells' farm. Where she said she wanted a partner who told her everything he suspected on a case. Who didn't hold back. Who was simpatico. She shoots right, and I duck the other way.

"Fuck both of your chatter." Tarticoft placed his gun against my right temple. "You tell me how you found me—or he's dead. In three—two—one—"

"Wait," Remy said, and she lowered her weapon.

And in my mind, I saw the future, lying just a few minutes ahead. With both of us dead at Tarticoft's hands.

But before she got to the ground, Remy lifted her Glock fast, and I moved the way I was supposed to.

A single shot rang out, and Tarticoft fell, a bullet right through the center of his forehead.

His body came down, atop mine, and I saw the dead blackness in his eyes. Remy had hit the inner ten at the shooting range. The center of the center.

She'd saved me.

There was only one problem.

Now Tarticoft could never tell me what happened with my wife and son.

48

It took an hour for us to contain Tarticoft's mother, get ahold of Chief Senza, and get a local team out to the cabin, which wasn't in our jurisdiction.

In the meantime, Remy and I searched the place and found a hoard of weapons and over two hundred thousand dollars in cash. We also found information Tarticoft had collected on Ennis Fultz's whereabouts and behaviors over a two-week period in April. The same existed on a dozen other men. Pictures and IDs. Other victims, filed away in boxes. Crimes that looked well planned. Perhaps made to look like others had committed them.

"You were sounding crazy when you talked to me," Remy said. "You kept saying Lena."

I looked at my partner. There was a good chance I was still losing my badge at the end of the night. And not every question of mine had been answered.

"Sorry," I said. "I don't know why I said her name. I was kind of all over the place."

I explained to Remy that I'd gone to the junkyard on a hunch about the El Camino that had gone in and out of the Tatham Arms Apartment Complex. That it might've been driven by our hit man. Then I'd traced the car to a machine shop in Burna and then to this cabin.

It was more or less what happened, except missing a few steps. Like when I sold out to Governor Monroe. Or when I found out how Tarticoft had killed my wife. And then got the shit beaten out of me by a handful of rednecks, who also stole my gun.

"Some of that money's mine," Tarticoft's mother hollered from where Remy had cuffed her.

"You're going to jail as an accessory," I said. "So don't worry about the money."

"The army made him that way," she said. "Before he came back, he wasn't like this."

"Tell you what," I said. I grabbed two stacks of cash. Maybe thirty thousand dollars. "I'll hide this here, under the sink. You can come back for it. If you tell us why your son did it. Why he killed Ennis Fultz."

I stuck the money up by the sink trap. The woman hesitated.

"Your choice," I said. "The offer expires when the other cops get here."

A few minutes later, she told us about how her son had gotten his first job, through a guy he worked in a factory with. Ten grand to hit the guy's wife. And when he told a military buddy of his, the work continued. Ten years now.

"They all done something wrong," the old lady said. "If Kian's hunting you—you had it comin'."

I thought about my wife and son and couldn't speak for a moment.

"Ennis Fultz," Remy prompted her, holding up a photo of Ennis that was with the money.

The old woman got back to her story. How Tarticoft would plan his hits out here where it was quiet. And that Cameron Fultz had paid Tarticoft twenty thousand dollars to kill his father, Ennis.

The cabin began to light up as police cars found a back way through the woods and came up on the rear of the place.

Patrolmen set up a perimeter around Kian Tarticoft's body, and evidence techs began looking through the cabin.

They separated Remy and me, and took my partner's weapon from her until a full write-up could be done.

"Take a look under that sink," I said, walking out the door to talk to the chief. "Up by the trap."

"You son of a bitch," the old woman came at me. A blue-suiter restrained her.

I handed my badge to Chief Senza and apologized about the mess that had happened out by the mini-mall in Centa. Also with the Meadows boys last night.

He hesitated, staring at me. To someone new—and maybe even open-minded—I might be an enigma.

"Right now, you're on unpaid leave, Marsh," he said.

Sarah Raines passed me on the way into the cabin. Her mouth formed a half smile as her eyes met mine. She looked away, but the feeling was clear. *She'll be okay.*

"Go home," Senza said. "Call your rep. There'll be an administrative hearing in the next week."

I looked around. Tarticoft was dead, and even though I didn't know everything, I felt a weight off my shoulders.

An ambulance tech cleaned me up, but I refused to go to the hospital, per usual. I could tell my ribs were just bruised, not broken.

When I was done, I walked up the forest path with Remy toward our cars.

"Good shooting," I said. "I imagine you think you're kind of a badass now."

"Forget badass," she said. "I just want you to admit you're the second-best shot in the department."

"There's nothing wrong with being number two," I said.

"You're talking about yourself, right?" Remy smiled.

I stopped and looked at her. "Today—standing here alive and breathing—I'm definitely talking about myself at number two. You tell me the day, and I'll eat tofurkey."

"You're welcome, boss," Remy said.

She looked at the ground and didn't say anything for a while.

"I'm taking a break, P.T. From homicide."

From me, she meant.

"I figured," I said.

Remy explained that she'd accepted that position as the humane law enforcement officer in the temporary department being built after the dogfighting scandal.

"It's a three-month assignment," she said. "They're bringing it back under county control at the end of the summer. But until they're done restructuring and hand it off, they want a cop in there."

We stood in the clearing where I'd dropped her rifle, and I grabbed it for her. Handed it back. "So the M Squad is no more?" I said, using the term that the real estate expert had said. "I'm sorry, Rem. For all the trouble I caused."

"Another big solve, though." She pointed at the cabin. "And who knows? By the time I'm back—maybe you'll be back too."

"Maybe," I said.

We stood there, and it felt like the end of an era.

"Hey, I know we'll get into the beat-by-beat details of this asshole," she said, motioning at the cabin. "But I'm confused. The connection here—from the junkyard to Tarticoft. How did you find this place again? That was straight from the junkyard? They had his address?"

I stared at Remy.

Tarticoft was dead, but I wasn't sure I was done looking for answers. And damn if Remy wasn't the smartest cop I'd ever trained.

"My head's kind of a mess, partner," I said. "You mind if we talk about it later? I assume you and Abe will clean this up and be bugging me for details."

"Sure," she said. "Probably Abe, not me. The guys in County want me to start Monday. Nine a.m."

"Chief knows?"

"He blessed it yesterday," she said.

So Remy had been holding on to news of the transfer for the last twenty-four hours.

"Good luck at the new gig," I said.

She gave me a hug. "Take care of yourself, P.T. I think this is good. For you to get away from work for a bit. Take a hard look at everything."

"Yeah," I said, grabbing the door to the Malibu. "And hey. Good shooting, Tex."

49

I spent the next morning cleaning up the house.

I'd remembered driving down to a package store and grabbing a fifth of gin Saturday morning after Sarah left. But there was evidence I'd bought more than just the gin. Or found other liquor around the house. A half-empty bottle of Dewar's was on the grass out back.

Loading up the trash, I told myself I was done with the poison, even though this is not the attitude they teach you in AA. Drinking is a lifelong symptom of a disease. "It's an illness that only a spiritual experience can conquer," my first sponsor had told me. But I wasn't much of a religious person.

When I was done taking out the trash, I loaded Purvis into my piece of crap Chevy Malibu. We drove to that junkyard up in Counsa County. Returned the old beater.

"Did you find what you were looking for?" Tommy Bogota asked.

"Some." I hesitated. "But I guess I'm still looking for the rest of the story."

I grabbed my truck from where Trevor and his dad had stowed it and wished the two of them luck. Loaded Purvis into the cab.

I drove into the nearest town and parked my F-150 right outside a Shoney's. I left the truck with the AC on for Purvis and sat in a booth where I could see my bulldog from inside. I ordered a piece of pecan pie drizzled in caramel while Purvis slept in the truck.

While I devoured the pie, I got on my phone and surfed the Net. There was a private investigator that I'd run into on an old case, a guy named Danny Cusumano. He'd been a cop in New Jersey when he was younger but had retired to Georgia.

All during the Fultz case, memories of my dad had been rising inside me. I had some time off and could do some looking around. But from what I picked up of the new chief's tone, me conducting another personal investigation might not be the best approach right now.

From the Web search, I saw that Cusumano's office was in a place called Broken Branch, about ten miles from Schaeffer Lake.

I finished eating and paid the waitress. Walked out to the truck.

Purvis and I drove then, cutting through small towns that no one's ever heard of.

I saw a sign that indicated I was entering Broken Branch, and I slowed my truck so as to not miss the place. The city was probably six blocks long.

In small towns in Georgia, the post offices and banks are of-ten located in historic buildings that bear ornate reliefs of men planting seeds or flags being raised.

I parked under a line of oak trees right near a shop that sold fancy soaps to tourists. A chocolatier was next door. And down the end of the same strip, a private investigation firm.

Cusumano was a small guy, maybe five foot four and at most a hundred and thirty pounds. He sat behind a giant steel desk and wore a weathered blue baseball cap on his head.

"It's good to see you, Detective Marsh," he said after some small talk. His New Jersey accent was strong on the word "you."

"It's *Mr.* Marsh this week," I said. "It's unknown if the Detec-tive title is coming back."

I told Cusumano why I was there. I'd lost track of my dad years ago and wanted to find him.

"Jack Marsh was his name. Jack Andrew Marsh."

"And what do you know about your old man?" he asked.

"He was a carpenter," I said. "Skilled enough to move around. Got work easy. Raised up here, twenty minutes west of Dah-lonega. His parents were Lee and Betty. Both passed when I was young."

Cusumano took notes. "When's the last time you've seen your dad?"

"I was in junior high," I said. "Something went wrong with him and Mom. I always assumed he screwed around. But lately, I got a whiff of a different theory. That maybe it was the other way around. My mom—"

I stopped talking, thinking of the conversation with Harmon.

About him being my mom's teaching assistant, back when my folks were still married.

"And you never used work resources to look for your old man?"

"Few years ago I got the itch and looked down a couple hatches," I said. "Didn't find anything."

Cusumano smiled. "Well, I got some special hatches other people don't know about. You got Dad's social?" he asked. "Date of birth? An old check stub or birth certificate?"

I took out a packet of papers I had on my dad. They were a random mix, but I'd found them in with my mom's stuff when she passed. Among them was a marriage certificate. A promotion letter from his work. And a note from her to him, saying she was sorry about something, without exactly saying what.

"Why don't you leave all that with me," Cusumano said. He pulled out a contract with his hourly rate on it. Other info about expenses. I signed it and left him a deposit.

"I'll get your originals back to you," he said. "Give me a week or so, and I'll call."

"Sounds fair."

I got in the car and drove back, my mind slowing and the countryside becoming rural.

Giant rolls of hay dotted grassy fields along the roadside, and the area looked depressed. Realty signs were stuck in the dirt every half mile, and faded UGA flags and cardboard-covered windows of abandoned homes.

After dropping Purvis at the house, I stopped by the mall and bought a big screen. It had been ten months since I put my boot through my old fifty-inch and nothing normalizes you in America like a TV.

Plus, I'd been told that the settlement with Tusila Meadows was wider than I'd realized. It covered me and the city in all civil matters relating to the case, which meant I could calm down about losing my place.

I got the TV going, connected my Netflix account, and sat for two hours watching that show that Sarah had finished without me.

50

The afternoon sun was falling, and I hadn't checked on Marvin since I'd gotten Exie's text in the morning, telling me she had to drive back home for a day. I grabbed my keys and drove to Mercy Hospital.

When I got there, Garva told me that my father-in-law had begun twitching his fingers a few hours ago. She'd tried me at my work number, but it just went to voicemail.

"Did his eyes open?"

"No," she said. "And we never know for sure. But we've been weaning him off the sedative. So sometimes when this happens, it means the toes come next, and he wakes up a day or so later." She hesitated. "I don't want to give you false hope, but—"

I almost laughed. "Give it to me," I said. "Any type of hope is good right now."

I sat down in a chair near the bed, reading to Marvin from a John Hart book called *The Hush* that Exie had left. I kept at it until the nursing staff changed over and the night shift came.

"Good night." I patted Marvin's feet. In response, his big toe flicked for a second and then stopped.

I waited, but nothing else moved. Still, I couldn't help smiling.

I went home and crashed, dreaming of a time when Lena and I rented a house in town for the week. A big spread with a pool and a waterslide. Jonas must've been six years old and demanded that we go down together.

Him on my lap. Then him on Lena's lap. Then the three of us, piled haphazardly together. I remember hitting the water and my eyes going wide, trying to find my son right away as we all plummeted into the deep end.

By the time I woke up and was dressed, Abe was at the front door. He came inside, and I made him a coffee.

"Yesterday was a bonanza," he said, sitting at the round table in the kitchen. "We got cops from three neighboring counties set up in the conference room."

"From the paperwork at the cabin?"

"Tarticoft killed thirteen people, P.T.," Abe said. "So we're closing cases that go back ten years. We're also unclosing cases. This guy was clever, so some folks got convicted for those murders. There's family members driving in from Alabama. From Tennessee."

"I wish I was there," I said. There was nothing better than seeing old wounds close.

"Well, don't worry," Abe said. "Your name's on everything. Lead detective, P. T. Marsh. There's a media tent being built in the parking lot."

"Yeah, well, I don't miss that part of it."

"I know that," Abe said. "But when your hearing comes up—it's gonna be hard to keep a hometown hero down."

I started making breakfast. "You want eggs?" I asked.

"Sure."

As I cooked, I thought of Tarticoft's connection to my wife. "Any local names?" I glanced at Abe. "Any of *our* old cases come up?"

"Lena's name is nowhere to be found in Tarticoft's papers," Abe said. "I've kept that away from the others. How you got to that junkyard. But I went through it myself and there's nothing, P.T. No Jonas Marsh either. I even checked on Marvin in case he was the target and Lena was an accident. Nothing doing."

I put some bread in the toaster. Flipped Abe's omelet.

I thought about Ennis Fultz. How, strangely, his death had delivered Tarticoft to me. I asked Abe about Alita and her mom. How they were doing.

"They went home yesterday," he said. "Moved into Ennis Fultz's place. Their place now. They're gonna make that land into some park, I guess," Abe said. "That's what the mom said."

"So what else?" I asked. "I can tell you're holding out. You got that look."

Abe reached to his waist and pulled out a Glock. Placed it on the table.

My Glock.

"Where you'd find that?"

"Heller in patrol found it." Abe took a sip of his coffee. "Patrol came upon a scene out in the numbered streets. Pretty grisly mess. Bodies everywhere. If this thing with Tarticoft wasn't so big, these murders would be getting a major play on TV."

I nodded. Listening as Abe described the scene. "Two dead Samoans. Three dead peckerwoods."

"The white guys," I said. "Was it an old man? And two guys in their thirties?"

Abe nodded. "Nesbit and Sanford Sorrell. And a guy named Vernal Wilkes."

"And the Samoans—both of them had the last name Meadows?"

"Daoto and Natche."

"Natche," I said. "I remembered Daoto, but I forgot the other one."

I buttered the toast and laid two plates down onto the kitchen table.

"Is this gonna make things worse for me?" I asked.

"I think you got lucky, P.T. Both sides were loaded for bear. Two .45s. Two .38s. Some knives. They all got records. And the Samoans," Abe said. "They had a stockpile of cocaine in the bedroom. Worth over six hundred grand. As far as it looks, they all killed each other over drugs. The last of them had been bleeding out for a day before a neighbor noticed," Abe said. "Just four guys that were shot. And one knifed to death. One guy on each side dead from exsanguination."

"Jesus," I said.

"And amid all of it"—Abe pointed at my gun on the table—"Heller in patrol finds a police issue. Shoved in a drawstring backpack. Never fired as part of the fight. Sees the two letters P.T. carved into the base, and calls me. Brings it to me. Real quiet like. Never hits evidence."

"I always liked Heller."

"Well, now you *love* him." Abe hesitated. "I figured I'd tell the new chief that I grabbed your piece yesterday. Been holding on to it."

My old partner dug into his food, and I put my head in my hands. If there were tears left, I'd cry. But there were none left.

"These guys were dirtbags, P.T.," Abe said. "The cocaine seized—it's off the streets now. The other fellas—they were gonna kill you."

"Does Remy know?"

Abe shook his head. "She's already off into her new gig. Stopped in for two minutes, mostly to tell me and Merle she's got no time to help with paperwork."

"She got tired of cleaning up after me."

Abe shrugged. He was never one to dwell on things. "You did good, podna. The new chief's holding a press conference tomorrow. We'll watch his body language and how he phrases things, but . . . I'm guessing he's gonna say you're on leave because of exhaustion."

"Does the chief know about the Meadows cousins?"

"He knows they're dead," Abe said. "And dead men rarely file police complaints."

"Still," I said. "I'm sure he's still sore about the city settling for that money with Tusila. What was it—four hundred grand?"

Abe finished and stood up. He had to get in to work. "That's what insurance is for," Abe said. "Plus, I think the thought process in retrospect is they should've let the city attorney solve the case against the department. Not Yugel. Cat Flannery's kind of a shark."

"Were you at the precinct when it settled?"

Abe nodded. "I was in with the chief, actually. Walking through the details on Cam Fultz's suicide. Cat stopped in for a victory lap."

I put away our dishes. "I'm glad I missed that," I said. "But it's a little pleasure knowing she had to split up her share. That other law firm from out of town . . ."

Abe cocked his head at me. "Oh, you didn't hear?" An odd look on his face. "Those people were working pro bono, P.T. Cat and Tusila got all that money."

I nodded, but was confused. "Johnson and Hartley?" I confirmed. "They worked for free?"

"That was their name, yeah. Funny thing—I don't think Cat even understood it. She said to me and the chief, 'Whatever did you boys do to piss those people off?'"

Abe headed for the front door. "I'll check in with you tomorrow."

He pointed at my living room before he left. "Your new sixty-inch wasn't lost on me, by the way. There was a time when you and me watched Falcons games here on Sundays."

"Just waitin' for the season to start," I said. "Course, we'll probably blow half the games."

"Don't *say* the words 'Super Bowl,'" he warned me.

Abe headed out the door, and I watched him get in his car.

I sat down on the steps outside, and Purvis came up next to me.

Let it go, my bulldog huffed.

And Purvis was right as usual.

But there's who you are, at your core.

And Johnson and Hartley working pro bono? It reeked of bullshit. And I had never been any good at letting bullshit lie.

51

My disciplinary hearing was the following Tuesday.

I put on my Class A blues and sat in front of a panel that contained two retired judges, a community member, and the new head of police, Chief Senza. Senza wasn't in uniform but donned a blue suit with a smart tie.

Both judges knew me, but the community member didn't. She was a blonde in her sixties and fixed me with a stink-eye the entire time.

I was questioned about what I did ten nights earlier, in attacking the vehicle registered to Daoto Meadows. And why I did it.

My SSPBA rep, Felix, handled most of the answers, explaining that I'd worked eighty of ninety-six consecutive hours on a case and was exhausted by the time I ran into the Meadows cousins.

"Is this true, Mr. Marsh?" the community member asked me. "You hadn't rested in four days?"

"I don't sleep much when a killer's on the loose."

"And with just four hours of rest after the car incident," Felix continued, "Detective Marsh discovered a trail that no one else in the department had noticed."

Felix had repped me once before, and he was the best.

He transitioned to how I'd connected Kian Tarticoft to the death of Ennis Fultz and Bill Lyman.

"The Fultz family was part of the civic trust," Felix said. "Without Detective Marsh, we'd all be fooled that they died accidentally and a killer would be free."

Felix ran through the benefits of overturning the four wrongful convictions. And how there were nine unsolved murders across three states that were now closed.

Then he presented interviews from neighbors that reported that the blue Mustang driven by Daoto Meadows had been outside my home on six separate nights—three more than I'd seen.

He turned his laptop and played a low-quality doorbell video from a neighbor's house, which showed Daoto Meadows getting out of his car. Stretching. Then walking alongside my property. You could hear Purvis barking in the background.

"If you're thinking these men look dangerous," Felix said, "you're right. A week ago they were murdered in a drug shoot-out, during which the city recovered thirty-eight kilos of high-purity, uncut cocaine with a street value of almost three-quarters of a million dollars."

I was asked to make a personal statement at the end of the meeting, and I stood up, flattening the wrinkles on my formal navy blue slacks.

"On a number of occasions I've made decisions that I'd like another shot at," I said. "Things that a simple word could defuse."

I stared at Chief Senza. Thinking of the conversation with Cat the Tiger and Tusila Meadows on the first day of the investigation. How I'd refused to apologize.

"Tell me what I can do to fix this and move on. Because I need this job. And I think this city needs me."

I was released to wait in the hallway and sat for a spell. Eventually Felix came out.

"Twenty-three hundred dollars in restitution for the car damage," he said. "That goes to a police charity. And thirty days' suspension."

"That's it?"

He bit his lip. "A pay decrease. Grade two," he said. "You can reapply next fall for your old pay. But you kept your job, P.T."

"You did great," I said.

Felix grabbed his briefcase. "I gotta go," he said. "Let's never do this again."

I waited in the hallway after the group filed out. Chief Senza came out last.

"I wanted to thank you in person," I said. "For fighting to keep me."

He walked with me toward the elevator. Saying nothing at first.

We got in and the door closed.

"I played football, about half my life," Senza said. "All the way through college at Auburn. I coached for eight years after. Community college. Division two."

"I heard that," I said.

"At State," he said, "I had this great quarterback. Young guy. Made lots of mistakes. And also this veteran. And the assistants would say—play the younger guy. Get him as many reps as possible."

"He's the future," I said.

"That was the wording they used." Senza nodded. "But if you really know about coaching, you know that recruits come for one reason: because you win. So it doesn't matter—young or old. You play the best guys you have. Every time. No past or future. Just today's win."

I started to say something, but he held out his hand.

"So here," Senza said, "I walked into a hiring freeze. The one spot I can create—I get by firing you. Except all I hear is you're a good man. And all I see—this Tarticoft thing. It's making us look good in the community. Healing wounds."

The elevator door slid open, and he walked out. "So I guess *effectively*—you're my first hire, Marsh. My first recruit. Don't fuck up again."

"Copy that," I said.

"Take the next thirty days," Senza said, "attend some meetings. And get your shit together." He stared at me hard, and I wondered how much he knew. About the truth behind the Meadows boys. How the rednecks had found them. Or even my own open questions still about my wife's death.

"If you got any unfinished business, P.T., now's the time to finish it, before you get back on my team. Or don't come back at all."

"Yes, sir," I said.

He turned and left me standing there.

52

The following Monday afternoon, the kitchen smelled of bay leaf and bacon. I had brought Marvin home from the hospital that morning to stay with me until he was healthy enough to be on his own.

"You and me—roommates?" he'd said at the hospital when I'd first brought it up.

"You got a better offer?"

"There were a couple candy stripers—"

We'd both laughed at that. "They're beating down the door to take some old man home, huh?"

Tonight I was trying to make one of Lena's specialties, Hoppin' Johns. My wife had grown up eating it on New Year's Day, and the dish was the go-to request, back when there were Sunday dinners at Marvin's house.

I'd begun by slow-cooking some bacon. Chopping it small so it got crispy. And when it was done, mixing in celery and green pepper and thyme. Eventually adding in a cup of black-eyed peas.

I turned on my Sonos speaker and found an old country station that Marvin would like. "Sea of Heartbreak" by Leroy Van Dyke ended, and Crystal Gayle's "I'll Get Over You" came on.

My thoughts went to Lena. A month into dating, we went with another couple to a country bar and danced to this song.

Marvin's home growing up was filled with music, and Lena could dance to nearly every song. She'd shift with ease from Willie Nelson to Jay Z. She could've done so much better than me.

Once the smell filled the house and the Carolina Gold Rice was puffy, Marvin found his way out of Jonas's room, where I'd set him up. He grabbed a glass of water and took a seat.

I was chopping some green onions and adding some more bay leaf when the phone rang.

It was Danny Cusumano, the private investigator.

"I don't have everything on your dad yet," he said. "But I told you I'd give you an update."

I stepped out the side door to talk to the P.I.

"Did your old man ever go by the name 'Andy'?" he asked.

"Not that I heard," I said. "But I told you Andrew was his middle name."

Outside the side door, my neighbor's slash pines had been trimmed, and I could see clear through into his house a hundred feet away. The TV was on in the dining area, a Braves game on it.

"I found a guy up in Chattanooga," Cusumano continued. "Andy Mars. No h on the end. Does that mean anything to you?"

When I was a kid, my father used to make up stories to get me to fall asleep. In one of his go-to favorites, I was an astronaut on the red planet. My name was Paul Mars. No *h*.

"No," I said to Cusumano. "Who's Andy Mars?"

"He works at a body shop in Tennessee. Place that services exotic cars."

"What put you onto him?"

"I got a friend at the IRS," Cusumano said. "I throw him some scratch once in a while, and he throws me a bone here and there."

"And this Mars guy?"

"Some dentist up north got audited and came forward with an additional 1099. You know—trying to claim an expense after the fact. But he never filed the paperwork originally. It was for this hand-carved sign for his office. You said your dad was a carpenter."

"Yeah," I said. "Lotta carpenters out there."

"Well, this carpenter's name was Andy Mars, but the social security number traced back to Jack Andrew Marsh."

I swallowed. Had to concentrate to do it. "When was the tax form filed?"

"Last year," Cusumano said. "I could drive up to the body shop. But I thought I'd check in with you first. I've also used up your deposit money."

The truth was that my dad had always been a car guy. Hobby, not employment, but he knew foreign cars. Some exotics. Porsches. Maseratis. Alfas.

I didn't say anything for a good minute, and Cusumano waited me out.

Coming off the case with Ennis and Cameron Fultz, I'd been hot about reaching out to my dad. But now I wasn't so sure it was a good thing. To find him at this point. To tell him everything that had happened to me in the last seventeen months.

Plus, I had Marvin back.

"Don't waste your time with this Mars fella," I said. "Let's consider things closed for now."

"You're the boss," Cusumano said.

I walked back in the house. Plated the stew and beans atop the rice and carried it over to the dining area.

In three weeks, I'd be back on the force, and who knows— maybe Marvin would stay here longer.

"What happened here?" my father-in-law asked, his hand tapping at a piece of wallpaper that was hanging free, just above his head.

This was a small test area where Sarah had peeled back the paper, to see what was underneath.

"Humidity," I said. "I'll put some adhesive under it tomorrow."

Marvin was happy to be here. I could tell.

I moved back to the kitchen to grab the greens.

I didn't fool myself this business with Kian Tarticoft was over. Tarticoft was dead, but he was a hired killer. And I had yet to find out who had hired him or why.

"Marvin," I said. "We never talked about the P.I. What'd he tell you before the gas leak happened?"

"Yeah," my father-in-law said. "So he'd tracked the car. I assume you've figured that out. The one I remembered from the accident."

"Dodge Aries," I said. "The car that saved Chrysler."

"A beauty back in my time," Marvin said. "But then Lucas had this other theory. About this guy over in Burna and this woman who had the shop next to him."

I sat down quietly. Not wanting to feed Marvin any answers. To hear them from him.

"What theory?"

"That maybe this guy stole her car. It didn't make sense exactly. More of a gut thing."

Marvin had been unconscious when the news of Tarticoft went down. I told him about how I'd found Tarticoft and connected him to the accident. To Lena and Jonas. I fudged a couple details to give Marvin some closure. In this version of the story, Tarticoft was a hired killer, but was not hired to get Lena.

"So he hit my girl and grandson by accident?" Marvin asked.

"He was rushing away from a crime scene," I lied.

Marvin nodded.

"We got 'em, Dad," I said. "Remy shot him. And your lead made the difference. That's how I found the guy."

Marvin went silent then, but his face turned red. Holding back emotion.

"Does Remy know?"

I shook my head, and he understood there were secrets, even from my partner.

I got up and refilled Marvin's drink. Put out a plate with three or four moon pies on them. When Marvin finished his Hoppin' Johns, he grabbed a pie.

"So it's finally over?" he asked.

I hesitated, knowing it wasn't over. That I needed to know who hired Tarticoft.

But at the same time, I wanted to give Marvin a gift I couldn't give myself.

"It's over," I said.

Marvin lowered his head and started rocking forward just slightly, his shoulders shaking as he cried. I put a hand on his shoulder, and he held on to me.

When he finished crying, I cleared his plate and finished my own food.

In a few weeks' time, when I was back working, I'd dig into Lena's death again.

I wasn't completely without leads.

There was only one case I was on seventeen months ago, when Lena was killed.

Thirty-three dollars was stolen from a liquor store called the Golden Oaks.

So if there was something more than just $33 at stake—if I'd stumbled into something without knowing it back then—then maybe coming after me or my family was a way to throw a determined cop off his game. If the stakes were high enough.

Right now I just needed some rest. To focus on other things. Me. Marvin. Sobriety.

"Food was great," Marvin said.

He told me that he needed to get over to his house this weekend. At least mow the back lawn and trim the roses.

"I'll do that," I said. "You can supervise. Tell me what I'm doing wrong."

We both laughed for a minute, because we knew how meticulous he was about his yard.

"I never told you this," Marvin said, "but the week you proposed to Lena—she knew it."

"Bullshit," I said. "*I* didn't know I had the balls to go through with the proposal. Or if she'd say yes."

"She said to me, 'Daddy, Paul's gonna ring you up to talk this week. You *better* be nice.'"

I smiled, remembering the conversation with Marvin. I didn't ring him up. I came by in person when I knew Lena would be gone. Got his permission.

"The smartest girl I ever met," I said.

Marvin told me he was tired and ambled off to Jonas's room.

I sat for a spell with Purvis on the porch, listening to the sounds of cicadas.

I closed my eyes, letting myself rest for a minute.

In my dream, I flew high above Mason Falls. Soared above a forest thick with six- and eight-story hemlocks, their bark the color of cinnamon and their needles dark green on top and lighter underneath.

I moved out east, where the dirt became as red as Georgia dirt gets. And the bushes became brown and crisp from lack of water. A flowing river slowed to a tiny drip, and I came upon the Condesale Gorge, in all its splendor.

Alita was there, living in her father's home and now older. Fifteen or sixteen. In my dream, the arborvitae had grown back, and Alita had long beautiful hair that fell past her shoulders. She wore a white polo shirt and a tan skirt with hiking boots.

She guided visitors through a maze of bushes to a bench where they could see out over the canyon to places far east, with the stretch of the gorge moving out in front of them without a single pumpjack in sight, even though the land below was thick with shale.

I thought of the people I had interacted with in the past month.

Kian Tarticoft was not just an assassin, but had used his own mother as bait. Nesbit Sorrell had never met me, but was ready to kill me with a baseball bat. And the Meadows cousins had the balls to stalk a police officer's house while they had three-quarters of a million dollars in cocaine back at their apartment.

The world was full of evil men, but there was good in it too: a goodness that flourished and survived regardless of circumstance. In fact, despite it.

Alita was a sign of that, and she was happy. She'd lost two members of her family, just like me, but had learned to survive. Which was inspiration.

I opened my eyes and saw Purvis had curled up next to me, my back against the wood of the house.

We can do this, P.T., he said. *We can move on.*

I rubbed the back of my bulldog's neck.

There was another lead I had to follow up on, other than the robbery at the Golden Oaks.

The attorney, Lauten Hartley.

Hartley had worked pro bono with Cat Flannery, to try and get me fired or sued. I'd also met him, a year earlier, on the Meadows investigation, out at some rich guy's mansion. Two strikes against him.

I pulled Purvis up into my lap. Watching as fireflies danced in the spring night sky.

I loved this house. I was glad I didn't lose it in some lawsuit with Tusila Meadows. Was glad that Lena's furniture and old things were exactly as she'd left them.

Even with Marvin staying in Jonas's room, I'd decided to put my son's old comforter back onto the bed.

I took a bite of my moon pie.

In moments of peace, I find that this area of Georgia is like heaven on earth, and I'm blessed to still be alive, here in Mason Falls, if even to just spend my days with Marvin and Purvis.

Lena forgave you, Purvis huffed. *Now you gotta forgive yourself.*

"Soon," I said to my bulldog. "Soon."

ACKNOWLEDGMENTS

I would like to start by thanking all the people who read *The Good Detective*, my first book. It's an honor to have your novel enjoyed by strangers. Even more so when some of those folks become friends.

I would like to thank my wife, Maggie, and my son and daughter, Noah and Zoey, for giving me the space and confidence to take another ride with my friends Paul Thomas Marsh and Remy Morgan. And Mark Tavani for reading an early draft of the book and advising me on rebuilding a new story spine.

To the folks at G. P. Putnam's Sons, many thanks for their outstanding work in marketing and publicizing *The Good Detective*: specifically Ashley Hewlett, Bonnie Rice, Emily Mlynek, Mark Tavani, Danielle Dieterich, Ashley McClay, Dan Musselman, Ivan Held, and others whose names I don't know but who hustle behind the scenes to get the book in the right people's hands. Last, a big thanks to the copyediting team, who work so hard to keep me honest and clean.

I'd like to thank my mom, Betty, who is the rocket fuel behind all the McMahons. Thanks to the Saturday-morning wrecking crew at Jerrilyn Farmer's workshop. To those who read early copies of the book for geography, legal, continuity, and medical expertise: specifically Kerry Archbold, Suzanne Miller, Allison Stover, Andy McMahon, and Bette Carlson. And to my cheer captain and super-agent, Marly Rusoff.

I would like to thank the writers who blurbed *The Good Detective*, my debut novel: John Hart, whose work is stellar; Glen Erik Hamilton, a fantastic writer and good friend; and Reed Farrel Coleman, a terrific author. To Marilyn Stasio of the *New York Times*, I am appreciative of the kind words in helping get publicity for an unknown writer. And to the folks of the great state of Georgia, for your continued hospitality as I visit, research, and write. Last one—to friends and clients who continue to cheer me on as I balance writing, advertising, and family.

To the folks who hosted me on my book tour: Jill at Fiction Addiction; Barbara at Poisoned Pen; John and Mckenna at Murder by the Book; Rob and Kelly at Mysterious Galaxy; Jen and Jackie at Vroman's; and Anne at Book Carnival. All these are great places to buy your next book or meet an author in person. Thanks to two great writers, William Kent Krueger and Matt Coyle, for their Q&A on tour. If you haven't read these guys, put them on your list.

One last thing—if you like the book, don't be a stranger. Shoot me a note at McMahonJohn@att.net and you'll be the first to know when the next one is coming out and read special advance excerpts.

P. T. Marsh will return with a vengeance. This is not over for him.